FINAL VICTIM

BOOKS BY GREGG OLSEN

FINAL VICTIM

GREGG OLSEN

bookouture

Published by Bookouture in 2025

An imprint of Storyfire Ltd.
Carmelite House
50 Victoria Embankment
London EC4Y 0DZ

www.bookouture.com

The authorised representative in the EEA is Hachette Ireland
8 Castlecourt Centre
Dublin 15 D15 XTP3
Ireland
(email: info@hbgi.ie)

ISBN: 978-1-83618-356-3
eBook ISBN: 978-1-83618-355-6

This book is a work of fiction. Names, characters, businesses, organizations,
places and events other than those clearly in the public domain, are either the
product of the author's imagination or are used fictitiously. Any resemblance to
actual persons, living or dead, events or locales is entirely coincidental.

PROLOGUE

WALLACE

He parks the charcoal gray Ford Transit cargo van in the garage. He'd stolen the van in Indiana. Random changing of license plates coming across the country made it all but invisible. He opens the back doors of the van and inside are shipping boxes stacked two high and a set of magnetic signs with the FedEx logo. He bought the signs on eBay for thirty dollars.

He removes a row of shipping boxes from the back of the van to reveal his latest work wrapped in a blue painter's tarp.

He climbs into the cargo area and drags the tarp toward the back doors. She's heavy for a small woman. But as they say, she's deadweight. He unfolds the tarp. The body is folded into a fetal position with the severed head tucked into it like a football.

Unlike some of his victims, this one had put up one hell of a fight. He still has the scrapes and bruises to show it. Not that it mattered in the end. But now he wishes he had been able to keep her alive longer. The eyes are so much like Rylee's. Same color, same intensity, same soullessness.

"One last thing."

He turns the head so it's facing up. He had broken a box

spring off a bed in the last motel where he stayed. He takes this from his pocket and corkscrews it into one of the eyes.

"Too bad I don't know which eye Rylee speared when she killed her father."

Rylee faked her own death and disappeared only to be reborn as several different persons. She's like a chameleon. He feels a chill of excitement at the thought of coming face-to-face with his creator.

"Wallace is here, Rylee. I've come for you like I promised."

ONE

The expanse of Drayton Harbor spreads across the horizon on my left and soon I'm crossing Dakota Creek, coming to the on-ramp for Interstate 5. It's a beautiful September morning. The rain has held off and the skies are swirls of red and white and blue. Very patriotic. A mile or so north is a shop called TOTALLY CHOCOLATE. I can really use a chocolate fix, but I take the ramp heading south toward Port Townsend, heading home. There's a chocolate PayDay candy bar in the console calling to me. *Megan Carpenter. I'm here, Megan. Don't feel guilty. You deserve me. Don't say no.*

"I deserve you, but I'm watching my weight," I say to the console. Yep. I'm watching my weight every time I look down. Since I started dating Dan, my metabolism has changed like fat on crack cocaine.

Who knew happiness can make you fat? Dan makes me happy, and so it's mostly his fault if I get fat.

I've just left the sprawling estate in Whatcom County where my detective partner, Ronnie Marsh, grew up. The estate was named Cougar Point by Ronnie's grandfather because it sits on the tip of a peninsula that looks like a cougar's head jutting out into the Strait of Georgia.

Ronnie is staying behind with her family. Her father has a corporate law firm and has tried for several years to get Ronnie to work for him. She turned it down to become a cop. She could have had a mini-mansion instead of living in a remodeled barn on the bay in Port Townsend. She could have had the best of everything, but she settled for the meager existence of a cop's life. Crazy, right?

However, Ronnie's sister, Rebecca, drank the family Kool-Aid and is a full partner in their father's firm. Rebecca is older and was the apple of daddy's eye until recently when Rebecca had called Ronnie asking for help on a kidnapping case. The kidnapped was Ronnie's mother. Of course, I helped Ronnie. She's my best friend.

As a result of our work, Ronnie and I were offered a job by the Whatcom County sheriff. We were both included in the offer, but I know the sheriff was particularly interested in hiring Ronnie since she was basically a local and knew the terrain. I wasn't interested anyway. I know where I belong. With my friends. My brother, Hayden, my boyfriend, Dan, Sheriff Tony Gray, and my other friends are all in Jefferson County. Ronnie has several reasons to take the Whatcom County job in and good for her. It's great. I'm very happy for her. It will be good for both of us if she takes the job.

When she first came to work with me, she was a reserve deputy, too pretty, too well dressed, too smart. I immediately didn't like her, but she was assigned to me. I didn't want her. I worked better alone. Some of the things I wanted or had to do didn't bear having a witness. But she quickly proved her worth and skill and became a full-time deputy and then a detective and my partner.

We've faced death together more than once and that kind of bond is forever. But I must be realistic. She may take the job in

Whatcom County as a sheriff's detective and stay near her family on Cougar Point. Family is important. My mother can go to hell, but I only recently was reunited with my brother, Hayden.

Hayden and I had been estranged for almost a decade and now that he's come back, if I had to make the same choice facing Ronnie, I'd take Hayden over my job any day. And then there's my boyfriend, Dan Anderson, the man I love. It feels strange and a little scary to think I could love any man again. The closest I'd ever come to a love interest was a high school crush on Caleb Hunter. He'd learned more about me than anyone. We were each other's confidants, but we never formed the bond Dan and I share.

Caleb. Thinking about him again, I think about another man in my life. My stalker: Wallace. The first time "Wallace" had contacted me was just after the first date I had with Dan. He called me Rylee, a name I'd given up long ago. A name I'd hoped to never hear again. Wallace knew things about me and my past. Things that could land me in prison or worse. The list of suspects was short. Caleb, my brother, Hayden, who still called me Rylee when we were alone, and, I'm ashamed to say, Dan Anderson. I've since eliminated Dan and Hayden, and that leaves me with Caleb who I haven't kept in touch with or heard from since leaving Port Orchard for good. It couldn't be Caleb. He would have no reason to blackmail or taunt me with my past. We'd only shared one kiss and that was in high school on the benches overlooking the track. Besides, even the thought of violence sickened Caleb. It was why we'd split up as a possible couple.

My phone rings, dragging me out of my reverie, and I tell Siri to answer. I hope it's Dan saying he's coming home early from San Francisco, but it's Nan, Sheriff Gray's secretary. I need to find out how to program my car to block calls from her.

"Megan?"

"That's who you called, isn't it?" I'm sorry I say this aloud.

"I wouldn't have called, but Sheriff Gray wants to be sure you're coming back today. He heard from Whatcom County Sheriff Longbow that you and Ronnie had success in that case and he's given Ronnie some extra days off."

"What's up?" I ask.

"I'll let him tell you."

Then why didn't he call? What the hell. I can hear the enjoyment in her voice at drawing this out. "Put him on."

"He's gone to a budget meeting."

Here we go. Round and round. "Okay. Tell him I'll stop by the office before I go home."

Her voice lowers to a whisper. "There's something else."

I hate it when people do that. Spit it out. "Okay."

"Actually, Sheriff Gray didn't tell me to call you."

I want to ask if she's hearing voices telling her to be annoying, but I don't want to make this conversation any longer than necessary.

In the same secret tone she says, "You had a mysterious visitor this morning."

I wait. I won't let her get under my skin, or I'll have to choke her.

"Do you want to know who it was?"

My hands clench the steering wheel, imagining it's her neck.

"He said his name is Wallace?"

My blood freezes. Nan is still talking, but I don't hear the words. It's easy to tune her out since I don't like her voice, but the name Wallace has just been in my thoughts. It's hard to forget someone who is threatening your well-being. I drift across the lane onto the shoulder and the stupid SUV computer voice tells me about my poor driving skill and corrects my steering all at the same time.

Nan's voice cuts through my consternation and I can't

ignore it. She says, "He didn't give a last name. Or maybe Wallace is his first name. He's very attractive. In a mountain man sort of way. He said to tell you he was sorry he missed you at the restaurant in Drayton Harbor, but he didn't want to interrupt you with your partner and her sister."

I can't speak.

"Megan?"

I don't answer. I drift across the lane again and the stupid computer voice tells me and corrects my steering. Thank God.

"Do you know who that is? He said you would know him?"

I do. He's my stalker. He knows things about me which could put me in prison. He's been able to keep track of my cases and never fails to let me know. But I don't comment. "Did he say why he was here?"

"No. He just said he would catch you later. He was looking forward to it." She pauses and I can imagine the smug look on her face. "You have an admirer, Megan. Is he single? I didn't see a ring. Does your boyfriend know about—"

I disconnect the call.

TWO

If I go to the Sheriff's Office now, Nan will be all over me like stink on sweaty socks, asking personal questions I can't answer. She wouldn't like me in this state of mind. I'd make sure of it. Instead, I head home to Port Townsend where I will have some privacy. Ronnie has taught me how to access the Sheriff Office surveillance video from my phone and home laptop. Normally, I would call Ronnie for her expertise in doing this. Ronnie can hack any system. She can access the office surveillance video from her phone or her iPad. But there are two reasons I won't call for her help. Number one, I'll never tell her about Wallace or involve her in anything that might introduce her to my stalker. And two, she's home and won't be back to work for at least a week. If she comes back at all, that is.

I live in an old Victorian house in Port Townsend that's divided into two apartments. I drive past my place checking out the street and empty lots where houses were razed. Wallace might be waiting; watching. I look for someone hanging around or sitting in a vehicle I don't recognize as belonging in my neighborhood. I'd picked this street primarily because of the lack of traffic. That and my belief that no one would come here to steal from poor and desperate people.

My gun is tucked under my leg. My heart is stuffed in my throat. My mind is whirling. What if I see someone matching the description Nan gave? What do I do? Do I get out and hold him at gunpoint until he proves he's not Wallace? Maybe that's exactly what Wallace wants me to do. A public spectacle of excessive police use of force will get a million hits on YouTube where he can expose who I really am. Maybe this is the confrontation he's promising in his emails? I find myself looking around, not for Wallace but for witnesses, hoping there are none. I want to deal with this guy once and for all, and witnesses will only hold me back. I don't take intimidation well, unless I'm the one putting it out.

Wallace knows Hayden is my brother. He knows Dan is my boyfriend. He called Dan Anderson my *lumberjack boyfriend* in one of his emails. He knows Ronnie is my partner and about Sheriff Gray. He knew I was just in Blaine at that stupid crab place. Was he there? Watching? Now he knows Nan. He wouldn't do anything to Nan after meeting her. But I fear for Hayden and my friends.

I cruise around the block in ever-widening circles, all the time anxious to get home to check the video feed of the Sheriff's Office. My heart pounds. If Wallace is on the video, I'll finally get a look at the bastard who has been stalking me. My nerves are overloaded with fight or flight but mostly fight. My phone rings and I kill it without looking at the caller ID. It's Nan, of course.

My regular parking spot is open. I can't keep circling the block like a shark. I'm home. If someone approaches me here, I have the right to defend myself.

Each apartment has a separate entrance off a common foyer. Historic usually equals quaint, but there's nothing quaint about this place. I've been the sole tenant until two weeks ago.

I've never seen my new neighbor, which I think is odd, given we live in the same house. I always lock the foyer entrance when I leave. Hell, even when I come home. But whoever this is invariably leaves it unlocked. It's unlocked again.

I know the thought is sexist, but I guess the person is a he because of the lingering smell of Old Spice. Both my stepfather and my friend Caleb, my almost boyfriend from high school, bathed in the stuff. My stepfather was my senior so I couldn't say anything to him, but I threatened to give Caleb a bath with a fire hose. Funny how the thought came back just now. The first time I smelled it in the foyer it made me think of Caleb. But Caleb would never move next door to me. Not without telling me. We parted ways many years ago after he saw who I really was. He was disgusted by me. Probably hated me. I have that effect on some people.

My pulse is racing, my gun is in my hand when I push the door open. This is ridiculous. I can't live in DEFCON 1 every time this asshole pushes my buttons. Holstering my weapon, I reach out with an unsteady hand and check the door to my place. Locked. I unlock the door and push it open a few inches and do a quick visual scan. Nothing. It feels empty. The lingering stench of the fish I had fried before leaving on the case with Ronnie is the only thing living inside.

I'm still not satisfied and go back outside and walk around the house. Nothing is out of place. The soft dirt and weeds under the kitchen window aren't disturbed. I run my finger over the shelf of the window that looks into my little office and it comes back coated with white chalky powder from the fading paint. There are no scuff marks on the wall or the windowsill.

I go back inside and think about knocking on my obnoxious neighbor's door to tell him to go easy on the aftershave. That makes me wonder what kind of smell he's hiding. Or maybe it's what spice smells like when it dies. Instead of Old Spice they should call it Decomposed Spice.

Ronnie had offered to put a Ring doorbell system on my apartment. She said I could access it on my cell phone from anywhere. I wasn't that paranoid back then but wish I had taken her up on it. As if she knew I was thinking about her my phone dings. The message reads:

Megan, call me when you get this.

I barely finish reading the brief text when I get a FaceTime call from Ronnie. I don't want to answer. She'll think something is wrong. But if I don't answer she'll think something is wrong. I accept the call.

Ronnie's smiling face fills the screen and I can see the waters of Semiahmoo Bay behind her. She's sitting on the bench outside the back doors of the Marshes home that's bracketed by a pair of monkey puzzle trees just above their private beach.

"Megan, I wanted to be sure you made it home."

I face the phone away from me and rotate it 360 degrees, showing her the inside of the room. "As you can see, I'm back home. Thanks for checking. I'm fine. I really am." I'm not. I can feel a tightness in my throat and I hope she doesn't detect my discomfort. She's a true friend. And the thought that she might no longer work with me deeply saddens me. I want to tell her about Wallace. That he's been stalking me for years and that he was watching me in Bellingham and then visited the Sheriff Office. But I won't try to lure her back with my problem. I've dealt with worse when I was alone. And I'm anxious to get off the phone and look at the office surveillance video.

"Megan, you really need to clean."

At first, I think she's said I need to "come clean." She's very intuitive, but I realize she's making a joke about my dirty house when she giggles like a schoolgirl. Her sister, Rebecca, has the same giggle. Kind of a titter. It's annoying. It's adorable. After the shock to my system from Wallace's sudden appearance in

Port Hadlock, I feel my eyes moisten from the comfort I feel
from that stupid giggle.

"I'll get right on it," I say and force a smile. "Did you need
something?" My question sounds like I'm trying to rush her off
the phone, but I don't know what else to say.

"I just wanted to tell you again I appreciate what you did
for me and my family. Here's Rebecca."

Rebecca's smiling face fills the screen and she whispers,
"Mom is not going through with the divorce."

"That's great," I say. I mean it. Victoria and Jack had
decided to get divorced just before she was kidnapped. The
trauma of that event put life back in perspective.

I hear Ronnie in the background saying, "It's getting mushy
around here. Mom and Dad are like high school sweethearts."

Rebecca says to her, "All the kissing and sweetness is a little
too much, but it's better than the quiet." To me Rebecca says,
"Thank you, Megan, for being there for us."

I'm eyeing my computer. Thankfully she doesn't notice and
the phone is handed back to Ronnie. "What's wrong, Megan?"

Shit. She's psychic. "It's nothing really," I lie. "Nan is at it
again. She called to see if I was coming back to work today. She
knows I hadn't planned on it, but it's her way of being
annoying."

"Ignore her," Ronnie says. "She's just jealous no men come
to see her."

I feel a new chill. "What are you talking about?"

Ronnie says, "I thought she called you about the man who
came to the office this morning."

"Nan called you?" Nan has gone too far this time. I feel my
hand tightening into a fist and I force my jaw to unclamp.

"You know how Nan is, Megan. She lives vicariously
through those of us with interesting lives."

I'm smiling by sheer force of will. "You're right. I feel sorry for her sometimes." Not. I want to kill Nan. But I don't do that anymore.

Ronnie nods. "Nan said you weren't answering your phone and she asked if you were still here at the house. She was curious who the guy was. She mentioned Dan's finding out you had an admirer. I told her you were on the road. Then she wanted to know all about what we had done and I told her I still needed to file a report with Sheriff before I could say anything."

"That's fine." It's not fine. "She's so nosey. I'll tell her the same thing. She can find out from the news media."

"So, Megan, who is this Wallace guy?"

"No one. Some guy wanting to ask about his background check for a concealed carry license."

Her look says she's not buying it, but like a good friend she doesn't pry. I want to ask if she's considering taking the job with Whatcom County, but I don't know if I want to know the answer. Best to wait and see what happens.

Ronnie says, "You're sure you're okay?"

I force a laugh. "You're wasting your time with me instead of spending time with your family. Go. Watch your mom and dad make out. Send pictures if you want."

She gives me a look of disgust, but I can tell she's ecstatic with the way things turned out with her parents. "Okay, Megan. But if you need anything, or just want to talk..."

"I'll call." I won't.

"Promise?"

"Cross my heart. Same goes for you. Unless it has anything to do with the folks having sex. In that case I'm unavailable."

Ronnie giggles and I can hear an identical giggle in the background.

We say goodbye and I sit on the edge of the chair. It's early. I'm hungry. Talking with the sisters has taken the edge off the shock of my stalker's appearance. But what I need more than food is to see who was at the office. I'll finally see what Wallace looks like.

My heart resumes racing and the anxiety doubles when I can't find the surveillance program on my laptop. *How did Ronnie do this?* I double-click the program and nothing happens. *Crap.* When I do manage to open it, I can't remember what to do to pull up the file I want. Ronnie said I couldn't accidentally delete any of the files, but my hands aren't doing what my brain tells them. I stop, sit back, close my eyes, and take a breath, let it out and examine the screen again, hit a few keys, and I'm successful.

The video files are in chronological order. Ronnie explained to me the surveillance system saves everything in four-hour increments. I find the file containing the video that includes the time Nan called. It starts thirty minutes before the call, so I only have to search a specific time frame.

On the video Nan is snooping around the inbox on my desk, getting coffee, fixing her makeup, talking on the phone. I'm about to open the file before, but I see the sheriff stop by her desk, tell her where he's going, and leave. A few seconds later Nan looks off camera toward the entry. The sound is weak and I can't increase the volume. What good is a surveillance system if you can't clean up the sound?

THREE

By the time I was eighteen, I'd already killed three people. All of them had tried to kill me and that experience ultimately put me on a path of loneliness and anger and loss. I was seventeen with forged high school graduation papers when I enrolled at Portland State University. I studied Criminology hoping to learn better ways to spot serial killers so I could put them out of my misery.

While I was there, I found and eliminated two targets. It seemed serial killers were following me around. I became addicted to caffeine and had a hard time sleeping. That was when my roommate had suggested a therapist for my insomnia and gave me Dr. Karen Albright's phone number. I always considered people who go to therapists as weak. I faced the situation and went intending to tell this woman as little as possible about myself, not even my real name. I ended up spilling my guts. Told her everything. Allowed her to tape the sessions and then became paranoid she would share them with the authorities. It turned out to be the best decision I've ever made in my life.

By the time I enrolled at the Police Academy and Sheriff Gray found me, I'd stopped several other killers. Sheriff Gray had taught one of my classes at the academy, and for some reason he was interested in me and hired me as a detective. I'd changed my name to Megan Carpenter and had fake credentials to get into the academy and hoped he wouldn't find me out. He must have sensed I was hiding some things, but he didn't ask questions, and I didn't tell him anything he would have to testify to in court. He was supportive, pleasant, and has been there for me when I need it. If I had to name two people most responsible for giving me a life, it would be Karen Albright and Sheriff Tony Gray. They fertilized the soil, and others since have nurtured and helped me grow.

And then I met Dan Anderson for the first time. It was during a spectacularly violent set of murders in Snow Creek, and he was possibly a witness. He was handsome, soft-spoken, accepted me without question, and for the first time I'd considered a true relationship. Not the one-night-stand kind. Afterward I went to see Dr. Albright. Relationships of the *Dan* kind scared the hell out of me and I needed her to tell me I was crazy. She didn't. I left in a little better frame of mind, less panicked, less angry, and that was the first time Wallace chose to contact me.

I've never wanted to talk to Karen Albright more than I do right now. Nan didn't tell me exactly what time Wallace was in the office and I hadn't asked. I dread calling her now to find out when he came to the office. If I show a modicum of interest, Nan will never stop the inquisition. I should look at the earlier file, but I don't want to search another several hours of video just to watch Nan snooping around the office. I know she goes through my desk if I leave it unlocked or leave anything on top. Reason tells me I'll have to call her to get a better description of Wallace than the one she's fantasizing about. Reality tells me to wait until I get my temper under control. No, I won't. I punch in her number on my phone. "Nan."

"I wondered when you would call, Detective Carpenter."

FOUR

Nan is like an alligator with prey in its jaws. I tell her the same lie I've just told Ronnie. She doesn't believe it, but I don't care. She gives me a description which to her is complete by saying "a hunk." I pressed and she added *male, youngish, extremely attractive, beard, jeans, and a hooded jacket.* She'd make a terrible detective.

Searching an hour from the end of the video file, I hit paydirt. The man she described approaches her desk at the time Nan told me, but all I see is part of his side and his back. The sound is better but not by much. It sounds like they're talking underwater, but I assume Nan tells him I'm not in and asks what he needs. He looks toward my desk and speaks so softly I can't hear what he answers. He stands there for exactly fifty-seven seconds and turns to leave revealing part of his front. I freeze the video. I guess his height at six feet. His age and weight are hard to define. He's wearing a gray Seattle hoodie sweatshirt with the hood pulled. Over that is a dark knee-length coat. A full reddish beard and dark sunglasses hide his face. I watch the video until he leaves, and although I never get a look at his face, his mannerisms seem familiar. He does know a lot about me so maybe that's why he seems familiar. Or maybe it's because he resembles Dan. Or maybe I've got Dan on my brain.

I ache for Dan, but he's in San Francisco meeting with some businesspeople interested in investing in a franchise. When I first met Dan, he was a neighbor I interviewed because of a family who had committed several murders. He looks a little like Paul Bunyan with his reddish beard and square jaw, but instead of an ax, Dan uses a chainsaw to sculpt wooden figures of every kind of wildlife. He bought a shop in Port Townsend after we started dating and branched out from wildlife to wood carvings of lighthouses and nautical things. His work has become so popular he's being approached about franchising his goods in Colorado, San Francisco, and, surprisingly, Baltimore.

He will come home a millionaire and forget all about plain old Megan Carpenter, although he swears it will never happen. Before he left on this trip, he told me he loves me and I could swear he was working up to something else. Like living together. Me. Megan Carpenter. Detective. Apartment dweller. Living with a boyfriend. I'm not beautiful. I don't wear fashion clothes or makeup or have my nails and hair done. If you look in my closet, you'll find seven dark blazers, seven pairs of slacks, two pairs of black work boots, one pair of high heels, and two or three good blouses I bought just to wear for Dan. I love him too.

And that thought brings me full circle to Wallace. Dan can never, not ever, find out who I was.

FIVE

WALLACE

Rylee is back in Port Townsend and didn't go to the Sheriff Office, so he followed at a distance and watched her driving around the neighborhood where she lives. He's known where she lives for some time and has even been inside her apartment several times when she was working. She's gotten soft over the years. And messy. It figures she'd live in this area of nondescript houses; some made into apartments; others ready to be torn down or bulldozed.

He's shaved the beard and changed into some comfortable blue jeans and a dark blue shirt that goes with the panel van. The sun is blazing overhead, so wearing dark glasses isn't suspicious at all. He's even honked at slow drivers while he followed her. Not what you would expect a serial killer to do. But then the most harmless-looking person can be the deadliest. Look at Dennis Rader, the BTK Killer, who was middle-aged, married, children, and worked for an alarm company. Or John Wayne Gacy, the Killer Clown, married, children, educated, active in the community, and performed as a clown at several children's wards in hospitals.

Serial killers are everywhere, but Washington State is rife

with them. Wallace is a needle in a haystack, like Rylee who now calls herself Megan Carpenter. Serial killers have one thing in common. They take on whatever role gains them access to their victims. Rylee is a detective. Armed. Licensed to kill. Like her, he's become a chameleon.

Rylee had gone inside the house over an hour ago. As much as he'd like to witness her panic after hearing from her secretary that "Wallace" had come for a visit, he has places to go, a body to dispose of. She'll get another call tonight and he'll watch her come. She's drawn to murder like a moth to a flame.

SIX

The apartment feels like a prison. I can't just sit here and wait for Wallace to show himself. I've watched the surveillance video time and time again, zooming in until the pixels became marbles. No luck. I've driven around the neighborhood in widening circles until I'm ashamed for my panic that has turned to rage.

At home I shower with my gun lying on the ledge with the shampoo. It's after midnight when I finally feel sleep coming on. I lie on my bed in gym shorts and long-sleeve T-shirt. My gun is tucked under my pillow, and I finally pass out but the dreams are vivid and tense.

I'm in a building, a hotel that turns into a house. No one is in the house, but I can sense I've brought someone with me. I have a knife. I'm Rylee again. I hear a child sobbing, but I can't get a direction. I'll have to search each room. I go through a door and I'm inside a child's doll house. The dolls are life-sized. A woman, a man, both dressed in formal clothes, but their hair is stiff plastic and changes color from blond, to black, to blood red. I hear the sobbing again, and the male doll's face contorts into an angry snarl. The woman doll sits on a sofa that has appeared and crosses her arm. She's indifferent to the child's cry for help. Her face goes blank and then changes into my mother.

The male doll reaches for me. He's going to strangle me. I shove the knife into his chest again and again...

I jerk awake; I feel my pulse in my temples. My gun is in my hand and I'm on my feet, sweeping the room until I hear my cell phone ringing. I sit on the edge of the bed and lay my gun on the mattress. My skull is shouting obscenities at me. I let the call go to voicemail. *If it's Dan, he deserves to be snubbed like he's doing to me. What am I thinking?* I roll across the mattress and look at the screen on my phone. It's not Dan. It's Sheriff Gray. I'm instantly curious. He wouldn't call at this late hour unless something has happened. *Wallace?* Tony didn't leave a message, but he knows I'll call as soon as I see this. I call.

"Megan?" Tony's voice eases my headache.

My heart settles a little. Tony doesn't sound like the world has ended. The dream blows away like a mist. "That's who you called, isn't it?" I can imagine him snickering. If I wasn't sarcastic, he'd think something was going on. It's going to be all right.

I'm wrong.

"I need you," Tony says.

I need you too. I need you to go away. "This isn't a social call, is it?"

"Hardly. I'm heading to the office now so meet me there."

"What have you got?" Which means, *what am I going to get?*

"I'll tell you at the office." He hangs up, and I look at the phone like it might give me a clue. It doesn't.

I look longingly at my bed, but Tony doesn't call for funsies. I slip a blazer and pair of slacks on along with a Portland State University long-sleeve T-shirt. He didn't say to dress up so I slide on my shoulder holster and an older-than-dirt pair of tennis shoes that were white in another life, and then I'm out the door.

The foyer door is not only unlocked now but is standing open. I look at my watch and see it's just after two o'clock in the morning. I've had an hour and a half of fitful sleep. When I come home someone's getting an ass-chewing. My key fob unlocks and starts the Explorer before I get to the vehicle. I'm starting to embrace technology. I climb inside and take a moment to make sure I haven't forgotten anything. Aspirin. I find a couple in the console and chew these. The bitter taste takes some of my mind off the headache.

A mile from the office Tony calls back. "Megan, forget about coming to the station. Go to Hood Canal Bridge and meet Detective Clay Osborne. You're familiar with him."

Clay is a Kitsap County sheriff's detective. I met him when Ronnie and I were working several homicides staged to look like accidental drownings. Come to think of it, I had just met Ronnie during those cases. "What's he got to do with this?"

Tony says, "It will be better if he tells you. I've only got a few of the details. After you talk to him give me a call."

"On my way," I say, and drive past the office, heading north on Highway 19. The Hood Canal Floating Bridge is the boundary between Kitsap and Jefferson Counties and the longest floating bridge in the world. In daytime traffic it can take as long as forty-five minutes to cross. This time of morning, ten minutes. With me driving it will take less than five.

Why is Tony being so mysterious? I don't like surprises. He knows that. But he's the boss and jumping back into a mystery may be just what I need to stop thinking about Wallace.

SEVEN

Emergency lights from a dozen emergency vehicles strobe and flicker through the mist coming off the Puget Sound on the far side of the Hood Canal Bridge. Somewhere on the bridge is the dividing line between Jefferson County and Kitsap County. I've never been sure where that line is but I guess it's close to the action ahead.

A figure emerges from the fog and flags me down. I pull off to the side and go to meet Detective Clay Osborne. The fog is thick as soup, and even with the lighting it's hard to see more than a few feet.

"Megan," Clay says, and gives me a hug. I allow it but only because we've been through some deep shit together.

"What's up, Clay? Sheriff Gray wouldn't tell me anything."

"Well, it's still a little confusing."

"Now I'm really confused."

"I'll show you."

Clay takes my arm and leads me into the mist. Shapes of officers emerge and disappear like ghostly figures walking through walls. I'm glad Clay knows where he's going. We stop and he points a few feet ahead of us, where a bloody object the size of a small melon is lying on the asphalt.

"Is that what I think it is, Clay?"

"It is. That's not all," he says, and once again takes my arm, leading me farther ahead. We stop maybe twenty feet from the other object.

A headless corpse is lying face down, arms and legs spread like a snow angel. Bizarre. Interesting. Crazy. But I still don't see why Tony wouldn't tell me about this. If Clay is here, it's obviously his case unless Tony knows something I don't.

I don't mean to sound uncaring, but I ask, "Why did you ask for me?"

Before Clay can answer a man wearing a yellow reflective vest, coveralls, and rubber boots comes up. Not the coroner obviously. "Detective Osborne," he says.

Clay shakes the man's hand and says, "Ernie, this is Detective Carpenter with Jefferson County."

Ernie shakes my hand distractedly, darting his eyes toward the body and away. Clay says, "Ernie is the Board of Public Works manager."

I'm confused. Why would a BPW manager be involved in this? Then it hits me like a brick in the stomach.

Ernie says, "You were right, Clay. That"—he nods toward the woman's body—"is in Kitsap County." He hooks a thumb over his shoulder. "The head's in Jefferson County."

I'm shocked. "Say that again."

Clay says, "Very inconsiderate of the killer to leave body parts in two counties, wouldn't you say, Ernie?"

Ernie nods like a bobblehead doll. He's nervous and out of his element here.

If this is a joke, it's not funny. I ask Ernie, "Are you sure about the boundaries? It's foggy. This is disturbing. Maybe you miscalculated." I may need the distraction from my stalker, but right now all I want is to crawl back in my warm bed.

"No, ma'am. Board of Public Works maintain this bridge. I know exactly where the line is between the counties. You see I have to know because of funding."

That makes sense and I hate him for it.

Clay says, "I guess we'll be working together." Then, "Not you, Ernie," and Ernie looks relieved. I know how he feels.

I say sarcastically, "Yay! The old team. Back together."

Ronnie and I worked a case with Clay last year. A cop friend of his and a detective from Clallam County were the killers. He's helped me with other homicides. One where a good friend was murdered and her daughter was marked for death because of their connection to me. A lot of people have died because of me, or by my hand.

I ask Ernie, "Did one of your guys find this?"

Clay answers my question. "Someone called Dispatch but hung up before Dispatch got their information."

He goes back to talking to Ernie, and I think word will spread like wildfire. Within the hour we'll have news crews and looky-loos gathering like a crowd watching gladiators dying. Nothing brings out the best in people like gore and death. It's cheaper than going to a concert.

Clay finishes talking to Ernie, who shuffles off into the fog. "Where's Ronnie?"

"Taking some vacation time." I don't want to explain Ronnie might be taking a job in Whatcom County. If I say it out loud, it might come true. I deflect his curiosity by asking, "How's Gabrielle doing?" Gabrielle Delmont is the daughter of my late murdered friend, Monique Delmont. Gabrielle's sister, Leanne, was an early victim of my biological father's killing spree. The connections between all the victims are hard to keep track of sometimes, but all roads lead back to me.

My father was married to another psycho, who turned out to be his accomplice. But my father also had a psycho girl-friend. I knew nothing about her until she started murdering people close to me to get my attention and lure me into a trap.

Gabrielle was a possible next victim of this bitch, and I had called on Clay to keep an eye on her. He was keeping more than an eye on her. I thought eventually I'd have to buy a wedding gift, but then I lost track.

Clay gives a lukewarm smile. "Gabrielle moved to Portland, Maine, to be with her son. They started a computer company."

"Good for her," I say, but the look on his face doesn't mirror my sentiment.

"We haven't seen each other for a while. You know how it is. Starting a business and this long-distance thing."

I have a clear idea of what he's talking about. Dan is getting his business off the ground and seems to spend more and more time away on trips. I say, "Yeah. That's too bad. I know you care for her."

Clay waves the remark away and says, "I can't blame Gabrielle for not wanting to live here anymore after what happened to her mother and her sister." He turns the conversation back to the task at hand. "The crime scene is obviously staged, but leaving body parts in two counties this close together..." His voice trails off.

"The murder took place someplace else. This looks like a dump site. Do you have an identification yet?"

Clay shakes his head "Forensics is still photographing the scene, and we're waiting for the coroner before we search the body. We're searching the area."

One of Clay's crime scene officers comes trotting up. There's no mistaking the look on his face. "Clay, you need to take a look at this. We have an ID on the body."

EIGHT

Kitsap Deputy Jesus Martinez recognized the victim as Detective Susan Dupont from Clallam County.

"Are you sure?" Clay asked.

"Ninety percent, Clay. She was in a knock-down street brawl in Port Gamble with a guy about a week ago. They beat each other up pretty good. I recognize the split on her upper lip and the cut on her forehead. She was gonna have a black eye and her nose was bleeding. But the guy got his ass handed to him and he was twice her size. It's her."

"Did you lock them up?" Clay asked.

"Both of 'em refused an ambulance and didn't want to press charges. She showed me her badge and asked me to just let it go. So, I just told them to leave. She was driving a Hummer and got in and left him standing there. He said he could get a ride. He called someone, and I went back by there about thirty minutes later and he was gone. I should have locked them up for disturbing the peace and battery."

Clay puts a hand on Martinez's shoulder. "You couldn't have known. Did you get the guy's name?"

Martinez takes a notebook from his uniform shirt pocket.

"John Duncan. He lives in Port Angeles. Said he was a cook or something. I didn't get much information because she acted anxious to get out of there."

I think, *And what you didn't know you wouldn't have to repeat to an Internal Affairs investigation. You were helping a fellow officer out. I would have done the same.*

"You couldn't have prevented this, Jesus." Clay put a hand on the man's shoulder. "Almost getting arrested should have scared them into straightening up. Hell, you scare me."

Martinez laughs. "You still got that Harley?" Clay nods. "You need to slow it down, buddy. I don't want to pick up pieces of you. This is bad enough." Martinez turns his attention back to the pieces he's referring to.

We walk a distance away while Clay calls a number and talks to someone for several minutes and then puts his phone away. "Clallam's desk sergeant says Detective Sue Dupont has been absent without permission for three days. They knew about the fight she had with Duncan and have him in custody."

"How did they know she'd been killed?"

"They didn't, but they were concerned. Officers went to talk to Duncan and arrested him for fleeing and battery on one of the officers."

"Case solved?"

"The timing sounds about right. I got the call from the Kitsap County dispatcher around midnight and called Tony as soon as I was sure this involved Jefferson County. Port Angeles in Clallam County arrested Duncan a couple of hours ago, and he's already lawyered up. They're sending a detective to make a positive identification on Dupont."

I was wrong about not wanting a part of this. An interesting case is just what I need. And to stop worrying over Ronnie's not coming back. I should just be happy for her that she's connected with her family again. She's never talked much about them except to tell me her father basically didn't approve of her choice of careers. Her mother and sister took that view as well. After all, her sister had fallen in line and went to work for the father's lucrative law firm. To be honest, I don't know what I would have chosen for a career if I'd had the opportunity to live a normal life instead of turning into a killer by my mother and biological father. I don't think I would have been a lawyer though. I can kill people but I draw the line there.

A figure emerges from the fog and Clay says, "Here's the coroner."

Kitsap's coroner is an elderly man, late sixties or seventies, overweight, long white hair, heavy full white beard, eyes that twinkle when he acknowledges Clay with a wave. He reminds me of the Jefferson County Coroner, who reminds me of Santa, except this one is wearing hospital scrubs. He goes directly to the body and then moves on to the head. Crime Scene assists him in doing his thing.

We're quiet for a moment as we watch the coroner. A police officer was murdered and that alone makes it personal. For us it emphasizes the vulnerability we try so hard to deny, try not to think about our own death, but the possibility is always the elephant in the room.

The coroner straightens up and his knees pop like gunshots. He winces as he stretches his back. I reassess his age at somewhere in his eighties. He spends a few more minutes examining the head and comes over, stripping his latex gloves off and putting them in the pocket of his scrub jacket. "I see you've brought help from Jefferson County." He reaches for my hand. "Detective Carpenter, if I'm not mistaken. I'm Doctor Reed, but just call me Sam." His grip is surprisingly strong. "I watch the news." He smiles and there are those Santa Claus eyes.

"What have you got for us, Sam?" Clay asks.

Sam shakes his head. "I guess you can rule out suicide."

He's not being insensitive. It's cop humor. We joke to deal with the ugliness and emotional hurt these types of scenes cause. From what I've experienced in my life, I should have become a comedian.

"That's easy for you to say, but we have to prove it." My attempt at cop humor.

He laughs. "I like her, Clay. My best guess, and it's just a guess, mind you, the victim's been dead for at least seventy-two hours. More or less. She was moved here. No blood at the scene. Do you have an identification?"

"Clallam County Detective Sue Dupont. They're sending someone for a positive ID."

Sam runs his fingers through his beard. "She's been beat up pretty good. The bruises and cuts on her face look to be the oldest ones. Maybe a week. There's a newer cut on the back of her head. I didn't see any cuts or holes in her clothing. I can tell you she wasn't killed where she lies, but I can tell you the head was chopped off. My guess is something heavy and sharp. It took one or more blows."

Clay asks, "Any idea when the autopsy will be?"

"Maybe later today. I still have the body your partner sent me from Port Orchard."

Another body? I've only been gone for a few days, but I see life has gone on—or ended—as usual.

"Anything else we should know, Sam?" Clay asks.

"Something metal was stuck so deep in her left eye socket that I'll have to retrieve it during the autopsy."

"The victim was in a brawl in Port Gamble a week ago according to Deputy Martinez. He recognized her because of the scar on her upper lip and the cut on her forehead. Could her facial injuries be that old?"

"Interesting." Sam shrugs and goes back to Dupont's head and motions Martinez over.

NINE

"Did Sam say he's doing an autopsy from a Port Orchard death?" I ask, and Clay nods. I hate it when someone should fill you in, but they just nod like it should explain itself. Why do I ask a question if I don't want an answer? "So, you have a partner now?" He was working solo last time I talked to him.

"Yeah. She's a transfer from Seattle. Poor Cindy. She's been here less than three months and catches something like that. But she has a lot of experience from what I gather, so she can handle it."

A female partner. Huh. Not that I'm interested. I might have been at one time before Dan and I got together. But I knew a relationship with another detective was a bad thing. They would ask too many questions that I couldn't answer, and I know Clay would notice a lie. Dan believes me and doesn't ask questions.

I have to get my mind back on the case at hand. Sam said an approximate time of death is three to five days. I'm thinking, *Dead for three days?* That means she was killed somewhere else and the body was stored. When the killer was ready, he left body parts in two counties. Which begs the questions... Why store the body? Was he waiting for the right opportunity? Is today something special in his mind?

There's an old saying. The right hand doesn't know what the left hand is doing, meaning if two or more people are working on something, none of them will know what the other is doing. Now we have three hands in the pie: Clallam, Kitsap, and Jefferson. Dumb luck? I don't believe in luck. Nor coincidence. The scene is too organized. The killer is doing this to hamper the investigation. He's knowledgeable of how police operate? Maybe he learned this from all the crime shows on television. I don't want to think another police officer is behind this, but it's happened more than once in my experience. My own biological father is an example. Detective Alex Rader was a cop. A rapist. A serial killer. I killed him to stop him. And for payback, truth be known. If this is a cop killer, I have to wonder why it's happening to me again. Do I attract sickos? Or does a higher power send them my way for my justice? In the past my brand of justice was permanent.

I'm lost in my thoughts when Clay says something that brings me back to the present and I ask him to repeat it.

"I said the murder victim in Port Orchard is a retired cop."

He's got my complete attention now. "What?"

"Retired Chief of Police Riley Denton. I don't think that case has anything to do with this case."

"Riley?" I repeat, wondering if the name can just be a coincidence.

"Riley Denton," he confirms. "The man was eighty-four and fell down a flight of stairs into his basement. It looks like he broke his neck. When paramedics got there, he still had a weak pulse so they took him to the hospital, where he was pronounced. The paramedic didn't think some of the injuries were consistent with a fall and called us."

Seeing the look I'm giving him, he adds, "Look, the guy had

a bad ticker and has been in the hospital several times. Cindy is calling it a murder. Sam's got the autopsy scheduled."

"Enemies?" I ask.

"What cop doesn't have enemies? According to Cindy we can take our pick. Cindy called his old police department and she said they didn't sound too broke up over his death."

We look at each other. Clay says, "Megan, there was no sign of a struggle. He was eighty-four and had a heart attack. We have something more serious to work on."

I ask, "When did this Port Orchard thing happen?"

"Yesterday morning."

"How did you get the call?"

"Cindy said it came in as an anonymous call."

"That's two in two days with an anonymous caller."

"Okay. Who called this one in?"

He's quiet far too long before saying, "Okay. I'll leave Cindy on the Denton death. Too bad Ronnie's on vacation. She'll be mad she missed this."

A knot forms in my stomach at the thought of Ronnie going to work for Sheriff Longbow. The thought of having to break in someone new makes me cringe. Worst-case scenario if Tony tries to give me a new partner, I'll fight it. I didn't want to work with Ronnie and look where that got me. She'll abandon me like everyone else I've ever cared about.

My real father tried to kill me. Hayden is barely talking to me. I sent my mother to prison. Dan is traveling all the time. It's like he doesn't want to be home. I know it's not true and I hate myself for being so negative. I don't want a new partner. Especially now when Wallace has come knocking like the big bad wolf and I feel like my protective wall is made of straw.

I deflect his comment. "Yeah. We should get T-shirts made." I hold my hands out making a frame with my fingers. "RONNIE'S HAVING FUN AND ALL I GOT IS THIS DISMEMBERED BODY."

He doesn't laugh. "Sorry," I say.

"No need, Megan. This stuff always makes me sick to my stomach. I don't know how you've handled some of your cases."

I stuff them in a box in the back of my mind.

TEN

"Here comes Clallam," Clay says as a beat-up, lime-green Yugo —one of those cars from the sixties that disappeared completely in a few years—comes slowly through the fog. I only know it's a Yugo because my mother had a used one when Hayden was wearing Pampers. It's the ugliest car I've ever seen and I wonder what the detective did to get this piece of junk assigned to them. But then I remember the broken-down Taurus I drove until I totaled it.

The woman who gets out of the Yugo is almost as run-down looking as the car. Mousy brown hair in a bun at the back of her head, too-big jeans, and a black-and-red flannel shirt with rolled-up sleeves, yellow Caterpillar brand boots. I guess her age as thirties or early forties. She's as tall as Clay—over six feet— and even under the baggy clothes I can tell she's sturdily built.

She sees me eying the Yugo. "Ain't she a beauty?" and sticks out a hand. "Detective Patterson. You're Megan Carpenter."

We shake hands, and when she releases mine from her "grip of death," I flex it and check for broken bones.

Clay says, "I see you're still driving that piece of crap."

Patterson feigns shock. "Watch what you say. Yogi has feelings."

"I thought you were going to restore it," he says.

"I did. It's got two new tires."

I'm starting to warm to her. "You named your car Yogi?"

"Yogi. It seemed to suit her. Let's get down to it, shall we? I see your coroner is here. My sheriff briefed me, but since you're standing around wasting oxygen, Clay, why don't you elaborate. And speak clearly."

Clay says, "Ladies first. And I use that term loosely."

Patterson chuckles and takes a notebook from her jeans and walks over to the victim, bends down, and looks the head over. She spends only seconds looking over the corpse then comes back to us.

"The head is Detective Dupont's. The corpse is about the right size." She casts a glance back in the direction of the head and grimaces. "Frankly, she was a bitch. Anyway, we have a suspect. John Duncan, white male, thirty-two. Master chef. Well educated. Master's degree in business. I haven't gotten his whole history yet, but I was told he came here from San Fran where he was fired after an altercation with his sous chef. My gal at the office is pulling the records and calling San Fran where he worked. We're also running all of Detective Dupont's arrests and sundry reports."

Clay gets on his cell phone and calls someone. "Bobby. Yeah, this is a mess. Right? Listen, I need you to pull everything you can on Sue or Susan Dupont. Yeah. The victim. She was a detective in Clallam County. Date of birth?" He looks to Patterson and she hands him her notebook. He gives Bobby the date of birth and the address in Port Angeles. "And I need anything you have on John Duncan." He reads the date of birth and address from the notebook and disconnects. To Patterson he says, "Continue."

I hold up a finger telling them to hold. I know my dispatcher can get police calls for service, but they balk at running complete record searches. So, I call Tony and he answers immediately. I briefly give him the names and information we have now and let him know Clallam Detective Patterson is with us.

Tony says, "Give Patterson the phone." I do and they exchange some unpleasantries, but she's laughing. She hands the phone back and Tony says to me, "I'll get someone in here to do your records search, but why don't I call Ronnie. You know she'd come right back."

"No," I say quickly. "Let her enjoy a few more days, Tony. If I get in over my head, I'll call her."

"It's your show, Megan. Keep your eye on Patterson. She might teach you a thing or two not to do."

I promise and disconnect. I was already going to keep an eye on her. She drives a Yugo so I doubt she can teach me much.

Patterson is saying to Clay, "You want me to do all your work, Clay? I don't know much more except she was in a fist fight with Duncan a while back and they beat each other up. She's a scrapper. Or was. In fact, she's had several excessive force complaints and is in the middle of a lawsuit."

The way she says this I can tell there's more. "What are you not saying?"

"I hate to speak ill of the dead, but, like I said, she was a bitch. I always thought there was something not right with her. She seemed to enjoy hurting people. She'd verbally abuse a suspect until they took a swing. Then she'd mop the floor with them. No pun intended, but Duncan bit off more than he could chew."

I'd sized up the victim and she didn't appear big enough to be that tough. Patterson must have read my mind.

"Kickboxer. Competed MMA. A bully. An expert marksman and a fair wrestler. Plaques and such attesting to that adorn her desk. She had T-shirts made that said, 'ASS KICKING... FREE DELIVERY.' You'd think someone in trouble for excessive force would wear white clothes and carry a Bible."

According to Patterson, Dupont was a hard-ass and had it coming just like the retired Chief of Police. I don't believe in coincidence and my gut is seldom wrong. "How long has she been missing?"

"She was gone the day of the fight, came in to work the next day, and has been gone for the last three."

"Have you searched her home?" If she has been missing for three days, it should already be in the works.

"We will now. Like I said, she's in a lot of trouble and could have gotten fired. I figured she'd just had enough, quit, and took off. I didn't want to risk breaking into her home."

"When are you going to search her home?" Clay asks.

"As soon as I got your call, I woke up a judge. I'll call again and add what we have here to the affidavit. If you two are done here, you can follow me. I have officers guarding her house, and I put crime scene tape on her office desk. We ought to do her place while we wait for the autopsy."

Oh boy! Can't wait. The last autopsy I attended, I spent most of it in the bathroom. Always-accessorized-to-the-nines Ronnie stayed for the entire thing. She has a stronger stomach. I hope I don't crap out on this one. Sheriff Gray taught me that witnessing the aftermath firsthand motivates a good detective to dig harder. I know he's right. *Damn him.*

Ernie, the Board of Public Works manager, who for some unknown reason hasn't already left, comes our way.

Clay says to me, "Let's not focus on John Duncan. Maybe the killer is someone who has knowledge of where the county boundaries are."

Or a cop. Great. That limits the suspects to hundreds of people if you count Kitsap and Jefferson County employees. All of which would have access to the same boundary details. And then there's the cursed Internet.

Ernie glances at his clipboard before speaking. "I've made a note to get you a complete list of my workers. If you like, I can get the info from Jefferson County too?"

I say, "Thank you, Ernie. You can give it to Clay."

Ernie stands with his hands on his hips and looks from one to the other of us. "I've helped with traffic fatalities, jumpers, and such. But nothing like this. I heard she was a detective from Port Angeles. It's just horrible. Catch this bastard." He turns to go and turns back. "And I hope you do to them what they did to her." He walks away, jotting notes as he goes.

Patterson says, "I take it you haven't called the Staties?"

She's referring to the state police. They will want a piece of this since it involves three counties and they have jurisdiction in each. It's good press. Unless it goes unsolved.

I say, "We can call them if we have to." And bringing more agencies into the mix will slow things down. Even if everyone shares, it will spread the case so thin the information won't be timely and we're on the clock.

Clay says, "Patterson may already have this solved, but until she gets a confession from Duncan, I want to get my people doing research. I have a couple of interns this week. One is supposed to be excellent on research. Not quite as good as Ronnie but he's thorough."

Patterson looks me over. "You've got some guts, girl. You arrested your own sheriff's cousin. He was a piece of work. No one misses him."

Ronnie and I had arrested Tony's cousin who was a detective with Clallam County. Tony wasn't happy, but he didn't care for the man.

Patterson asks me, "Ronnie Marsh isn't working with you on this?"

"She's on vacation."

"Too bad. I've heard good things about her."

Me too.

ELEVEN

We follow Patterson to her office in Port Angeles. Clay rides with me so I can show off my new Explorer SUV. He's not impressed. *Jerk.* The little Yugo has surprising speed and scoots right along leaving a cloud of exhaust behind. I snicker at her name for the car.

The Clallam County Sheriff Office is in a sprawling brick and glass building in downtown Port Angeles. A patinaed copper cupola of an old-timey courthouse is visible behind this. I've never understood the purpose of a cupola. Then again, before I became a detective, I hadn't understood the need for a courthouse. In the olden days they'd hold court in a tavern and a guilty plea would end in a hanging. I used to think finality was justice, but I've changed.

A half dozen marked sheriff SUVs and an equal number of personal vehicles—all pickup trucks of course—are parked in front of the office, and the place is lit up inside like it was dayshift and not a little after four o'clock in the morning. My own Sheriff Office will be a beehive of activity too, now that I've informed Sheriff Gray what we have. In a case like this, deputies will work extra shifts if needed.

Patterson takes us inside where a dozen pink sticky-notes are on her desktop. "Coffee before we go?" She indicates a double Bunn coffee maker behind her desk. Clay and I both pour a cup of the overheated remains. It tastes like jet fuel, but I have a feeling I'll need it. I add a lot of sugar.

Patterson has a ceramic mug that reads, PEOPLE ARE DYING TO MEET ME. The public would be offended. She reads the notes then says, "A file is being prepared for each of you. We can get them when we come back. Most of what we know is in those folders. I haven't had a chance to talk to Duncan, but we're trying to find an attorney who will come in for him. The county doesn't pay the public defender much, but I'm guessing when word gets out a detective was murdered, the sharks will be circling." She leads us to the parking lot.

"Do you have search warrants for Duncan and Dupont?" Clay asks.

"They're bringing them to Dupont's house."

Outside I look at the Yugo and I don't want to squeeze into it. It brings back memories of Mom driving, Rolland riding shot-gun, Hayden sitting on my lap in a soggy diaper while everything we own is piled on the back floor and the seat next to me.

I offer to drive, and Patterson pats the hood of Yogi affectionately before she climbs in. Like Clay, she's not too impressed with my ride. What the hell?

Heading east out of town, I notice Port Angeles is a ghost town this early in the morning. Patterson gives me directions to a residential street paralleling Marine Drive, also known as Harbor Road to the locals because it follows the northern coast of Port Angeles Harbor. Regardless of what the street is called, the town is zipped up tight.

We've been driving along stretches of single dwelling houses and have come to what appears to be a forested park on my side. "Turn left," Patterson directs. I turn but don't see a driveway until I'm right on it.

"Pull in."

The driveway is under a canopy of trees that create a tunnel into the park-like setting. Farther in, some crime scene tape is strung between the trees. The tunnel opens up and a marked Clallam County unit is parked partially blocking entry. He backs up and waves at Patterson. Ahead is a three-story plantation style home with a black Hummer parked like a monument in front.

"Ritzy, huh," Patterson says.

"Detective Dupont lived here?" Clay asks, and I gawk along with him.

"This must have cost a pretty penny."

Patterson grunts in response. I stop a good distance from the ornate double doors. There's no way a cop can afford this. "Are we waiting for Crime Scene to bring the warrant?"

Patterson opens her door and gets out. "They know I want to go through it first."

Clay and I get out but stand by the car doors. "Crime Scene?" I ask to be sure I'm not going to be charged with breaking and entering. My sheriff might frown on that.

"They'll be along shortly," Patterson assures us.

I interpret that to mean she didn't really have a search warrant yet and is waiting to call Crime Scene. I've done this on several occasions.

Patterson says to Clay, "I hear you've got an ugly one in Port Orchard."

"Yeah. We're waiting for the autopsy, but it might be an accidental or natural death. Cindy is working it," Clay says.

Patterson lifts the edge of the WELCOME mat and picks up a key. "Trusting bitch, ain't she?" She unlocks the door and gives us paper booties and gloves. "Don't touch anything. That's the deal I've got with Crime Scene. They let me look without them watching over my shoulder."

I say, "I'd like my forensic person to do a walk through with your people if it's okay? Do you know Mindy Newsom?"

"Already called her. My guys have worked with her before."

I'm not surprised Patterson knows Mindy Newsom. Mindy sees things no one else does, but maybe I'm prejudiced because she's my friend. That thought makes me realize I've not spent as much time with Mindy as I did before Ronnie came along. Mindy was the first real friend I made when I came to Jefferson County. We'd spent many an evening at the Tides in Port Townsend, having drinks and talking about anything but work or my personal history, which I didn't offer and she didn't pry.

Mindy was hired as a Forensic Specialist for the Sheriff Office where she had her own lab in the building. She was invaluable in sorting through evidence and connecting small pieces of clues. Then the budget cuts made her superfluous since we already had a Crime Scene Unit and the city fathers didn't want to pay a civilian contractor.

Now she and her husband operate a flower shop, but she still does some private consulting for Sheriff Gray and apparently for other departments as well.

Patterson pushes the door open and goes in first, announces our presence, and then motions us inside Dupont's house.

TWELVE

The inside of Detective Dupont's house is breathtaking as far as décor and disappointing as far as any signs of a crime scene or obvious clues. We spread out and I cover the home office. It's as big as my entire apartment and better furnished. One entire wall is floor-to-ceiling wood shelves filled with criminal-justice type books. The ceilings are high enough to require a rolling ladder to reach the topmost volumes. Some look to be collectors' items, leather bound, heavy. I browse the row I can see without climbing and see titles such as *Criminal Investigations* and *Washington State Law* and *Evidential Documents*. I remember being told about the last one in the police academy. It talks about typewriter and handwriting comparisons. Another book is well used and titled *Courtroom Survival: The Officer's Guide to Better Testimony*. Several other books on criminal evidence and interviewing and interrogation techniques. And one on the BTK Killer, Dennis Rader, along with several others I remember from my psych class at Portland State University having to do with serial killers. I wonder if she's read all of these. If so, we have an interest in common.

The desk is tiny and new and out of place in this huge

office, dwarfed by the tomes surrounding it. The desk calendar is open to the Thursday that Patterson said they lost contact with Dupont. She hadn't touched it for two days. Three now. Nothing is written on Thursday. I'm about to flip some pages when Patterson comes in and catches me. *Crap.*

Patterson moves beside me and slowly flips the pages. There are notations on each page but nothing telling. Nothing suspicious except for two capital letters seeming to repeat themselves on random pages. *RP and JD.*

Patterson smiles. "JD. John Duncan. RP. Roast Pig. That's where Duncan works."

The calendar dates show the initials frequently until the previous Monday, and then cease. "She showed up at work with a black eye on that Tuesday. She missed her shift at work on Thursday and Friday. The fight in Port Gamble was on Monday."

I confirm, "That's what Deputy Martinez told us."

Patterson looks like the cat that ate the canary. "Duncan was the last one to see her alive." That's not damning evidence, but it's good enough for me.

Clay comes into the office. "I didn't see any blood or signs of a fight in the kitchen or in the other rooms down here."

We're only doing a walkthrough so we can't turn the place upside down, but Patterson says, "Let's go upstairs and split up. Crime Scene will be here shortly and I want to be outside."

Patterson doesn't have a deal with Crime Scene. Clay realizes this too and says, "I'll wait out front."

"Me too." I don't know her guys and they won't cut me any slack.

"Suit yourselves. I'll be out in a minute."

Clay and I go outside and strip off the gloves and booties. The deputy guarding the scene doesn't even look our way.

"Megan, I should have warned you. Patterson doesn't do things by the book."

Me either. So?

Patterson comes outside a minute later and pulls the door to, locks it with the key, puts the key back under the mat and strips the gear off. "We didn't touch anything so no prints. We weren't inside."

Clay asks, "What *didn't you find* upstairs?"

"Nice house," she answers. "I didn't go upstairs because we were never inside. Crime Scene is here."

Headlights shine through the trees and soon two SUVs and a white panel van sporting a flower-shop logo on the side drive up to the house. Patterson goes to talk to her crime scene detectives and I meet Mindy at the van.

Mindy smiles and gives me a hug. "Hello, stranger."

I hug her. I've come a long way from the girl who doesn't like being touched by anyone. "We need to get together soon. And not like this."

"I agree. You know my number."

I think I've been chastised. "What's Patterson like to work with, Mindy?"

"She's very thorough. And smart. She sounds tough but she's really nice. You two are very much alike. You'll like her, Megan."

I already like her.

Mindy asks, "What should I pay special attention to?" She knows we've been inside because she knows me. And apparently, she knows Patterson too.

Patterson has returned and answers Mindy's question. "I don't know what you're talking about." Mindy looks at me and I say nothing, which says a lot.

Patterson tells her, "The victim is a missing detective. Her beheaded corpse is on the Hood Canal Bridge. Have you been there?"

Mindy answers, "I've talked to Sheriff Gray. I don't think I need to go to the bridge right away, although I don't suppose they will be able to keep the area locked down for much longer?"

"Saturday commuters," I point out. "They can probably get away with opening one lane each direction."

Mindy looks around the property and whistles. "Nice place. Let me know about the bridge. I'd like to see for myself."

"I'll see if Tony can send some deputies to help Kitsap out and direct traffic on the bridge," I say.

Mindy slips on a coverall and other gear. Clallam's Crime Scene Unit is geared up and waiting at the front door. She says, "I'd better go."

"If I'm not here when you're done..."

"I'll call you."

I thank her and she trots off with a camera slung across her shoulder and lines up with Crime Scene, reminding me of a SWAT entry team. Minus the flashbang and yelling.

Clay comes over. "Your Crime Scene and some deputies showed up at the bridge in case you were going to call them."

I'm embarrassed I hadn't thought to call earlier. I'm starting to slip. My personal life is casting a shadow over my duties and I can't allow that. I need to focus, but I didn't even notice Clay is holding three paper cups of coffee from a Dunkin' Donuts until he hands one to me and one to Patterson.

"Patterson's guys brought enough for us," he says. "There's donuts in their SUV if anyone wants one."

"You have them trained well," I say to Patterson.

"Won't happen in Kitsap," Clay says. "I'm lucky if they bring a good attitude."

I chuckle. Clay's a good guy and that makes me think of Dan and wonder where the hell he is right now. I excuse myself and walk away dialing Dan's number. The call goes to voice-mail. I disconnect without leaving a message. He's probably sleeping. Patterson motions us over and my phone rings. It's Dan. I hold up a finger and take the call.

"Hey, beautiful," he says. He sounds like he's just come from a deep sleep. I can feel my face do that thing it does before tears start to form. The last thing I want is to be *that* woman. Needy. Clinging. I'm disgusted. I love him. I miss him with all my heart.

"Did I wake you, Dan?" I still call him Dan, not honey or babe or handsome. Even when we're alone. I'm trying, but it's hard to let myself relax.

I can feel the smile in his voice. "Best thing that's happened to me since the last time we talked. How are you doing?"

Damn. He can feel my need. "I'm fine. Just wanted to hear your voice."

"You've got another bad one, don't you?"

This time a few tears run down my cheek and I'm glad we're not on FaceTime. Outside of Hayden, Dan is the only one that can do this to me. I don't know how I deserve him. I only know I need him. And he needs me. A feeling completely alien considering my past.

When I find my voice, I say, "Yeah. I'm in Port Angeles with Clay Osborne and a Clallam detective."

"I can come home," he offers.

I turn my back so Clay and Patterson don't see me struggle with my emotions. Why does he have to be so damn kind? "I've got it under control. You have work to do there. You need to pay my brother's wages so he won't run off somewhere." He's hired my brother to help run the store in Port Townsend. Hayden has become a dab hand at wood carving and painting the finished products.

Thinking about Hayden I realize I didn't call him during the entire time I was in Semiahmoo helping to find Ronnie's mother. I had thought about him quite often but just couldn't, or wouldn't, pick up the phone and call. I still feel like he doesn't welcome my attention, but that's me being paranoid.

Dan's quiet for a long moment until I say, "Really. You finish what you started. Not that I wouldn't welcome you home."

"Are you sure?"

"I'm sure. I've got to get back to work."

He sighs. "I worry about you, you know that, right?"

"I know."

"You still wearing that gift I got you?"

"Sure. Wearing it now," I lie.

"Good," he says. I can tell he knows I'm lying, but he's too nice of a guy to call me out.

"I love you, Megan."

"Love you, too, Dan," I say, disconnect, and run my sleeve across my eyes.

Patterson and Clay are behind me when I turn around. I don't like people sneaking up on me. I don't like not being aware when they do. I don't like flaws or weakness.

"Dan?" Clay asks.

"That was the president. He needs some advice on climate change. I told him to quit farting."

Patterson snickers. "Good one. Now, let's get our heads back in the game."

THIRTEEN

There is no reason to stay at Dupont's house so we go back to Patterson's office where we sit and look through the file she's prepared. Someone has made fresh coffee and brought donuts, and I'm on my third one for the sugar fix.

Patterson's first name is LaToya, but everyone calls her Patterson. She seems to prefer it.

Clay asks her, "Tell us again why Duncan is our killer?"

Patterson looks impatiently at him over the rim of her mug. "Okay. One more time and then there will be a quiz."

Clay laughs. "I just want to go through this one more time to be sure we haven't gotten ahead of ourselves. I'll go first. We got a call saying there's a body on the bridge. Now you."

Patterson sets her coffee down. "This started with Dupont not showing up for work. She hadn't asked for days off or called in sick. Like I told you, she's being sued for excessive force and facing disciplinary action here. I thought she could have just flown the coop."

"Yesterday the sheriff had a car go by her place. Her Hummer was there, but there was no answer. I wasn't too concerned at the time. Like I said it was kind of a break not having her in the office. But she'd been in the fight with Duncan a few days before and was trying to hide a black eye with makeup. She had some cuts on her face too. Everyone here thought she'd gotten the injuries at the gym."

I ask her, "You said she was badass. Did she ever have those kinds of injuries from sparring in the past?"

Patterson patiently says, like she was explaining something to a child, "She's a kickboxer. I figured she finally found someone who could kick her ass. There's always someone tougher. But word got around the troops and I heard about the fight in Port Gamble. I was about to run Duncan down when we got a call saying someone was climbing in an apartment window. Dispatch knew I was looking for Duncan by then and said the apartment was Duncan's."

"When we got there, I knocked and heard something inside. A deputy was at the back of the building and saw someone climbing out of the window. I kicked the door in and saw his butt before he dropped to the ground. He tried to run but my deputy caught him and there was a little tussle. Duncan lost. He had blood on his hands and more blood smeared on his blue jeans.

"In his apartment, a meat cleaver was on the floor by the window. It looked like blood and hair on the blade and handle. The hair on my arms stood up. All I could think was that he'd done something to Dupont. But all I could arrest him for at the time was for taking a swing at my deputy and scuffling on the ground. I had him brought here, but he didn't want to talk. Just kept saying he was being set up. I reminded him of the meat cleaver and that he'd struck my deputy, but he kept repeating himself. I asked him where Susan was and he looked funny. Scared maybe. I thought for sure he'd done her in. He finally said he wanted a lawyer, and I stopped asking him questions.

"So I applied for a search warrant for his place, but before I got it I was informed you had a body on the bridge. A woman tentatively ID'd as Dupont by one of your deputies."

Clay asks, "Has Duncan gotten an attorney yet?"

She shakes her head. "He won't talk to us without one and they'll tell him to keep quiet most likely. I've contacted the public defender's office, but it may be later today before someone shows up."

I ask, "Does he act like he wants to talk if he gets an attorney?" If he does, I get one out of bed and drag them down here.

"He acts scared. He's aware he's in deep doo-doo. Dupont had kicked his ass good. He's a walking bruise. I'm asking him if he knows where she is, so he had to know something was up. But one thing bothers me."

She gets up and refills her coffee. "Refills?" We both decline. She empties the last of the pot in her mug and sits again. "That's better. One thing bothers me—" She's interrupted by her desk phone ringing. She talks for a minute then informs us, "Duncan's lawyer is here. He's already in with Duncan and I know this guy. He may let us talk to him. Want to wait?"

Of course, we do. I prompt her, "You said one thing bothers you."

"Not bothers me, but my gut isn't easy. You know?" Clay and I nod. "Well, the anonymous call came a couple of hours before you found her body on the bridge. The blood on the meat cleaver looked too fresh. Duncan was in jail several hours before the body was found."

I suggest, "Duncan makes the perfect scapegoat. But let me put this in the mix. What if it wasn't Duncan climbing in the window?" Patterson raises an eyebrow. "What if someone else climbed in the window. The caller was anonymous. Maybe the caller climbed in the window to plant evidence?"

It's a stretch and I know it, but I have to look at all the angles.

Patterson's expression hardens. "Or what if no one was climbing in the window?"

I think she's agreeing with my theory until she says, "What if aliens transported the cleaver? What if he teleported down from the Enterprise?" With a glum look she says, "I'm sure he's our guy."

Everything points to Duncan. And maybe that's the problem. The anonymous call said someone was climbing in his window. When Patterson gets there he's climbing out of his window covered in blood. I understand him going out of the window, but why would he climb *in* his window in the first place when he has a key? Is it possible he came home, found the bloody cleaver, picked it up, and next thing he knows the cops are beating on his door? In my mind I see him scared and confused, he drops the cleaver and instinctively tries to get away. The look on Patterson's and Clay's faces tell me they think I need a shrink.

My phone rings. It's Mindy.

FOURTEEN

"I'm with Clay and Patterson," I say, and put it on speaker.

Mindy can't keep the excitement out of her voice. "I have something."

Clay and I look at each other, but Patterson is smiling tightly in anticipation. I'm thinking, *The room Patterson hinted at but denied looking into.* But I'm wrong.

"There was a basement of sorts. More like a root cellar. It was accessed from the back of the house. I guess they used it for a storm shelter as well. I took Patterson's guys down there and I think we found the murder scene."

"Tell me," I say.

"I'll do better than that. I just sent some pictures to your phone."

Mindy has taken quite a few pictures of the storm cellar.

"Megan, send those to me and I'll pull them up on my computer screen."

Patterson gives me her email, and after I forward Mindy's email, we gather around to view the pictures. There are no windows in the cellar, just the entry door with a set of concrete block steps leading down. The cellar is dirt floored, hardpacked by years of foot traffic so there are no shoe prints that I can see even when Patterson zooms in on the ground. There are smudges of what looks like dirt or dried blood on the concrete steps, but it's impossible to tell if they were entering or leaving. The size of the cellar is hard to determine in the pictures, but it feels spacious, like the rest of the house.

Along both side walls are deep wood slat shelves, some still containing mason jars of canned vegetables. The concrete block walls are stained from water damage, but the floor looks dry. More cement blocks are stacked against the wall at the back of the room, and one of these blocks sits on the ground in the middle of the floor. This one is covered in what looks like dried blood. The dirt floor around it has turned dark brown where it absorbed a magnitude of the blood, and the surface of this spread looks congealed.

The next photo is a close-up of the block and I see several deep indentations that scar the top. I can imagine the meat cleaver hoisted high and coming down with such force it goes through the neck and hits the concrete. A close-up photo shows something in the dried blood on the block. Hair. The same color as the victim's.

Patterson calls Mindy. "Mindy, a meat cleaver was found in our suspect's apartment. Could a large cleaver have made those marks? The blade was about eight inches."

"It's possible."

"But?"

"Well, to me it looks like something a lot heavier than a cleaver did this. Maybe an ax. One of these guys said he saw the meat cleaver and he didn't think it would match. But who knows? Don't hold me to any of this. We're collecting the block."

Patterson hands the phone to me and says, "Well, we should be able to match the cleaver to the cement block when we get the two here in the lab. The blade should be dulled.

Duncan handed us a slam dunk. Crime of passion. Or revenge."

"Thanks, Mindy. I'll be in touch." I disconnect. I'm not convinced. If Duncan was stupid enough to leave all these clues, why would he stage the body? The homicide class I took at the police academy taught that a murder falls into two categories. Organized and disorganized. I never agreed with that. It was like a weatherman saying, "Today there's a fifty percent chance of rain." It can be both. I know from experience.

"Do you know Duncan?" I ask Patterson.

"I've seen him around. I've eaten at the Roast Pig a few times. Arrogant but a great chef. The last chef they had didn't know a roast rump from a roast asshole."

Clay asks, "What's wrong, Megan?"

"Nothing." And now Patterson is looking at me.

She says, "Give."

I collect my thoughts, organize them into something that makes more sense than saying it's a gut feeling, and say, "It looks pretty pat."

Patterson gives me an askance look. "You don't think it's him."

"No. Maybe. I guess we'll wait and see if he'll talk to us."

Someone has brought ice-cold spring water and I down a bottle. Clay takes one and twists the top off. "If he doesn't talk to us, should we go back to Dupont's?"

Patterson is still a little tiffed at me for raining on her parade, but she'll get over it. "I don't see any point. Mindy and Crime Scene techs will tell us what they see."

Clay's question was really his opinion that the evidence speaks for itself. He's right. I'm sure Dupont was murdered in her cellar. I'm sure she and Duncan had been fighting and the issue was bad enough for it to come to fisticuffs. I'm sure the body parts were staged to be found, and separated by enough distance to ensure a part was in each county. Add to that the victim was from a third county. But if Duncan is that smart, he would have to know we would search her house and find the murder scene. Duncan was caught with a bloody cleaver in his apartment. And I can't get over the anonymous call saying someone climbed *in* the window.

Clay says, "Megan, he was caught red-handed."

"I get it. He panicked and tried to flee." I can't believe I'm going to say this. "But I'm not convinced. I want to hear his story."

A deputy sticks his head in the door. "The attorney wants to see you."

"You're about to get your chance," Patterson says, and walks us down a corridor to the holding cells. A uniformed deputy and an older gentleman in a tight-fitting suit are sitting at a desk in the hallway. The older guy turns and sees us and he's not as old as I first thought. His hair is white and down on his shoulders, but he looks to be no more than thirty.

"Detective Patterson," the look-alike says with a fond smile and takes her hand in both of his. "I guess breakfast is off this morning?"

Patterson says, "You're pretty intuitive for an attorney."

She introduces us. His name is Paul Chamberlain. He's met Clay in the past and they shake hands and exchange niceties. He doesn't offer to introduce himself to me. I'm the red-headed stepchild.

"I would say it's good to see you, Paul, but under the circumstances..." Clay says.

Patterson is growing impatient. "Enough chit-chat. Can we talk to him?"

"You don't waste words, do you, Toy?" Paul looks toward the closed steel door and lets out a deep breath. "He's innocent."

Patterson puts her hands on her hips. "You won't mind if we investigate this murder, will you, counselor?"

"I'm just stating what he told me, Toy."

"I told you not to call me that."

Paul grins. "Her first name is LaToya, but back when we were in school, her nickname was Toy. She doesn't want anyone to know, but I think it's a beautiful name."

"Stop," she says in a dead serious tone. "Now. Will he or won't he?"

"First tell me exactly what he's being charged with."

Patterson says, "I'm going to add some things if you don't answer my question, Paul."

"He admits he was in a fight with Detective Dupont a few days ago. He got worse than he gave from the look of him. He came home late and found one of his meat cleavers on the floor in the kitchen with blood on it. He naturally picked it up."

"Naturally," Patterson says, sarcasm dripping.

"You were forcing your way into his apartment. He didn't know it was police. He thought it was whoever had left the meat cleaver, so he tried to go through the window and the deputy outside roughed him up."

Patterson's cheeks are flaming red.

Paul backs up a step. "He's going to sue Detective Dupont for battery and causing bodily injury. He's got a pretty good case, Toy."

I ask, "Did he say where the fight with Dupont took place?"

"I guess you already know, but yes, he said it was in Port Gamble. They'd agreed to meet there to talk."

"Did he go to the hospital after the fight?" I'm hoping he did so there's a record of something at least.

"I didn't ask him. I doubt he took pictures of his own injuries, but he says there are witnesses. One is a Kitsap deputy. He shouldn't be hard to find."

"He's right, Paul." Patterson's blood pressure has settled, or she's a good actor and manipulating him. "We've talked to the deputy."

Paul spreads his hands. "No charges were filed and he wasn't arrested by the deputy. This has all been a misunderstanding. I can ask him not to press charges if he's released now. He'll probably want an apology."

"I have a few problems with doing that, Paul," Patterson says.

FIFTEEN

A deputy brings chairs into the interview room while another leads the prisoner in. John Duncan is in handcuffs hooked to belly chains and ankle cuffs. The first thing I notice is he has to duck his blond head to come through the door. He's built like an NBA player, thin and lanky and far too old to still be in the game. Maybe mid-thirties. His hair is long and looks like he wears it in a ponytail that is now down around his face. He shakes it back and I see his cheek is swollen and red. Older bruises are on both sides of his jaw. Black-and-blue circles surround his crooked nose that looks broken. Deep lines around his mouth identify him as a serious smoker. The eyes are a dirty gray with flecks of gold. I try to imagine Dupont dating this guy. The pictures I'd seen of her showed her to be a beauty.

Patterson pulls a chair up to the table and tells the deputy, "Get those off of him," indicating the cuffs and chains. The deputy looks defiant but takes them off. I can see his point. This is the guy that killed a cop. One of theirs. He would have brought Duncan in a collar and leash if he'd had one. I have no doubt the swollen cheek was the result of an "accident."

Patterson walks the deputy to the door, and I can only

imagine the ass-chewing she's giving him. She dismisses the deputy and takes a seat across the table from Duncan and his attorney. Clay and I sit against a wall. "Thanks for agreeing to talk to us, John."

Paul gives the customary caution. "Don't answer questions if I tell you not to. And you don't have to answer any question you don't want to." Duncan nods and his eyes go to each of us in turn. To me he doesn't have the look of a guilty man. He's definitely worried, but there's a tinge of anger just beneath the surface.

Patterson says, "John, I'd like to video record this conversation. Do you understand?"

I notice she avoids the word "interrogation."

Duncan nods and she says, "John, I need you to say yes or no."

"Yes. I understand you're recording everything."

I remember my therapist, Karen Albright, asking if she could tape our sessions. She promised the recordings would never be heard by anyone else. The opposite is true here. These recordings will be played for a jury if this goes to trial.

Patterson reads the Miranda Rights waiver form, and Paul passes it to Duncan. Duncan signs, hands the form and pen to Patterson, and looks directly at her. His back is stiff, but his hands are on top of the table and he's not giving clues he intends to lie. Like tapping a finger or a foot or crossing legs or arms. I can tell Patterson has noticed this as well.

He answers the preliminary questions such as name, address, date of birth, phone number without any hesitation.

She asks, "Where are you employed?"

He half smiles. "How quickly they forget. I cook for you a couple of times a month. You know where I work and what I do. You take your filet medium rare but with a lot of pink."

"Humor me, John."

"I'm the chef at the Roast Pig. Have been for three years."

"And you're an excellent chef, John. But I'm not ordering steak right now, so please stick with answers to the questions and this will go a lot faster. I'm sure you want to go home and we have a lot to do."

"Or what? You get out the—"

Paul puts his hand on Duncan's. "Just answer the questions, John. We talked about this."

Duncan takes a deep breath and lets it out. "I apologize, Detective Patterson. Ask your questions so I can go home and clean up the mess in my kitchen. Have you found out who broke in?"

I have to give Patterson credit because she doesn't even blink. "We'll get to that later. I promise to find that person. And by the way, you do make a mean filet."

I watch his expression carefully and if he's putting this on, he should get an Academy Award. Her praise makes him sit taller and the pleasure of the compliment is forming a smile on his lips before she says, "Dupont's dead."

His expression freezes and then he shakes his head in disbelief. "Susan? Dead? No... no."

"Susan Dupont is dead, John. Why did you kill her?"

Paul interrupts. "Turn the camera off. Turn it off now."

Patterson motions to the camera operator to stop recording. "Paul, you know I have to do this. Don't you?"

"What? Blindside me. Blindside my client. This interview is over. You've gone too far, Detective Patterson. Too far."

Paul starts to get up, but Duncan takes his wrist. "Sit down. I'll answer her questions."

Paul stammers objections but takes a seat. Duncan says, "Turn it all back on and tell me how she died. You think I killed her or I wouldn't be here."

Patterson speaks to Duncan, but her eyes are on Paul. "This is a murder investigation, John."

Duncan stares at the top of the table, and I see his nose

begin to run. Paul hands him a tissue, but Duncan holds it on the table. "Murdered? How can it be? We just talked a few days ago. We had a fight. I told Mr. Chamberlain." Tears puddle under his eyes and spill down his cheeks. "I can't believe it. I just can't... Susan... Dead..." Patterson hands him another tissue, but he doesn't take it. His hands cover his face and his chest hitches. "Who? Why?"

Patterson's voice softens. "That's what we're going to find out, John."

He sits up straight and sniffs. "I want to see her."

Patterson pauses for only a split second before saying, "I'll see what I can do. She's with the coroner now."

Duncan wipes at his eyes and then stares into space.

Without missing a beat, Patterson switches gears. She's asking hard questions now that the cat's out of the bag.

"You said you and Susan were in a fight. What was the fight about?"

"You must ask. I know. She's one tough lady, my Susan. You can see what she did to me. But it was my fault. Totally my fault."

"Tell me."

In a trembling voice he says, "She just wasn't ready."

"Ready for what, John?"

"I asked her to marry me."

SIXTEEN

Jefferson County Sheriff Tony Gray pauses before getting out of his truck at Moe's Café. He's called Ronnie and she agreed to meet him here. He thinks about calling Megan to let her know Ronnie will be in town, but first he wants to hear what Ronnie has to say before he gets Megan's hopes up that Ronnie is coming back to stay.

Ronnie seemed excited on the phone when he'd filled her in on what they had working. He hoped she wasn't taking the job in Whatcom County. If she did, Sheriff Longbow would be getting a good detective and he would be losing one of his best. It bothered him more than he thought it would.

He'd promised Megan he wouldn't call Ronnie, but this was serious and they could use the help. He'd find out what Ronnie wanted to say in a bit and he couldn't worry about it when there was coffee to be had. No cinnamon rolls. No double cheese and bacon burger.

His wife, Ellen, has more and more been hinting at his retirement. He's well past retirement age and has been in law enforcement for over forty years, most of them good years. He loves his job. And if he retires, he'll get to spend more time with family. But...

Heck, he's only a few pounds overweight, but Ellen calls it Dunlap Disease. She's teasing—he thinks—but she's become like a diet Nazi that doesn't care to include any of his favorite foods. If he was a rabbit, he'd be in heaven. What the hell is paleo? It sounds like something prehistoric, but cavemen ate whatever the hell they wanted if it didn't eat them first. He knows he's gone soft around the middle and he's not quite as fast as he once was, but her remarks hurt him. He's not washed up. He can still go out with his troops and help make a difference. He loves his job and his people, but he loves his wife more than he loves donuts and bread and sugar. He releases a soft sigh.

He was never this negative. Now his mind is going down a path, thinking his two best detectives might go somewhere else to work. They were temporarily deputized by the Sheriff Longbow in Whatcom County to assist in finding Ronnie's kidnapped mother, and he's not surprised they were the ones to find her. Longbow's detective was crooked and a murderer. He thinks, *When one of ours turns bad, it looks bad on all of us.*

Megan had come back from Whatcom County and he'd put her right to work, but he wasn't sure she'd stay. He sure had needed both of them this last week, what with the discovery of a body washed up on Indian Island, a cop no less, a state trooper. The death was ruled a boating accident after the state police investigation. That case should have been Jefferson County's, but with Megan and Ronnie gone he was glad to let state police handle it.

And now Megan informed him of a suspicious death in Port Orchard. Also a cop. Retired, but nonetheless a cop.

When he'd taken Ronnie on as a reserve deputy, he had very little hope she would remain in law enforcement. She came from a wealthy background and he hadn't told her, but he'd gotten a call from her father wanting him to wash her out of the program. Her father had told him Ronnie could "do something better with her life." That had decided him to keep her. So, he'd assigned her to Megan because he wanted to see how she'd do working with someone of the opposite personality. He knew he was throwing Ronnie in the deep end, but he figured it would toughen her up. And if she quit, it would be her own doing and not her father's machinations.

Ronnie was book-smart, top of her class at the academy, a never-stray-from-the-book type. Megan was a smart aleck, rarely went by the book, was not afraid to get her nails dirty or fight. Megan wore appropriate clothes and boots to work. Ronnie, on the other hand, dressed like a fashion model while assigned to plainclothes detectives. But he'd seen something in her right away. He'd seen the same thing in Megan, and the decision to hire and mentor her had turned out to be the best decision he'd ever made. Both were tough, hard workers, intuitive. Where Megan would sometimes recklessly charge ahead, Ronnie was the voice of caution and finder of information.

The front door of the café opens and Moe sticks his head out. "Coming or going?"

Tony waves at Moe, goes in, and sits at his usual table. Most of the tourists are still asleep at two in the morning, but there are a few at the other tables, chatting, smiling, some arguing or giving and receiving the cold silence of disagreement, and Moe nods at him as he pours a coffee and brings it to his table.

"Your usual, Sheriff Gray?" Moe asks.

"Just coffee this morning, Moe," he answers, and sighs.

"Fresh cinnamon rolls? I just took them out of the oven."

"Sounds wonderful but I'd better stick with coffee for now."

Moe puts a sad face on. "Your wife still got you on the paleo diet?"

"I'm limited to one grass-fed hamburger a week, no bun.

Salad, fruit, nuts, no donuts or fried anything, and a big helping of guilt and fat-shaming."

Moe laughs. "You're a riot, Sheriff."

One of the couples gets Moe's attention and he hurries off to wait on them, leaving Tony to ruminate on life. He's been doing a lot of that lately and it's the same old thing.

Too many tourists. Too many drunks and fights and wrecks. This was a happy and safe place before the county councils advertising campaign. "Visit Jefferson County. Your new home."

The population was growing everywhere and Jefferson County's ad campaign was bringing in its fair share of tourists and new residents.

More people meant more problems, more stretching of already overburdened resources. Deputies were leaving or retiring faster than they could be hired and trained. That was another reason he couldn't afford to lose Megan or Ronnie, or both. He didn't want to dwell on it like a sore tooth, but it was troubling. He was getting old. He wanted a cinnamon roll. He wanted a hamburger with bacon and cheese and onion rings. Bottomless pit for a stomach.

The job had changed so much over the years. First, policemen started being arrested for murders, and now policemen were increasingly being murdered. Sheriff Longbow was replacing one of his detectives who had been complicit in the kidnapping Ronnie and Megan had just worked. He was not only a murderer, but a dark stain on the reputation of all law enforcement. A life sentence was too good for him. This year alone three more officers in Tacoma and one in Auburn were charged with murder. Last year Megan and Ronnie had arrested Tony's cousin—a detective in Clallam County—for rape and murder, and he hoped the bastard would never see the outside of a prison.

He worried that if he was this disaffected by the changes in law enforcement, how long would it be before Ronnie and

Megan sickened of the job? He wouldn't blame them if they transferred somewhere new. Or left the job entirely. It made him sick that they'd never had a chance to see the good side of being a cop. Always the bad. And it was just getting worse. Those girls were too good to keep working for the wages the county pays. They could get a job in any large city and make twice the money with less work and worry. The irony was he'd put them together with no real belief they'd ever get along, but they'd grown on each other and become a team. He'd never known Megan, a self-proclaimed loner, to take to someone like she had done with Ronnie. *If Ronnie goes, Megan goes too. Maybe I will retire.*

SEVENTEEN

An earthquake couldn't have shaken us any more than Duncan's revelation. The items Duncan had on his person when he was taken into custody are spread on the table in front of us. Patterson opens a small silk-lined box and inside is a gold engagement ring with at least a two-carat diamond.

Patterson is robbed of speech. Her slam-dunk case has just grown wings. Duncan may grow wings soon and fly away from here. But we're not done. Duncan wasn't just rejected by Dupont, she humiliated him and beat him severely. Her murder could be a crime of passion. He admitted he lost his temper and struck her. He could have easily gone to her house, continued the confrontation, and then killed her. But we need evidence to prove that.

I ask, "John, where did you buy the ring? Can you provide any witness that you bought the ring for Susan?"

His hope deflates. "I've got the receipt. I didn't tell anyone I was going to ask her because I was afraid she'd say no. I don't have any close friends so I don't have a witness."

Clay speaks for us all. "Mr. Duncan, John, you know you'll

be kept in custody a while longer while we investigate and make a decision."

Duncan looks relieved. "You believe me. Don't you." It's not a question. "You don't have to answer. I want to help in any way I can. But please let me see her." His face starts to turn ugly, but he sucks the emotion back and watches us. Paul doesn't interrupt again. He's satisfied his client has exonerated himself. To tell the truth, I'm leaning that way myself.

Patterson puts the ring box back in the property envelope and says, "It may not be up to us, John. But I'll do what I can." It's a lie. He won't want to see the body even if she could let him view it.

I attended a police conference on the east coast once where a detective there told us about a case he'd worked. The suspect cut his wife into pieces and spread them over five counties. When he was caught, he cried and asked if there would be an open casket viewing at the funeral. The detective thought it was funny. I didn't think it was in the slightest bit funny.

"Do you promise, Detective Patterson?"

"Pinky swear," she says, and Duncan tries to smile, but it falls flat.

"I love her. I knew it from the first time I saw her. She was giving one of my dishwashers a grilling at the restaurant over some silverware she said was dirty. I tried to cool her down and she threatened to arrest me." He smiles at the memory. "Got handcuffs out and everything." He pauses a moment. "I said to her, 'How about a nice meal on the house.' She said, 'Are you trying to bribe me?' and I said 'Yes.' She laughed and it was the most beautiful thing I'd ever heard. I fell in love right there." Tears well in his eyes. "I'll never hear her laugh again. Promise me you'll find the person who did this. It's what she'd want."

It will be my life's mission. I've seen this kind of hurt on other victims. Now I'm convinced John Duncan is a victim.

Patterson looks at Clay and then me for other questions we

might have. I say, "That was quite a fight you two had in Port Gamble."

"To be totally up front, I got really pissed at the way she was acting when I asked her," Duncan says. "She didn't just say no, she told me to shove the ring... you know where. She said she'd never marry a loser like me."

"How did that make you feel?" I ask.

"I wanted to die. I was humiliated. I mean, she comes from money. I come from dirt poor. She has a big house. Have you seen it?"

I nod but say nothing.

"I live in a shitty apartment. I've got a little money saved, but it took almost everything I had to buy the ring. I thought it would show her how serious I am. But she seemed to be expecting me to propose and had her answer ready."

I say, "I'd be mad too. You hit her and I can't blame you."

"It wasn't like that. She knocked the ring out of my hand and it almost went down a storm drain. I picked it up and tried to put it in her hand. When I touched her, she decked me. She just kept hitting me and kicking me." Duncan stands and pulls up his shirt. There are bruises on his stomach and rib cage turning yellow as they fade. He pulls a pants leg up and there are more bruises on his calf. "I tried to get her to stop, and when she wouldn't I hit her. I didn't mean to hurt her. I never hit a woman in my life." His hands go to his face. "Oh God! Oh God. I did that. I hate myself. And now... And now..." He leans forward and hangs his head. "What have I done? Did I cause this?"

Patterson jumps on his words. "Did you? Did you kill her?"

Duncan looks Patterson in the eyes. "I did not kill Susie. I would never. No matter what she did to me. You've got to believe me, Detective Patterson. I'd trade my life for hers if I could bring her back."

Patterson never breaks eye contact. "She's dead, John. You

have to tell the truth. If you ever loved her, you owe her that. You know that, don't you?"

His face contorts into a mask of deep hurt and rage. "I know she's dead, you bitch. Why are you doing this to me? Just put me in jail. I deserve it. I failed her. I should have protected her. I wasn't there when she needed me. I'm to blame somehow. Things like that don't happen to people like Susie."

Paul says, "If you're finished, Toy, I'd like a few minutes with alone with my client."

"Sure. Take as long as you want. You have ten minutes."

We get up and go into the hallway. Clay's phone chimes with a text. He shows it to Patterson and then me. The autopsy is about to begin. Patterson goes back to the interview room and calls the deputy over.

"Give them ten more minutes and then put Duncan up. Bring him something to eat and drink and I better not see any more marks on him. Understand?"

The deputy knows when to shut up and just nods.

We go back to her office and she asks, "What do you think?"

"He's very convincing," I say.

She pauses. "Before we go to the autopsy, I have a question for you both. Do either of you think Kim Kardashian's are real?"

I can't be mad at this woman.

EIGHTEEN

We drove to the Hood Canal Bridge where Clay picked up his car. Then the three of us caravanned to the Kitsap County Morgue in Bremerton. I'm surprised at the modern style of the building every time I've had the unfortunate circumstance of being here. Jefferson County still has a serious-looking brick building that resembles a reformatory with a basketball court on the grounds. This one is beautiful and looks more like a tourist attraction than a place where bodies are dissected.

Clay punches in a code on the keypad, the lock buzzes, and we enter. Clay leads us past a door marked PRIVATE and says, "That's cold storage."

Got it.

At the end of the hallway is a door marked AUTOPSY ROOM. The last autopsy I attended had the bathrooms in the basement. I'd spent a little time in there during the autopsy. The door beside the autopsy room is a unisex bathroom. *Thank you, Lord.*

Clay knocks and a man's voice says, "Just a minute." The door is opened for us by a thirty-something ebony-skinned giant. He makes Shaq look like a midget, and he smothers my hand with his own. "You must be Megan Carpenter. Sam told me you'd be coming. So glad to finally meet you. Where's your partner?"

"Do you mean Detective Marsh?"

"Who else?" the gentle giant responds with a smile. So Ronnie has another admirer. Good for her. Yay.

We enter a room where the shelves are stocked with surgical gowns, gloves, booties, caps, and full-on Hazmat-looking gear. We dress out, and the giant leads us into the autopsy room.

He says to me, "My name is Cedric. Detective Carpenter, if you feel sick, I will give you a sick bag to take with you."

My reputation for vomiting at autopsies has preceded me. I shake my head. "Not necessary." I notice he brings one with us anyway.

I've killed with a knife and a gun; done horrible things to another human being and never felt squeamish. But here, watching the body opened, the smell of innards, hearing the squishing sound an organ makes when it is cut free and dropped onto a weight scale just sucks the dignity out of the room.

Patterson and Clay stand to one side to get a good view of the procedure. I stand a little farther behind them. Laid out on one of the stainless-steel tables is the naked body of a frail elderly man. The blood has already been washed from his body, and the distinctive Y-incision has been roughly stitched closed. This autopsy is at an end, but the preternatural stillness in the room makes me uneasy. The body remains but the spirit is free. My take on death is if a person dies a natural, expected death, the spirit is at peace. The ones who are murdered are angry. When I'm dead I'm going to be really pissed off.

Sam motions us over to the table. "Riley Denton," he says. The retired Chief of Police. Sam turns the body's head completely to one side. "Broken bones in the neck."

Clay looks satisfied. "From the fall down the stairs, right?"

"No. His neck was twisted until the C1 vertebrae was separated from the C2."

Patterson whistles softly. "Commando style."

Sam says, "Exactly. His head was twisted to each side. There are bone fragments on the X-ray. You can break your neck in a fall but not like this."

Patterson's phone rings and she moves away to talk.

"Instantaneous?" I ask.

"Unfortunately, no. The break paralyzes the subject and stops their breathing. Oxygen doesn't circulate in the brain. If he was fortunate, he was unconscious for the two or three minutes it would have taken to suffocate."

Like drowning slowly in a room full of oxygen.

"He has other injuries you'd expect with a fall. Scrapes, contusions on knees, bruises on upper chest, and swelling with some bleeding on the back of his head. I would say he probably fell down the stairs, but there is something else that makes me think it was deliberate." Sam turns Denton's hands over showing the palms.

"What are we looking at, Sam?" Clay asks.

Sam manipulates the pads of the palms. "He has deep tissue bruising on his palms. The cut on the back of the head might not be from the fall. It looks like he was defending himself from a blow and was then struck on the back of the head. Your partner is on to something, Clay."

"So the cause of death was... what?" Clay asks.

Sam sighs. "Massive coronary and broken neck. With the broken neck he would have died in just a few minutes. All of this combined may have been the reason for the coronary. For all we know he was beaten and thrown down the stairs. Who called the police?"

Clay gives me a look before saying, "Anonymous call, Sam."

"It would be nice to know if the body was moved." He tells

Cedric to take the victim back to the cooler and prepare Dupont.

Cedric takes the body away, and a chill runs up my spine as an unbidden thought runs through my mind. The whiteboard behind the table gives the victim's name. Riley. When I was a hunter of serial killers, my name was spelled R-Y-L-E-E. Not many people knew that. Probably a coincidence. But I can see me lying on the table, the top of my skull removed, my chest cut open and spread wide.

I'm not a hunter any longer. I gave that life up when I stopped being Rylee and became a cop. Megan has to bring killers to justice the legal way. Rylee brought the killer to an end. I shove the thoughts away.

What's getting into me lately? I'm almost certain the brooding thoughts of my past have been brought on by the visit to prison to see my mother. I've tried hard not to think about her. About what she did to Hayden. What she did to me.

Or maybe the reappearance of my long-lost brother Hayden has set this in motion. His return was a complete surprise after being incommunicado for so many years. The reunion started off rough, but now that he works with Dan, it has smoothed out. I've introduced him as my brother, and Hayden has somehow obtained or created a new driver's license and birth certificate showing his name as Hayden Carpenter. It's as good a name as any. We've both gone by so many names it's hard to keep them all straight.

My mother and I still share a secret. Hayden and I are the blood children of a serial killer. Hayden is still under the impression our real father was a war hero. I've never corrected him and apparently my murdering mother hasn't either.

Cedric comes back rolling a gurney with Susan Dupont's body. She's naked now. Her head is on the gurney and placed where it would be if it was still attached. Clay steps forward to help Cedric transfer the body to the autopsy table, but Cedric easily moves it and positions the body feet down where there is an industrial steel sink. The head rolls to the side and the eyes face my way. One eye is a black hole.

A sick feeling forms in the pit of my stomach and I'm tempted to take the sick bag Cedric had offered, but I know I'm just overwhelmed by this situation. This is the second cop in as many days and that fact isn't lost on any of us. My gut tells me we have a cop killer. A serial cop killer. Are there connections between the two victims, other than their choice of careers? If so, who else shares the connection? As far as I can tell, these two worked in different states before coming to Washington State. Both ran afoul of the same killer—or killers. I don't know much more than that right now; except I know there will be more. Washington State is a breeding ground for those types of mentally deficient animals.

Dr. Karen Albright, my therapist, once told me society has tried to come up with a global definition of serial murder. She said you can't define something as intangible as evil. And she shared something else with me that has bearing on my current thoughts that the victims are somehow connected. She said, "Why should all the victims of serial killers be strangers? Why should killers only operate alone or in pairs? To understand the serial mind, you have to think outside the box that current law enforcement theory has built. When we restrict our speculations, we skew the data and create a false definition. It's like theorizing that 'only bad dogs bite.'"

One thing is for certain. Serial killers don't stop. The first taste of blood leads to the next and the next. Who will be next?

NINETEEN

It's becoming hard to focus on what's before me and leave speculation behind, but I'm pulled back when Sam speaks into the mic suspended over the table, giving the date, time, victim's name and description, and the names of those present. He then says, "Crime Scene have already been here and have all the photos and clothing and other items. The autopsy is filmed and recorded so I can give you a copy if you like."

Great! Now I won't have to rent *The Ted Bundy Story* on Hulu.

Sam says, "She's been dead for forty-eight to seventy-two hours. I'm basing this on the condition of the body and the police report saying no one had contact with her for that period of time. After the murder she was kept somewhere cool and moist."

He sees us giving him a curious look. "I was just showing off. Actually, I was told by Detective Patterson's people the victim was killed in her root cellar, so I'm guessing she was kept there until she was dumped on the bridge."

I have to ask, "Was she...? You know... before?"

"She was dead before her head was removed," he assures

me. "The weapon used to take the head off was something heavy and sharp. You said the suspect was a chef."

Patterson nods.

"And you have a meat cleaver from his home."

"We do."

"Did you find any other heavy-bladed weapons? A machete or an ax perhaps? Or was an ax found on her land?"

Now Patterson shakes her head. "We didn't find anything like an ax."

Sam points out the clean-looking cut on the neck. "A knife, even a large one like a chef would use, wouldn't have been able to make those deep cuts. I count at least two blows, maybe more. It's not as easy to behead someone as people think."

"She might have had an ax. She lived on a large, wooded lot," I say.

Sam pauses and thinks. "The weapon was extremely sharp, and judging by the depth of the first blow, I doubt it would have been a meat cleaver or even a machete. The first blow severed the epiglottis"—he touches the bony prominence on the front of his neck—"but not the cervical vertebrae. An ax is your best bet."

I ask, "Cause of death?"

"The cause of death is a toss-up. Beheading is number one, but I told you something was shoved into one eye socket."

He did.

"A coiled wire was shoved through the left eye socket into her brain. She could have died from the brain injury, but it would have taken longer. It's possible the wire was twisted in and then her head was hacked off. In any case I think she was unconscious while this was happening. The back of her skull was caved in. She may not have felt a thing."

A memory is triggered and I feel a chill but shake it off and listen to Sam.

Sam continues, "Her torso still shows healing bruises from the fist fight you say she had with this guy Duncan."

We thank Sam and I escape from the room, peel my Tyvek suit and gear off, and throw it in a Hazardous Waste container. The sun has come up while we were inside. Taking several deep breaths of outside air, I let the morning sun burn the sweat from my face and neck. I'm nauseated, but I didn't need the doggy bag Cedric had left within reach in the autopsy room.

Clay catches up with me. "Patterson will be out shortly. Are you okay?"

"Why wouldn't I be? Two dead cops. One of them beheaded and a wire shoved through her eye. Happens every day." I immediately regret the sharpness. "Sorry. I hate these things."

"This is the part of the job I hate too. Always makes me a little queasy," he says, and puts a bottle of ice-cold spring water in my hands. "Splash a little on your face. It helps."

I do and he's right. "Thanks, Clay." My skin feels like it's on fire, and fingers of heat crawl up my spine and into my skull. The autopsy itself, watching a body dismembered with the cool calm of a professional, is disgusting but is only part of my unease. Goose bumps cover me. I'm all too familiar with the sharpened wire Sam had removed from Dupont's skull. I'd broken one exactly like that from a box spring mattress where my mother and I were being held captive and shoved it into my biological father's eye before I shot him to death with his own gun. The gun he intended to kill me and my mother with. Not only did I shoot him in the chest, I pulled his pants down and blew his manhood off with two more shots. Asshole.

I'd killed Alex Rader because I thought he'd killed Rolland and taken my mother prisoner—but I was wrong. Wrong about so many things. My mom had been an accomplice to other murders. I was only seventeen when she'd let him take me prisoner, hoping that in doing so he'd truly release her. Bitch. I should have let her die when he had her. But she's my mother. As far as I knew then, she and Hayden were my only living family. Then I found she had a sister, Ginger, living in Idaho. Her sister was a lying manipulating bitch like my mother. It must run in the gene pool because I've become a master liar and manipulator myself.

Clay is saying something that pulls me back from my rumination. "I'm sorry," I say.

Patterson has come outside and is standing looking at me like I'm a smear on a slide. "Are you okay?"

"I'm fine," I say. I'm not. "What are we doing next?"

Clay says, "If it's all right with both of you, I'm going to instruct my Crime Scene people to let Jefferson County take all the evidence they collect on the bridge." To Patterson, "Megan has a good rapport with the crime lab for Jefferson County. She can get things faster than we can."

Patterson nods. "If your lab will take our evidence, I'll do the same. Is that okay, Megan?"

"Sure," I say, and hope I'm not overstepping. I've got to call Tony and the lab to get their approval, but I'm almost sure Marley will prefer to look at everything instead of piecemeal.

Clay has a brief conversation by phone, and then says, "My sheriff agrees."

I ask Patterson, "What was the call about? You know, when we first got in here."

"That was my Crime Scene guy. He said the meat cleaver we found at Duncan's only had animal blood on it. The blade wasn't dull. He's going over the cement block now. The blood on it matches Dupont. He's hoping to find traces of metal from the weapon."

"I'll call and make arrangements for all the labs," I say.

Maybe I've just made this case exponentially more difficult. But given the circumstances it's the right call. I'll have to call Tony and I need to call Ronnie to have her light a fire under

Marley Yang at our lab. I haven't spoken to Marley since before Ronnie and I went to her parents' house on Cougar Point to find her mother. I wonder if Ronnie has called to tell him her news. Those two were getting pretty serious and I figured any day she'd either come to work wearing a ring or have kicked him to the curb. In which case Marley might not want to help me.

TWENTY

The sun is unusually warm when I leave the morgue heading for the Sheriff's Office. The meat cleaver has been ruled out as the murder weapon. Patterson will have no choice but to release Duncan.

There's nothing I can do until the evidence is sent to the lab and fingerprints, blood, and DNA can be compared, and even then it may not tell me anything helpful. Whoever the killer is has the luck of the Irish or they're very methodical.

Clay will try to find someone who witnessed the fight on the street in Port Gamble just to tie that end up tight. Good luck with that. Patterson has deputies doing a door-to-door canvass of Duncan's apartment building to try to find the anonymous caller. She is also checking to see if Dupont had any visitors or deliveries, but the house is surrounded by a forest of trees so I won't hold my breath. Patterson is new to me. Maybe she's too much like me in her willingness to skip a few legalities.

Clay said he will bring Cindy, his new partner, in on this investigation now that the two cases have enough similarities to link them.

I have nothing but a head. I'm glad I'm working on this, but this has opened doors to memories I've tried so very hard to stuff down deep.

I call Sheriff Gray, who is waiting for an update. He answers on the first ring.

"Megan. Where are you?"

"I'm on my way in. I'll fill you in when I get there, but I need to ask something."

"Shoot."

"This murder happened in Port Angeles. The only suspect we had has an apartment there."

"You said you 'had' a suspect."

"Patterson likes him for the Dupont murder, but he's not a suspect in my view anymore." I hear a snicker and wonder what that's about. "We don't want to spread the evidence over three counties' labs. We've decided to have everything taken to Marley Yang in our lab, if it's okay with you?"

"Have you called Marley?"

"Not yet."

I don't know why I'm surprised when Tony says, "Well, I have. He's agreed and is expecting your call."

"Thanks, Tony. That's a big help. And Mindy is working on this, but she's on Clallam County's payroll. We might need her here."

"I've called Mindy," he says. Sometimes I forget how long Tony has been on the job and that he was a top-notch detective before becoming sheriff. "Have you called state police, Megan? I've waited to do that."

Smart. He knows me. "We don't need them yet. I might need some help with records and things like that."

"Ronnie should be here."

No. She shouldn't. Wallace is here and I don't want her near him. But I'll have to tell her at some point. "I'll think about it."

"Megan, she won't take the job in Whatcom if that's what

you're worried about. Don't you think she'd love to get involved in this?"

"You're right, Tony. But let me see what I get into today." *I'll wait as long as I can to drag Ronnie into this.*

"The bridge is open to traffic, Megan."

"Okay."

"When you come in we need to talk a little more. I'm sorry I had to pull you out of bed. I know you hadn't been home long."

"No, you're not," I say, and hear him chuckle.

My thoughts drift back to my own problem. Namely Wallace. He knows me. Knows how important my cases are to me. He's as much as said so in his emails. Is he involved or just watching me?

My phone rings before I can call Marley to thank him. It's Mindy.

"Megan. Just wanted to tell you Clallam Crime Scene techs let me take the desk calendar from Dupont's home office. It was open to this last Thursday."

As if I didn't know, I tell her, "Patterson says that was the last day anyone had with her."

"Well, I randomly checked some calendar pages going back a month and there were several initials on pages. Does JD or RP mean anything?"

"Our suspect was John Duncan. He is a chef at the Roast Pig and Dupont had been dating him. But we have all but dismissed him as a suspect at this point. The meat cleaver Patterson found in his apartment had blood on the blade, but it was an animal's blood according to her Crime Scene techs."

"I've talked to them. I think the weapon was something heavier anyway. Like an ax. Do you believe he's innocent?"

"I do, but I think he knows more than he's saying. Mindy, he's so pitiful I can't see him killing her."

"I see. Well, I looked ahead on the calendar like I said and there are several pages missing."

I had only checked from Thursday until today, Saturday. I ask, "What pages?"

"This coming Monday until Sunday have been torn out." An entire week. "I wouldn't have noticed except I saw a scrap of paper in the binding area."

Of course. Another mind lapse on my part.

She says, "I'll run an ESDA on it."

I have no idea what she's talking about.

"Sorry," she says. "That's an Electrostatic Detection Apparatus."

"Right." I still have no idea what she's talking about.

"I recently went to a Questioned Document School at the Secret Service Academy in Georgia. I haven't had much use for the training yet with all this digital crap. No one writes anymore, but this is right down my alley"

"So this ESDA does what?"

Mindy takes a breath.

"I can take a blank page from the desk calendar and use the machine to lift indentations of the words written on the pages above it," she says. "Dupont used a ballpoint pen and so I can find the writing ten to twenty pages deep."

"That's crazy," I say.

"Yeah. I bought one a while back and I'm anxious to use it. I've told Clallam Crime Scene techs to keep an eye out for other paper documents. Notepads, envelopes, bills, that sort of stuff."

TWENTY-ONE

When I get to the office, I see Nan has come in early. The top of my desk looks like a suicide bomber exploded on it.

"Coffee, Megan?" Tony asks.

"Thanks, Tony." My phone dings with an email from Patterson.

I open the email on my desk laptop and pull photos up. Tony comes around the desk to see what I have on the computer screen, and I advance through the photos slowly.

"That's John Duncan," I say. The picture shows a scowling man in his mid-thirties. The gray eyes are creepy and set deep into his lined face. I go through the other pics and a new message pops up. Mindy has sent a file. Tony examines each picture carefully, only stopping me to clarify what he's looking at.

Nan is glaring across the room and I'm sure she has ants in her pants to talk to me about Wallace. Not gonna happen.

Tony closes the lid on my laptop and pulls a chair around facing me. "Megan, we need to get something straight about Ronnie. What's your problem with calling her? Is it because you don't want things to change here? Or is it because of this Wallace character?"

I swear he's psychic sometimes. "Not at all," I lie.

"Then you won't mind that I've called her and she's in Port Townsend."

I can feel tightness in my chest. I've been awake a long time and had more than several cups of coffee. That must be it. I want to say, *You don't trust me to handle this alone*, but I find my mouth saying, "Thanks, Tony."

"Megan, she's not taking the job Sheriff Longbow offered her. I called him. Woke him up in fact. Told him I'd start bussing our troublemakers and homeless to Blaine if he kept trying to filch my best people."

I'm one of his best people? My eyes moisten and I say, "You're stuck with me, Tony."

He says, "You think I'm talking about you?"

"Jerk."

"She'll meet you at Moe's. You need to go eat and get your eyes off this for a bit. And, Megan, Nan is bursting at the seams wanting to know who Wallace is. It's your business, but I'm just preparing you."

So that's why my desk is messier than usual.

Tony turns to go back to his office and I put a hand on his shoulder. "Thanks, Tony. I mean it. I'd give you a kiss, but your wife would flatten me."

"She probably thinks kisses are fattening," he mutters, and I run for the door before Nan can catch me. Outside I wipe the moisture out of my eyes so I can see to drive.

* * *

Something smells wonderful when I get out of the car at Moe's. He's wiping a table when I come in.

"Detective Carpenter. Have a seat. Your usual?"

By *usual* he means whatever he feels like giving me, so I just say, "The usual." Moe doesn't charge me for meals even though I've tried to pay. So, I leave a tip equal to the price of the meal.

Minutes later Moe sets a platter of fried eggs, bacon, and toast in front of me. I smell fresh bread. "Do you make your own bread now?"

"You got a problem with that, detective?" he says and chuckles. It's a game we started playing, so I take my handcuffs from my belt, and set them on the table with a clink. Moe raises his hands and pretends to run away.

"Are you arresting Moe again?"

The voice comes from behind me. Ronnie has snuck up on me again.

"Quit doing that."

"I think you're getting deaf in your old age," she says, and takes a seat across from me. "My usual, Moe."

"I'm only a couple of years older than you, Ronnie. But I'm wiser than my years."

She looks concerned. "How are you, Megan?"

"You didn't have to come, Ronnie. I could have handled this."

"Of course, you could have. But I'm here. Besides, I've had my fill of family time. I think I liked it better when my parents were fighting."

"Change is hard." I know. I'm struggling with the changes I've made in my life. I don't want to need anyone. When I was alone, I didn't have to worry about anyone else. I'd lost all I could lose. Now I love so many people and they've changed my world and opened me up to new feelings and experiences. Some good. Some bad.

When I was alone most people were bad or very capable of it. So, I felt no guilt using, manipulating, and, sometimes, killing them. I'm too young to have PTSD, but my therapist has hinted at it being something I'll have to deal with eventually. I don't want to go back in therapy. I always leave feeling like shit. It takes a few days to clear the things I've told her out of my head and accept her kind way of pushing me into considering why these things still bother me. Karen is the only person who knows how far I've come.

"Megan," Ronnie says. "You were somewhere else."

Moe brings her a Greek yogurt and a small bowl of blueberries. I look at her minuscule meal and then at my platter of heavenly grease.

"Eat up, partner. We have a lot of catching up to do." I won't tell her about Wallace until, and if, I have to.

TWENTY-TWO

Ronnie slides beside me in the booth.

"Here's what I've found so far," she says, firing up her tablet and pulling up a shitstorm of records.

"Wiki version please," I say.

She nods and goes to a full-screen photograph of a man in a blue police uniform with what must be premature white hair. He could be a stand-in for Anderson Cooper, the cable TV news guy. She flips to another photo. This one not so pleasant. The face is flattened, making the nose, mouth, and eyes into slits in a wide face. He's lying face up on a steel table.

Autopsy photo.

The hair is snowy white, but it would take a DNA match to identify this one as the first one.

"I assume this is the same man as in the first picture."

"Detective Robert Spradley from Idaho. Five years ago, he was found stabbed to death in his home. No suspect. I don't think the PD worked too hard to find the killer. There was a lot of evidence in his house pointing to his being a predator who was into child porn and bondage. Some of his victims were under five years old."

Fingers run up my spine again. When I was seventeen, after I'd killed my bio dad and his freakshow wife, I'd had to disappear and my friend Caleb had gone with me to St. Marie's, Idaho, where I'd found a twelve-year-old girl who was kidnapped by a sick son of a bitch named Ted Duggan. Caleb and I had freed her, but that wasn't enough for me. Ted Duggan was a normal guy with a normal job and nice neighbors who never suspected a thing. At least not until the police found him stabbed to death. The walls in his office were covered with photos of naked children, boys, and girls. I'm sure they found the child-sized doll-house in a bedroom where he'd kept the children as sex toys.

Ronnie races through some crime scene photos and goes to a new case file. She stops at a photo of a woman about my age, late twenties, blond hair twisted into a bun, sharp features, attractive, especially the eyes. They remind me of my mother's: beautiful yet hard.

"What police department did Spradley work for?"

"Wallace, Idaho PD. Why?"

That revelation floors me. When my mother had disappeared, I tracked down an aunt that I never knew existed. Aunt Ginger lived in Wallace, Idaho.

"Wallace," I say under my breath. It can't be a coincidence.

"What about him? Is that the Wallace Nan was talking about?"

Now I've done it. "It's nothing. He's a nobody. I don't know why I said that."

"Megan's got a secret admirer," Ronnie says, and tries to smile.

"I promise I'll tell you all about it later." I won't. "One thing at a time."

"Okay, but is the Wallace guy from Wallace, Idaho, or is that his name?"

"You'll have to ask Nan. She's investigating like a pro." This seems to satisfy her that nothing will be forthcoming. "So, who is the woman you were going to tell me about?"

"Sally Coleman. Campus Security at Portland State University."

Another hammer blow drives into my chest. Portland State U is another place where I caught up to two serial killers. Lars Nielsen and his son, Dan. Lars was a professor of Psychology at Portland State U, and his son, Dan, was a student who helped his father kidnap and kill. And all because the professor's wife was going to leave him. The wife was his first victim.

While looking for these sick bastards, I was led to believe the killer was a security officer for the campus named Jason something or other. Now this.

"Portland State," Ronnie is saying when I zone back in.

"What about it?" I ask sharper than intended.

Ronnie gives me a curious look.

"You have one of their sweatshirts. Didn't you go to school there?"

Did I put that on my application to the Sheriff Office? I can't remember. Lies have a way of catching you out. You tell one lie and have to tell another to cover your tracks. I change the topic.

"What happened to her?"

"She was found on campus in an empty dorm room. Her throat was cut and she was stabbed through both eyes."

"When was this?"

"Coleman was killed last year about this same time. Spradley was killed five years ago this month. I've been searching for other murders of law enforcement that are unsolved, but so far, these two are all I've got."

She's only been looking for half an hour.

"Good work."

The food tastes like paste in my dry mouth. My mind is circling, traveling from one murder to another, making comparisons, connecting the dots, knowing I may be completely wrong in my assumptions. I've been blind to several things since leaving Ronnie's parents' house. I'm more certain that ever that Wallace has something to do with these murders.

TWENTY-THREE

We wave goodbye to Moe and go to our cars.

"Megan, Tony said you are to go home and get some rest. I'm on this and I'm fresh."

"Okay," I say, and surprise her. My batteries are dangerously low; my clothes smell like yesterday's laundry. Maybe they are. I'm even too tired to look for the boogeyman as I drive home. But as I go to the front door of my building, the adrenaline kicks in. The outside door is unlocked and my anger is replaced by fright as I find the door to my apartment unlocked and someone is moving around inside.

I push the door open with the muzzle of my .45 and pray the hinges don't squeak. My rational mind tells me it might be my brother. If so, seeing me with a gun won't freak him out. Hayden is a combat veteran and very little seems to disturb him. If it's Dan who has come home without telling me first, it will come as a surprise, but I can explain. If it's anyone else besides them or the landlord, I'll give them the surprise of their life.

The .45 leads me into my front room and I search for a target. Nothing. Nothing out of place. The noise is coming from the kitchen. Shuffling. A huff of air startles me. You'd expect the noise to come from a bear or a moose or some large creature searching for food.

The .45 muzzle blades around the door to the kitchen but stops when it acquires a target. A very large target. A man standing at the kitchen sink with his back to me.

He's as big as Dan or Hayden, but it's not one of them. My landlord is an eighty-year-old widow. I grip the gun in hands to steady them and suddenly the whole world has slowed down and I can see everything around me: the curtain in the open kitchen window is moving with a breeze, fresh coffee is brewing, the man's left hand holding the blue coffee mug Hayden made for me. From behind his hair is cut short and blond, his skin is deeply tanned, the knuckles on the hand holding the mug are rough.

Wallace! The age may be right, but the clothes are different from what I saw on the video, and I don't see evidence of a beard. I take a step back, getting into a shooter's stance.

"Put your hands up. Slowly. Don't turn around. I'm a cop and I have a gun pointed at you." My training has kicked in and I'm relatively calm considering that I've caught a stranger making coffee in my kitchen. My voice has changed and I sound like the Terminator. Later on, I might laugh about this if I don't have to kill him.

The man puts the blue mug down on the counter and raises his hands to shoulder height. The knuckles on both hands are bruised and scraped. *Fighter.* I take another step back. He's much bigger and has at least seventy pounds on me. Muscles stretch the sleeves of his buffalo-pattern red flannel shirt.

"Yes, ma'am. I'm not armed. I come in peace, Rylee. Or Megan if you prefer."

I've heard that voice before. "Name?" I order him. "Now. And what are you doing in my apartment?"

"Which one do you want me to answer first?" There's that chuffing sound again like this is a joke.

"Answer now or let's see how funny you feel with your butt cheek blown up."

"It's me, Rylee. If you let me turn around, you'll see."

I back another step and lower the gun, pointing at his waist in case he ducks and comes at me. "Slow. Hands in the air. No funny stuff or I swear I'll kill you."

The man turns slowly, and my breath stops, replaced by my heart pounding so hard I can feel it in my temples. My voice doesn't sound like the Terminator now. It comes out like a little girl in shock. "Caleb?"

He smiles and I'm sure it's him. Caleb Hunter. My friend, my almost boyfriend, from South Kitsap High School in Port Orchard.

His eyes narrow when he sees the gun. "Can you please not point that cannon at me?"

The gun goes back in its shoulder holster, but I stay where I'm at. His smile falters and his hands turn palms out, as he says, "Hey, I'm a friend, remember."

"I know who you are. I don't know why you're in my apartment."

"I was making coffee."

"Back up. How did you get in my apartment?" My hand goes back to my gun, but I don't draw it.

"The door was open, Rylee. I swear. The kitchen window was open too. I came in to check on you. Everything was okay and I just got nosey and found the nifty blue mug. I thought I'd make coffee and wait for you to get home. I'm sorry I didn't come over sooner, but I was hesitant. You know?"

I never leave a window unlocked, much less open. He's lying. "You found the window unlocked and open?" I say this with my most sarcastic voice.

He smirks. "You got me. I opened it after I came in to air it out. It smelled like stale pizza and cheap wine." He looks around at my messy room. "But the door was open. I swear."

"I swear" usually means "I'm lying." But I may have been so distracted last night that I didn't shut it properly. And he was right about the smell.

"Did you go to the Sheriff Office yesterday and talk to Nan?"

He gives me a questioning look. "Nan?"

"Answer the question?

"No. I haven't been to the Sheriff Office and I don't know who Nan is."

My hand relaxes. I believe him. Tears flood my eyes and I see he feels the same. I cross the room and hug him fiercely. Out of happiness at seeing him as much as relief. We stand like that a long time, arms around each other, my face on his chest, his head resting on top of mine. The smell of Old Spice is now overwhelming, like he's taken a bath in it. I should thank him for opening the window.

My stepfather, Rolland, wore Old Spice. Not a bathtub load like Caleb, but I always thought it was pleasant and, well, Rolland-y. I push away from Caleb. Adrenaline rushes through me and I feel the pulse in my neck pounding again. I can't afford to become complacent. A cop killer is at large and it appears he's hungry and shortening the time between killings. There was five years between the killing of Detective Spradley and the killing of Sally Coleman. A year after her murder, he kills Denton and Dupont. Where was the killer for five years? Prison? Out of the country? Military service? There aren't any military bases near Wallace, Idaho. But there is an Army Reserve base near Coeur d'Alene.

"How did you get in the lobby? That door is always locked." That's a big fib, but he won't know it.

He shrugs. "It wasn't today, I guess somebody must have left it open. Your neighbor, I guess?"

That part checks out at least.

"What are you doing here, Caleb?"

"I don't understand, Rylee. You're glad to see me, aren't you?"

I don't answer that because the answer is complicated. I know Dan sure as hell wouldn't like me to be glad to see him. But that doesn't mean I'm not.

"It's just kind of out of the blue. We haven't seen each other in..."

He looks puzzled. "But... you asked me to come."

"What are you talking about?"

He shrugs and pulls out a small postcard from his back pocket and hands it to me. It has my address on it, spelled out in disturbingly neat handwriting.

"I didn't send this."

"Are you sure?" Caleb asks. "Look on the back."

I turn it over and my blood chills. It must have drained out of my face too, because Caleb asks if I'm okay.

"I mean, that's an M for Megan, right? I heard you'd changed your name."

Maybe it looks like an M for Megan to him. The way I'm holding it, it looks like a W.

"Where did you get this?"

Caleb shrugs. He doesn't realize the gravity of the situation. If Wallace brought him here, he doesn't have anything good planned for him. "It came in the mail the other day. I figured you were being mysterious."

"Listen to me, Caleb, you need to leave now. You need to..." What? Go back home? That won't help, not if Wallace knows where he lives.

"What's wrong?"

"There's a guy who's been sending me messages. Calls himself Wallace. As in 'W'," I say, holding up the card. "He's bad news. You could get hurt."

"I can take care of myself. And it sounds like you need someone to watch your back."

I sigh. "Where are you staying?"

"A hotel in town. I booked a couple of nights, I wasn't sure if..." He trails off, and I realize I really don't want to get into this now. Maybe he has a point about someone else to watch my back. And it'll be easier to keep an eye on him here rather than worry about Wallace waiting for him when he gets back home.

"I have a boyfriend," I blurt out before I think about it. "His name is Dan."

"Oh," Caleb says, looking taken aback. "I mean, I didn't come here because... That is, I'm not..."

The adrenaline is wearing off and exhaustion rolls in like a wave. "Caleb, I really want to catch up, but can we do it tomorrow? I haven't slept for almost a day."

"Of course, Rylee. Whoops, I mean, Megan. I know your job keeps you busy." He shakes his head. "I never would have believed you'd become a cop."

His dismissive tone pisses me off. "And why is that?"

"I'm sorry. You're very good at what you do. I've done some Internet surfing and you've become quite the local celebrity."

"Yeah. I get my coffee and donuts for free."

He smiles and I can't help returning a small one. "I've really got to sleep."

"Sure. We can do this later." He pats down his pockets until he finds a pen. He takes the lid off with his teeth and scrawls his number on the back of the postcard he showed me. "You can tell me what you've been up to and how Hayden is doing."

Did he meet Hayden? I don't remember. Hayden might remember. But I'm sure Dan won't be thrilled an old boyfriend has come back.

TWENTY-FOUR

I stand at the door and watch as Caleb walks down the street. He turns to wave as he reaches the corner, and I return the wave hesitantly. I forgot to ask him where his hotel is, but I guess it must be close by if he's on foot. It would have been nice to spend more time with Caleb, but I'm so wiped out that in another minute I will be drooling and snoring.

I skip a shower, kick my boots off, and lie down in my clothes. My gun goes under my pillow and I try to shut my mind down. Not going to happen. My mind is trained to solve problems, put missing parts back together, make connections between events or people or things that don't connect, like a thousand-piece puzzle.

By the time I was seventeen, I had faked my own death and then went on the run. By the time I was twenty, I was registered in Portland State University with forged credentials and started tracking down another set of serial killers. During my time at the university, I met Dr. Karen Albright. She changed my life and I hated her for it. But only for a while.

She had sat patiently supporting me through the many sessions where I poured my soul out and told her things I believed I would never tell anyone. These sessions were recorded and when she thought I was ready, she gave the cassette tapes to me. I didn't want them, but she insisted I would want to listen to them to remember how far I'd come from that confused, angry, homicidal young woman that came into her office. She didn't know I would use them to help me solve other problems while tracking down more serial killers and currently to find this asshole killing cops.

I've since transferred the cassette tapes to an encrypted digital format on my phone and laptop, but the originals and a cassette player are locked in my apartment desk drawer. I'm drawn to the recording about a serial killer working the Portland campus. It turned out to be two killers, a father and son, who were killing athletic and beautiful female students out of a twisted sense of justice and revenge. I get the player and find the cassette and hit play. Dr. Karen Albright's voice is pleasant, non-judgmental, but to the point.

> *Dr. Albright: You say that serial killers often hunt for a specific type of victim.*

> *Me: It's true. But it's not what I'm getting at here. I'm wondering about her day-to-day routine.*

I'm talking about the victim here.

> *Me: I'm wondering if she did anything out of the ordinary or said anything that you later look back at and, you know, think, is that a piece that doesn't fit?*

Pausing the recording I remember Karen had served tea that day. Heavy with cloves and cinnamon and raw sugar. I thought I would taste the spices for the rest of my life. I hit play.

Me: My roommate, Annabelle, told me the campus police were investigating the last student's disappearance. The student, Addy, had been Annabelle's roommate at the time of her disappearance. Annabelle said a rent-a-cop weirdo named Jason Lemmon came to her room and interviewed her twice.

I stop the recording. I remember this.

That was the name I couldn't remember from earlier.

Jason Lemmon. At that time, I was working for the college newspaper, *The Vanguard*, and the editor had given me a list of names of possible people to see the missing girl last.

Lemmon's wasn't among them. I told Annabelle maybe the campus police should leave the investigating to someone with a real badge.

Annabelle had already talked with a Portland detective and told him she thought Lemmon was acting inappropriately. When I asked her why, she thought that she told me that the first time he visited her room he'd asked questions about when Addy had last been on campus. That sort of thing. But then he came back and wanted a piece of Addy's clothing for their K-9 team. I thought that was weird because campus police don't have a K-9. I was on the crime beat of *The Vanguard*. I told her Lemmon was maybe trying to act important to impress her.

She told me she didn't think so. The first year she was in the dorms, all the girls on her floor noticed underwear missing. Bras and panties. They had joked it off but thought some creep was stealing out of their rooms. She acted like they had a suspect. I asked who and wasn't surprised to hear the creep was Lemmon.

I had asked her if they ever caught the creep stealing their underwear and she said they did. It turned out to be the boyfriend of a resident aide on the floor above them. He was a cross-dresser and panty hoarder. They had caught him on a webcam.

At the time I'd thought Lemmon was in the clear, but

Annabelle said Lemmon had come back and told her he needed a piece of Addy's clothes. Something personal.

Annabelle said Lemmon had asked for a pair of Addy's panties. A thong. She'd said she knew she shouldn't have given them to him because he didn't put the thong in a bag. He stuffed them in his front pocket.

She'd called the Portland detective and told him about Lemmon, and that led to Lemmon being questioned and shortly after he was made to leave the university. I'd asked if she'd seen Lemmon again, thinking someone like that would retaliate. Annabelle said Lemmon had come to her room and yelled at her, called her names, and blamed her for his firing from the university. She saw him a while later working security at Macy's in the Lloyd Center and he'd given her threatening looks.

I drift off to sleep thinking about Jason Lemmon.

TWENTY-FIVE

Three hours' sleep was it, and even that was fitful with dreams, nightmares, anxiety. Monsters really do exist. In life and in dreams. Dreams are a way to learn from your mistakes so you can defeat the real monsters. The monster that killed Dupont and possibly Denton and others is on a mission to kill law enforcement types. Retired, active duty, men, women; all like bugs to him. What Ronnie turned up convinced me the killer is fighting monsters. Police had let down society in some way. Instead of protectors they had betrayed the public trust and abused their authority.

I'm good at putting puzzles together, but some pieces are missing. For instance, Detective Spradley of the Wallace, Idaho PD was into child porn and bondage of small children. That was his sin. Sally Coleman, security officer at Portland State University, had her throat cut and her body dumped in an empty dorm room. What was her sin? Riley Denton, retired Chief of Police from St. Marie's, Idaho. As Chief of Police I imagine he'd made enemies. And Dupont was a bitch. She'd beat her boyfriend, John Duncan, up for asking her to marry him. But my gut tells me when we start digging into these victims, we'll find bigger sins and a clue to the killer's identity.

Before I leave my apartment, I open my laptop and enter the name *Jason Lemmon* in the search engine. A Portland Oregonian Newspaper article from seven years ago pops up. The headline reads:

MALL SECURITY GUARD FOUND DEAD

Jason was found in the security office when a call came in from an unidentified caller. Police arrived and found he had hung himself with his belt. The article doesn't say much more except he had been employed last at Portland State University as a campus policeman. I looked up the obituary, but no next of kin was named. Foul play was not suspected. It may be related, or maybe not. I've got the Portland PD phone number in my contacts at work. We need to check with them about Sally Coleman anyway. I shut the laptop down and get dressed for work. *Another creep bites the dust.*

The front door is unlocked again. If I ever meet him or her, my neighbor and I need to have a serious conversation. Circling the blocks a couple of times around my place and satisfying myself nothing is out of order, I head to the office to see what Ronnie has come up with. The thought of Ronnie staying with Jefferson County makes me smile. Tony must have put a real bug in Sheriff Longbow's ear, but I don't think Ronnie ever intended to take the job in Whatcom County.

When I arrive at the office, Nan is waiting by the front door. I'm in no mood for her inquisition. I greet her and brush past, motioning for Ronnie to meet me inside Tony's office. I hope he's in or I will look silly, but at least I'll have a closed door between me and Nan.

Tony's in. A bag of powdered sugar donuts is on his desk. In his hand is the remains of one. "Don't you ever knock?"

"Can I have one?" I counter, and he pushes the bag toward me as I slump in a chair across from him. His fingers are coated with sticky white powder and there's a ring of it around his mouth. I take one I don't really want, but I might need to put something in my mouth if they start up the Wallace thing. They don't.

Tony finishes his donut and says, "Ronnie will fill us in. Go ahead, Ronnie."

It's my lucky day. Ronnie doesn't preface the results of her online search with "Guess what?" or "You'll never guess what I've found."

"I've got a file for you, Megan, but to save time I'll just brief you."

I nod. This is a good start.

"Detective Robert Spradley, age thirty-two, Wallace, Idaho PD, ten years on the job. Spotless reputation. At least it was until they discovered the child porn in his home after he was murdered. This was five years ago this month. He was found in his backyard. Stabbed twenty-three times in the back. The scene looked like the stabbing started in the storm cellar and he was dragged outside and stabbed in the back. The coroner report said the stabbing in the back occurred after death. The cause of death was stab wounds in both eyes that were so deep the blade, probably an ice pick, chipped the bone in the back of his skull. The killer had twisted it around, shredding his brain." She pauses to see if I have questions. I'll wait.

"Sally Coleman, age thirty-one, Portland State University Campus Police. An unidentified caller reported dead body and police found Coleman stabbed to death in a dorm room. That was one year ago this month. The killer must like September. The weapon was similar to the one in the Spradley murder, but Coleman's wounds were only in the eyes and face. She must have put up more of a struggle because there were penetrating wounds on her forehead and cheeks."

She pauses. "In case you're wondering, I said Coleman must have struggled harder than Spradley because he was a small man and Coleman was almost six feet tall and a weight-lifter. Spradley was five seven and spindly.

"The Kitsap coroner put Dupont's death at about two to three days ago. Denton's was newer by at least twenty-four hours. Dupont was killed first so her corpse must have been kept somewhere cool until the killer wanted it to be found. It's highly possible the body was kept in her root cellar."

"Ronnie, did you find out who the anonymous callers were?" I ask.

"I wasn't able to."

"So far we've had no luck either," I say. "All of these happened during the first week of September, right?"

"Yes. I'm looking back beyond five years for others, but so far nothing jumps out. Can you think of anything else I can search for?"

Wallace. "There is one thing." I want to tell her about Caleb surprising me. Arriving in town without telling me, then suddenly appearing in my kitchen. But I can't think of a way to do that without revealing my past. Besides, he may be moving on before long.

It's not fair for him to do that to me. It's not fair that he meant so much to me all those years ago. It makes me feel unfaithful to Dan. I wish Dan would come home, but how would I explain Caleb to him? I'm getting ahead of myself. There's no reason I have to introduce him to anyone. Caleb knows the beginning of my past. He has no reason to out me. Surely he's not still upset about Ted Duggan's death. I need to think this out before I meet him again.

"Can you call Portland police back and ask about a Jason Lemmon?"

"Was he murdered?"

"Maybe. According to a news article, he was working security at Macy's in the mall in Portland. He was hanged by his own belt in the security office. The news article didn't say much more, but it's worth a look."

"I'll call the detective back, Megan."

TWENTY-SIX

My phone dings. The sender's email address chills my blood and I need get away from my desk. A trip to the restroom will attract less attention from Ronnie or Nan so I head there and lock the door behind me. With shaking hands, I open the email and read it slowly.

> Rylee, have you gotten my message yet? You're a smart girl so I know you'll put the clues together. I want you to know how disappointed I am in what you've become. I had such hope for you. I thought we were the same, but I can see now that you've gone soft. You've given up the mission. I haven't. I'll be in touch.
>
> Wallace

Wallace. I know who the killer is now. And he's been killing people for at least five years. Maybe as far back as seven if Jason Lemmon is another victim. A lot of good the idea does since I haven't been able to put a face to the name. I take deep breaths to slow my pounding heart and splash cold water on my face, flush the toilet, and wash my hands.

When I open the bathroom door Nan is staring at me from her desk. If she asks about Wallace, I'll... I'll make an excuse and leave. She doesn't but she says, "Megan, Detective Osborne sent an envelope."

"What is it?"

She looks offended. "How would I know. The envelope is sealed."

Thank you, Clay. I want to distract her from asking questions so I decide to recruit her. "Nan, we're really covered up here and I hoped you could give us a hand." That hit home.

"Of course, I will. That's what I'm here for, Megan. What can I do?"

You can go away for a few weeks. Months even. I say, "Can you open the envelope and see what Clay has for me? I'm checking on some other things." I know if I'd stayed in the restroom any longer, she would have steamed the envelope open.

Nan carefully slits the manila envelope open, and I see Ronnie giving me a curious look. At my desk I quickly read the email again. My laptop has a dozen or more emails that need to be read. Most of them are marketing related. I can get smoother younger skin in only ten days. One wants to increase my business reviews. One wants to boost my sex life. I can boost it myself if Dan ever comes home.

Police records give me nothing on Caleb Hunter. Without a license plate number or date of birth, I can't search for vehicle registration. I know his birthday is in September, but it's been many years since I knew the day. He's one year older than I am, but that won't get me far. As a Hail Mary pass, I check Washington State prison records. Nothing. I run NCIC and get three hits on Caleb Hunters. Two are much older than my Caleb and one is only nineteen years old.

I get a coffee and go by Nan's desk, smiling, and ask what she has for me as if she's a detective now. She holds up a finger, her focus on a police report. I wait. Impatiently. At least she's forgotten all about Wallace for the moment. Finally, she taps the papers back in order and looks up at me. I want to laugh at the seriousness on her face but don't dare.

"I don't believe there's much more in this that you don't already know, Detective Carpenter. This is very interesting. And disgusting. And... And..."

Looking at her more closely, I can see I've mistaken her serious look for one of distress. Tears well in her eyes and she takes a tissue from the dispenser on her desk and dabs at them, smearing her eyeliner. She slides the envelope across the desk with the tips of her fingers as if it is contaminated. In a way it is: with sickness. Nan has been doing this work for quite a while and seeing her react this way makes me realize how callous I am, and my heart goes out to her. I'd always seen her as a tough-as-nails, selfish, nosey bitch. She is, but she's hurting and it's not even selfish hurt. I never imagined I'd feel anything for her so maybe I'm not that broken. But I'll get over it.

An idea hits me. "Nan, I have another project for you if you're not too busy."

She doesn't look as eager this time. "Megan, I don't know if I can."

"It's not like what you've just done. I promise. I just want you to do some research. Internet, news, YouTube, news articles, that kind of stuff."

"Well, I guess I can do that. I'm not too busy."

"You'll be searching the Port Orchard area from..." I have to think about how far I want her going back. There may still be pictures of a young Rylee in the news from when I was a suspect in my stepfather's murder. I've been gone for over eight years so I tell her to check back five years. I'm careful to tell her

I already checked the earlier dates. "Can you get me anything you find on families named Hunter. It may take a while, but as soon as you finish, let me know."

"Of course, Detective Carpenter."

TWENTY-SEVEN

I start my computer search with the year I was seventeen and a South Kitsap High School student. The cool thing is Ronnie taught me how to get into newspaper archives for free. Nan doesn't know how to access those archives so I don't expect her to find anything. But if I find something that incriminates me, I'll give her a different urgent task.

My mind goes back to a past lesson my mother taught me. Indoctrinated, really. I was a pre-teen and we hadn't moved to Port Orchard yet. I don't know where we were then, we moved around so often, but I remember wanting to play with some neighborhood girls. Mom had said no. "We can't trust anyone, honey. No one." And she'd asked me if I understood. Of course, I didn't understand. I was a kid. I wanted to have friends. But she'd ingrained in me we weren't like everyone else. We could never get close to anyone. I never did. Not until I was seventeen, named Rylee, and going to South Kitsap High, where I met a boy. Caleb Hunter. If I had been a normal girl, with a normal family, I think things might have gone further with us, but we never really dated or made out or anything that he was used to doing with other girls. It was against our house rules.

So, Caleb and I talked in the cafeteria or on the high school track. I was a runner then and he was too. I remember thinking he had the most beautiful eyes and a way of making me feel special with just a look or the way his hand touched mine. My first crush. My last one until Dan came along.

Caleb had said, "This school sucks," and his eyes gave mine a searing look that made me turn away. Even with the most innocuous statements or questions, Caleb had that kind of effect on me. Like he was reading me. I hoped he liked what he was reading, but I wasn't a good judge of what others thought back then. I assumed, and still do, to some extent, that people were being as deceptive as I was.

I'd agreed with Caleb about school sucking, although I was glad to be there, in high school, instead of rotting in my prison at home.

It was the first time Caleb and I really had the chance to talk. He was getting his driver's license soon and I'd told him I was jealous. He'd said, "Yeah. I can get out of here and leave this town and my dad and his girlfriend in the dust and never, ever come back."

He'd lied about his home life. He'd told me his mother had died that summer. I was later to find out she had just abandoned him and never told him goodbye. Now I wonder if he'd ever tried to find her.

"I'm sorry about your mom," I'd said, and allowed my eyes to look into his for as long as I could manage without being weird. He said, "Thanks. Dad doesn't want to talk about it, about her, and of course, that bitch he's about to marry doesn't allow her to be discussed either. All of Mom's pictures are gone. Her clothes are gone. There's nothing left of her. Just a bad memory."

Not knowing what to say I let his words hang in the air and avoided his eyes. He'd asked me if I ever just wanted to disappear.

"Totally." The truth was I'd been disappearing all of my life. In Port Orchard, I was finally beginning to feel that I had a home. Part of that was the boy I was sitting with right then.

He'd nodded, happy I'd agreed with him. A kindred soul and all that. He'd said, "Sometimes I just want to fill up my backpack and leave. For good." He'd looked at me. Reading my response, then said, "If you could go anywhere, do you know where it would be?"

I'd already been a lot of places by then. Mom used to move when she felt we'd been in one place long enough, or when she felt we were in danger of being found. By who? I didn't have any idea back then. Off the top of my head, I'd told him Paris. Not the one in Texas. The one in France. He'd broken out in a huge smile and said, "I figured that out on my own."

The bell had rung and we parted, going in different directions, him to Algebra, me to Computer Science, and then his hand touched mine. It had sent a volt of energy through me. I didn't know if it was on purpose or it had been an accident, but I was glad of it. Now, thinking about all this, I can feel Caleb's touch on the back of my hand and can't help but sigh.

"Are you okay?" Ronnie asks. She's come up on me like a ghost and it's her hand on mine and not Caleb's.

"Can't a girl sigh?" I ask a little too testily, and soften my tone with, "I was just thinking of something happy. You know, to break up the tension."

"I do that sometimes," she says, and smiles and nods her head toward the exit. "Let's get some fresh air."

I was so lost in the past, I hadn't even begun my search. I cast a glance at Nan. She is bent over her computer like a heart surgeon and doesn't notice us leave.

TWENTY-EIGHT

We leave the office while Nan is head down at her computer like a Neanderthal distracted by fire. Ronnie leads me outside to a picnic area we'd taken to using for breaks and lunch.

"Megan, I think I might have come across something. Susan Dupont isn't her real name."

"How's that?"

"The date of birth and Social Security Number Dupont gave came from a dead person."

"Are you sure?" I ask unnecessarily. Ronnie doesn't make mistakes.

"It's the one she used when she worked with Cleveland PD. The SSN was issued in Loveless, Ohio. The Susan Dupont in Loveless, Ohio, died when she was seventeen."

Dupont has been graveyard trolling. Graveyard trolling is when a scam artist finds death records for someone and uses them to create a new identity for themselves.

I say, "Do you think our victim knew the real Susan Dupont?"

"Not necessarily. But she didn't make up the SSN because it's in the system and there *was* a real Susan Dupont."

"Good work, Ronnie."

"And there's more. Her personnel record from Clallam shows she had a Bachelor of Science Degree in Criminalistics from North College of Idaho in Coeur d'Alene."

There's that ping again of some memory at the back of my subconscious raising its head. When I registered at Portland University, I was still seventeen, and since I hadn't graduated from high school, I had obtained forged credentials. In my case I was looking for someone, a serial killer. It became my mission in life to end as many of these monsters as I could find. The hunt gave meaning and purpose to my life.

I was studying Criminal Justice, and if I had graduated, my degree would have just touched on the criminalistics aspect. In one of my classes, I had read a book on Sherlock Holmes that referred to him as a criminalist, which is a person who solves crimes by studying the evidence. Sherlock Holmes trusted evidence, clues, facts. I trust my gut. It's seldom wrong and right now it's screaming at me that Dupont is evil. She was someone I would have hunted in the past.

No wonder Clallam hired Dupont without checking her background more thoroughly. She had law enforcement background, a bachelor's degree in criminalistics, so she was extremely qualified. So am I.

Ronnie touches my shoulder to get my attention and I say, "I'm sorry."

"There's no Census record of our Susan Dupont in Loveless, but not everyone reports on the Census. I'm going to call North College to see if anyone remembers her."

"Call Loveless PD too and see if they know her."

"I've got their numbers in my phone." She takes out her cell and calls North College first. She talks to the registrar and there is no record of a Susan Dupont ever attending the college. Ronnie calls Loveless PD. I nudge her and tell her to ask for the nosiest person working there. Everyone has a Nan.

The call is answered and she puts it on speaker phone.

"Loveless Police Department. Sergeant Phillips. How can I assist you?"

Ronnie advises him who we are and that we are investigating a murder in our county. They may have some needed information. I thought that would get his attention and cooperation but he sounds bored. "Me and the secretary are the only ones here today. Tell me what you need and I'll have someone call you back."

Ronnie says, "This is about the death of a seventeen-year-old girl about twenty years ago."

I hear a sigh. "Let me connect you with Gladys. She knows everything about everyone."

There's a click and I think he's hung up, but then a woman comes on the line. "This is Gladys. Personal Assistant to Chief Roberts. Sergeant Phillips said you needed to talk to the person that knows the most about the people in this town. Who am I speaking to? A person can't be too careful nowadays. You're not a reporter, are you?"

Ronnie identifies us and tells Gladys she's on speaker phone. Gladys asks for the Jefferson County Sheriff's Office phone number. Ronnie gives it to her and I sigh. This is Nan to the Nth power.

"So, if I call your sheriff, he'll vouch for you?" Gladys asks. She even sounds like Nan. But maybe that's just my impatience showing.

"Gladys, this is Detective Carpenter. We're in kind of a hurry since we're investigating multiple homicides of police officers. One victim was beheaded. This is very important." I refrain from raising my voice and I'm glad because her tone changes to one that tells me we have the right person. If she knows anything, she'll tell us.

"Sorry, detectives," Gladys says. "We've had some big

crimes here recently and the news media won't leave us alone. What do you need to know?"

First of all, I want to ask what type of "big crimes" a little township like Loveless, population five hundred, can have. But I don't go there. I turn the conversation over to my partner who is more patient than I am.

"Gladys, this is Ronnie again."

"Yes, Ronnie. Go ahead. I'm recording this call. I don't want to miss a word."

Ronnie and I glance at each other before Ronnie begins. She tells the nosey Gladys only what she needs to know and I can hear the greediness in Gladys' voice. This will feed the gossip mill in Loveless for at least six months.

Gladys remembers the Dupont family, but the parents passed away shortly after their daughter died in a car/train accident. The parents also died in a car/train accident. She says both incidents were actually suicides because they drove onto train tracks and waited for the train. Ronnie manages to get Gladys back on track when Gladys starts to describe the accidents in great detail.

When we've wrung all the information out of Gladys, Ronnie thanks her and is about to disconnect when Gladys throws us a zinger.

TWENTY-NINE

Ronnie goes inside and comes out with two mugs of strong coffee. She's drinking hers black now, like a grownup. I'll start drinking my coffee with cream and sugar just to keep her from being too much like me. No one should be like me. I sip my coffee and we're both silent. Ronnie grimaces at the strong coffee like a person smoking their first cigarette.

She takes another sip. The girl's got grit. I have to give her that. Ronnie asks, "Do you think Dupont was the one trying to get information on the family deaths?" Ronnie's referring to the phony Susan Dupont. The one resting in pieces in the coroner's refrigerator.

"I do. It fits."

Gladys of Loveless Ohio PD had shared with us that the seventeen-year-old Susan Dupont had driven her brand spanking new Chevy convertible, an early graduation present from her parents, onto the Ohio-railway line tracks just outside of Pattersonville. The car's gearshift was still in Park when it was examined. The death was ruled a suicide by the coroner, but the facts were kept from the media. Two months later the parents parked their car on the same railroad tracks with their lights off and followed their daughter to wherever she was. That time the news media got the story and it hit national news. Death, misery, especially the death of an entire family, is always good for a headline. I remember a journalist once saying they were "privileged" to have been at the scene of mass carnage. How sick is that?

Gladys had told us after the clamor of news reporters had died from a roar down to a growl, she received a call from a woman saying she was with a college newspaper. She claimed to be doing a story about suicides of students and the grief it causes the parents. She said she was doing this piece as a wake-up call to other students who were considering suicide to prevent them from doing so. Gladys has a good nose for bullshit. She asked the name of the school newspaper and was told *North College Campus Times* in Coeur d'Alene, Idaho. Just like she'd done to us, Gladys had asked for the phone number where she could verify this and was given a number. She told the woman to hold on the line while she contacted the school. The caller had identified herself as Lois Dupont, no relation to the victims.

Gladys put the call on hold while she called the school. They'd never heard of Lois Dupont, and their newspaper had shut down the year before for lack of readership. Gladys said the woman had hung up before she could get back to her. Gladys thought it was a reporter lying to get more information than had been released. I changed my mind about Gladys being a busybody in this case.

We're still trying to absorb what Gladys told us when Nan comes across the parking lot at a trot.

"Detective Carpenter. Detective Marsh." Nan is out of breath when she catches up. "I think I found something. It may not be connected to the murders but I thought it was worth telling you about." She hands me a sheet of printer paper with a newspaper article from the *Seattle Times*, dated from seven years ago. The headline reads:

MURDER-SUICIDE IN PORT ORCHARD

The article is about Caleb's father and the new wife Caleb had told me about all those years ago. Ronnie is looking over my shoulder as I read and Nan is standing so close, I can smell her shampoo. I need body space.

Interspersed in the article are pictures of the happy couple; one a wedding photo where they are both smiling brightly and, in the background, I see Caleb with a defeated look on his face. Another picture shows crime scene tape across the front porch of Caleb's home. At the bottom of the article there is a black-and-white high school yearbook photo of Caleb. My heart goes out to him. In the high school photo, he has that dazzling smile and good looks that always made me wonder why he would talk to someone like me. I wasn't a cheerleader. I wasn't anything special. But he sought me out because he felt a kindred spirit in me. We were both having a rough time. He told me his problems with his dad and new mother. I told him lies.

The article is a long one, hyped by the reporter to sell papers. I fold the article up and put it in my jacket pocket and thank Nan for the good work.

"I'll put this in our folder, Nan. I owe you one." I don't intend to pay off. I'm just thankful she didn't find any pictures of me.

THIRTY

Ronnie's never met Detective Patterson and I want her to see I'm not the only one that cuts a corner here or there for the purpose of getting to the truth. I must have been driving on autopilot because Ronnie jabs me in the arm. "Hey, don't go to sleep on me."

"I'm not. Just thinking." It's the truth, but I'm not thinking about the case. I'm thinking about the Caleb from my past. I have to stop this, but it's like a song going through your head.

"You should let me drive, Megan. You haven't had enough downtime."

"I'm fine, Ronnie."

"How many fingers am I holding up?"

I glance at her and say, "Four and a big toe," which cracks her up. I crack myself up sometimes.

"Do you think the article Nan found has anything to do with this?"

I give her the look. The one that says: *Seriously? Did you really ask that?*

She leaves me alone the rest of the way to Port Angeles.

Patterson is waiting by the Sheriff Office main doors and comes down the walk saying, "Lying bitch!"

Ronnie gives me a startled look and I put a hand on her arm. "She's not talking about me." I hope.

We get out of the Explorer and meet Patterson on the walk. She says, "Sorry. Been a bad day. I'm Patterson."

"I'm Ronnie Marsh."

Patterson steps back, eying Ronnie over, and says to no one in particular, "I thought she would look more like a nerd. Clay calls her the computer guru."

"I get that a lot." The two shake hands. "Pleased to meet you."

"Cut your vacation short, did you?" Patterson asks, but doesn't wait for an answer. "That's good. We need you on this."

What am I? Chopped liver. "Ronnie has something interesting on Dupont's past."

Patterson nods and opens the door for us. "I've heard. Your secretary called me. I knew Dupont was trouble from the get-go and my feelings are almost always right. Looks like I'll have to start an investigation with her as a suspect when this is over. Who knows what she was into."

My secretary? What the hell? Nan wasn't outside when Ronnie told me about Dupont's identity theft. How could Nan hear that. I say to Ronnie, "Remind me to check the parking lot for listening devices when we get back."

"Let's talk." Patterson takes us to an interview room that's more modern than ours. A booster seat is in a corner of the room surrounded by a stack of toys. A magnetic chalkboard is on one wall with colorful plastic letters spelling out foul words. Most are misspelled.

"Sorry," Patterson says, and mixes up the letters on the chalkboard. "You've seen our adult interview room with the steel tables and chairs and everything bolted to the floor. This is our juvenile room. We need the whips and thumb screws in here."

Ronnie has brought copies of the Dupont's Social Security information for Patterson and lays these on the table where we're seated.

"I guess we'll have to work on our background vetting for applicants. Hers probably was only a cursory one since she came to us from another police department. Still..." She looks down at the pages as if they embarrass her.

Ronnie reaches across the table and puts a hand on Patterson's. "You didn't do the hiring. It's not your fault."

This is why I work with Ronnie. Men love her. Women want to be her. "She's right. Now, what are we going to do with this?"

"I've ordered her personnel file—including the fingerprints she gave when she was hired—to the National Database. We should hear something shortly." The usual hiring process requires that the applicant's fingerprints are run through the FBI Database. "But after I talked to Nan, I asked my guys to compare the fingerprints from the morgue to the ones we should have had in her personnel file, but those prints are gone."

Ronnie's eyes widen.

"How is it possible?" Ronnie asks, but I'm pretty sure I know. The fake Dupont got into the files and stole her fingerprints before they were put into the database. Pretty smart.

"But Dupont's prints from the morgue are interesting. Those fingerprints match some taken at the scene of a robbery/homicide in St. Marie, Idaho, five years ago. I'm waiting to hear from them."

A knock comes at the door and Patterson goes to answer and talks to someone. She comes back in with her cell phone in her hand and takes a seat. "St. Marie is calling."

THIRTY-ONE

The fingerprints Patterson had sent to St. Marie, Idaho, resulted in a call from one of their detectives. Patterson puts the call on speaker. "I have Detectives Carpenter and Marsh of Jefferson County with me."

"This is Detective Thompson, St. Marie PD. I've been waiting for this call for a very long time."

"Go ahead, Detective Thompson," Patterson says.

"The fingerprints you sent my agency match some taken at a homicide scene I worked five years ago. This is the first lead I've had. One of our detectives was murdered. Do you have the person in custody?"

Patterson lets me take the question. "Detective Carpenter here, Detective Thompson. Are you referring to Robert Spradley?"

"How did you get the information?"

"Detective Marsh was looking into similar murders to the ones we have here. She came across the Spradley case, but we didn't have much info."

"Do you have the person in custody?"

"The fingerprints we sent you were taken at the morgue in Kitsap County." I can hear a "Well, shit!" from the other end.

"So you have identified them?"

"Not exactly," I say, and this time I hear the phone hit something hard. I hope he hasn't smashed his phone. "Detective?" The line is silent for a long minute.

"Sorry. I'm just disappointed."

Who wouldn't be? But we have a name to go with the body. And a head. That might cheer him up. "We know a possible name that belongs to those fingerprints, but we think it's a fake. I'll tell you what we have and then we have some questions. Are you sitting down?"

"Shoot."

"Okay. Here goes." I tell him about the discovery of the dismembered body on the Hood Canal Bridge and how that led to the identification of Susan Dupont, detective from Clallam County. He doesn't interrupt once during my recounting of the case. When I'm finished the only question he asks is, "What can I help with?"

I give him all of Dupont's information including where the name Dupont was stolen from, Gladys's contact information in Loveless, Ohio, and the college angle in Coeur d'Alene.

When I finish, he says, "I've got another case involving those fingerprints and another victim from seven years ago. I'll send the file." He gets Ronnie's contact info. "It may take a while to send it. I'm not good with computers. I can get a hard file to you."

I say, "That's not necessary. Just email the file to Detective Marsh. What can you tell us about the other murder?"

"Okay. We had another murder that might be related to your Dupont, but the murder didn't happen here. It was in Wallace, Idaho, seven years ago. A guy named David Ludwig was murdered in his home. Bound to a chair, beaten, and stabbed through the eye. They have fingerprints from the scene, but they had no luck with identifying the owner of them. We only made the connection because Spradley was found to have a computer filled with child bondage and child porn. This Ludwig guy had been selling this crap. Spradley was one of his customers. The detective in Wallace wasn't too broken up. But we had an officer killed and I pushed it all I could. It ended up being a dead end. I think the Wallace detective was chasing down the porn victims."

I ask, "Do you have the Ludwig file available?"

"I can get it. I'll have the fingerprints from the Ludwig case compared to the ones you sent me."

Ronnie texts him Dupont's Clallam personnel photo, and he doesn't recognize her. He promises to send her photo to Wallace PD. All the excitement has drained from his voice like sand through an hourglass, but he promises to get back to us quickly. We exchange some other ideas before Patterson disconnects.

She says, "I guess we're not on his Christmas card list this year."

I respond, "He's on mine if he has something else for us. It's been a long time since those cases were looked at."

Det. Thompson agreed to run Dupont through their system and post her picture and info around the police station and give it to all the officers on duty.

Ronnie's phone dings. "That was fast. It's the case file from seven years ago." She sends the file to Patterson's phone, and Patterson goes to make print copies for us. The file is not very big. Ronnie reads from her phone. "The Wallace victim's name is David Ludwig. Age fifty. Black male. Worked as a corrections officer at Pee Wee Valley Correctional Center in Indiana before he moved to Wallace, Idaho."

Dupont doesn't have any connection with St. Marie that we know of. Minus the prints at the scene. But Ludwig has a strong connection.

Ronnie says, "He was selling fake passports, birth certificates, death certificates, driver's licenses, diplomas, and such. He was into selling child porn like we already knew."

Ronnie and I lock eyes. There's our connection. I say, "Dupont was using fake credentials. I'll text Detective Thompson and ask him to go through Ludwig's computer to see if he has a picture of Dupont on any of the hard drives." I begin texting, and Ronnie continues reading.

Until now Thompson had fingerprints but no physical suspect. Dupont might be his killer, but then again, she might have only been buying fake IDs.

"I think Thompson will accept Dupont as the doer of the deed," Patterson says, and lays a print copy of Thompson's file in front of me. "As for me and mine, we will keep open minds. I mean, why would Dupont end up dead as a result of killing some sick psycho seven years ago? She's on my shit list, but the big kahuna turd is still out there."

Ronnie thinks that's the funniest remark she's ever heard. I don't like to be upstaged, but I say, "Good one."

* * *

On the way back to Port Hadlock, Ronnie takes her iPad out of her messenger bag and touches and swishes and pinches and does other weird things people do to those tablets. She turns it toward me and I slow down to look. She has pulled up a map of Washington, Oregon, and Idaho and highlighted the locations where murders took place.

She's been counting the murders and the trajectory of the killer's travels.

"Whoever this is covered a lot of ground," she says. "From Portland to Port Angeles is over two hundred miles. From Portland to St. Marie and Wallace, Idaho, it's more than four hundred." With the tip of her finger, she draws lines between the cities in the order the murders were carried out. "If Lemmon was killed by the same killer eight years ago, he waited a year and went from Portland to Wallace, Idaho, and killed Ludwig. Then, two years after killing Ludwig, the killer goes to St. Marie, Idaho, and kills Spradley. He stopped until a year ago when Coleman was murdered in Portland. And now he's killed Denton in Port Angeles, and Dupont was found on the Hood Canal Bridge. Those were within days of each other."

This guy is killing cops that he's judged guilty of heinous crimes. Wallace has been sending progressively threatening emails to me. Am I next? I feel an ice-cold fist in my chest thinking that Hayden and Dan both have access to my apartment. My friends have been targeted in the past to get to me. Are they in danger? Wallace is here.

Dan had given Hayden a job, mostly because Dan could intuit how much I wanted Hayden to stay in my life. Hayden had rambled around the country after separating from the military and I feared he would pick up and leave again. We got off to a rocky start, but things have gotten so much better. He's working. Happy. And although I know he'll never forgive me for leaving him behind, he still cares for me. If Wallace is a danger to me, he's a danger to Hayden. I'm done with being stalked, threatened by psychos from my past. If anything happens to Hayden, or Dan, or anyone I've gotten close to, I don't think I can do the right thing. I've worked very hard to put my past behind me, but I can still feel the old me, Rylee, just beneath the veneer of civil.

"Megan. Where are you going?"

"Huh. I'm just thinking."

"No. I mean, *where* are you going. You missed our turn."

She's right. I've become so distracted by the appearance of Wallace that I'm not myself. I have to think of something credible to tell her since I can't exactly tell her about Wallace or anything to do with my past.

"I didn't tell you this, but Jason Lemmon was killed in September, just like the others. According to my friend at the university, Lemmon was a self-absorbed asshole and pervert. I can't feel sorry for any of these victims." *And I won't even try. They got what they had coming. The difference between this killer and me is that I only killed murderers. This guy is killing any cop he deems to be dirty.*

I get off at the next exit, and as I turn onto the right road, a silver Caddy with dark-tinted windows and wire rims blows past us heading toward Port Townsend. I can't see the driver, but I know the car.

"Was that Nan?" Ronnie asks, and twists in her seat to watch the car disappear around a curve. I could care less about Nan right now.

I park outside the office and I take a breath. I have a lot of information, but what I don't have is a way of identifying the killer. Sheriff Gray is standing in the door to his office with a concerned look on his face.

"Where's the fire?" I ask.

Tony's expression is tight. "What? Oh, you mean Nan. Megan, do you have Nan working on these cases?" His voice sounds a trifle angry.

I say, "I gave her some busy work to keep her out of our hair. Why?"

"She's driving me crazy. Been in my office a half dozen times wanting to brainstorm."

First, she'll need a brain. But that's unkind. She has a good mind. It's just devious and nosey.

"Sorry, Tony. I just thought she'd be better off doing some small things and keep out of my desk. Did you give her a Junior G-Man badge?"

"I had to get rid of her before I did something unpleasant. I sent her to Moe's to pick up some things. It looks like this day is going to never end." He pauses and I know he's not done venting.

"She salutes me now." He gives us a serious look and adds, "She calls me sir and it's all your fault, Megan." He tries to keep up the stern look, but a tight smile forms on his lips and soon we're all laughing.

I give a smart salute and Ronnie comes to attention and joins me.

"Smart asses."

"We do our best, Sheriff Gray, sir." I know it's insensitive to laugh while people are dead, but it's either that or scream obscenities.

When the laughter dries up, Tony says, "Tell me what you've learned before Nan comes back."

We tell him about fake Dupont and what we learned from Detective Thompson. When we're done, he says, "Another serial killer? Golly-dang gee-whiz. Why pick on my little department? If this keeps up, we'll take the title of Murder City away from Gary, Indiana. Or Chicago."

Ronnie reminds him, "Washington State has the most serial killers per capita."

"Tell me something I don't know." He motions us into his office where a bag of fries is open and ransacked like a drug raid took place.

"Help yourselves. I can't eat all this."

Liar, liar, pants on fire.

I hadn't realized how hungry I was, but my stomach gurgles loud enough that it brings a snicker from Ronnie. We sit around, chomping and licking the salt and grease from our fingers.

We demolish the food, and Ronnie gets up. "I'm going to degrease and get us coffee."

"Thanks, but none for me," Tony says.

"I'll take some with a lot of cream and two packets of Sweet 'n Low."

"Right," she says, then, "You're kidding. Right? You always take it black."

"Do I look like I'm kidding?"

"Well, Okay."

Ronnie leaves the office, and Tony leans toward me. "Are you okay, Megan?"

The sincerity with which he says this catches me off guard. Maybe I'm still exhausted, or the love in his voice has gotten to me. I'd take a bullet for this man. He holds out a box of tissues and I wave it off. I'm not all right. Not by a long shot. But I say, "I'm fine, SIR..." and give a curt salute. Just then Ronnie comes back in with coffee.

"What'd I miss?"

Tony and I say, "Nothing."

THIRTY-TWO

Sheriff Gray taps a pencil on his desk. It's a nervous habit he's developed lately. His chair used to squeak every time he shifted, and he shifted a lot. But we were all given new desks and chairs so now he taps his pencil loud enough to cause me a distraction.

"So, our victim, this Dupont woman, is a suspect in a homicide in St. Marie, Idaho, back some six years. And possibly in Wallace, Idaho before that."

Ronnie pulls up the police report on her iPad and reads out loud. "David Ludwig was found tied into a chair and tortured. His penis was removed. His skull was caved in and an ice pick was driven into his brain through his eye. Evidence at the scene included hundreds of child porn videos found on his home computer. Also, on the computer were programs used exclusively to make IDs, such as passport, drivers licenses, business licenses, birth and death certificates, and other items like letters of recommendation and such."

Tony holds up a finger. "And our victim, Detective Spradley, was one of Ludwig's child porn customers."

"Yes. And we believe Ludwig is possibly where Dupont had her fake IDs made. Detective Thompson, St. Marie PD, is going to check through the computer data again and look for Dupont on any of the IDs."

Tony sips his coffee, grimaces, and pushes it away. "Dupont might be involved in the killings in St. Marie and Wallace, Idaho. Spradley was a dirty cop. And the retired Chief of Police, this Denton guy, is being investigated by DEA for drug dealing and possibly something worse. And we know Dupont isn't really Dupont. Is that about right?"

"There's something else, Sheriff," I say. "This may have started eight years ago with a security guard named Jason Lemmon. Lemmon was fired from Portland State University where he was a campus officer and went to work as a rent-a-cop. He wasn't the type to kill himself according to my sources. He had some of the same injuries as the others, and the call to the police was anonymous. He worked the same university as Sally Coleman. They may have known each other, but we're not able to determine that."

"Jeesh! This just gets worse and worse. Is that it?"

Isn't that enough? "That's what we have so far. If we can find someone who all the victims have in common, maybe we can get some traction."

We leave Tony's office and Ronnie says, "I like Patterson. She reminds me a little of you."

"You'd better take that back."

"No. I mean..." She punches my arm. "You're pulling my leg now."

I was. Caleb had a saying about this type of joking around. "Never try to fool a fooler." It seems like everything reminds me of Caleb lately and I feel a little shame for my disloyal thoughts. I have a boyfriend. Dan is caring, loving, talented, supportive, and all the things I could want in a relationship.

Then I remind myself that another man in my life is somewhere around—Wallace. That puts any impure thoughts right out of my head.

THIRTY-THREE

We left Tony communing with a stash of cream-filled donuts he thinks he's hidden in his lower right-hand desk drawer behind some files. His wife is going to kill him if the sugar and grease don't. Ronnie goes to her desk to work her magic, and I go to mine where I plop down in my comfortable chair and rummage in my jacket pocket and find two Aleve, coated with pocket lint, but I don't care. I pop them in my mouth, down them with a sip of cold and disgusting black coffee, and lean my head back and close my eyes.

I can feel my computer screen saver staring at me, reminding me I've come up blank. I've got nothing. I've got less than nothing. I've got a headache and that adds to the turmoil my mind and emotions have suffered since coming back from Cougar Point in Semiahmoo. It's hard to believe that all this has happened in less than twenty-four hours.

I feel helpless. Ronnie is doing what needs done here and faster than I ever could. Patterson has her own intel person and the benefit of local files and other police officers who knew the victim. Patterson has people to interview and has already been able to eliminate Dupont's ex-boyfriend. Of course, he couldn't be the killer because that would be too easy.

Clay has his own investigation working on Riley Denton in Port Orchard and half of Dupont, literally. And Dupont's argument with John Duncan, the late boyfriend, happened in Port Gamble; also, Clay's jurisdiction. His researchers haven't come up with squat, but they seem less than motivated. Jefferson County has the victim's head. A head. But I've got Ronnie, thank goodness.

Nan has returned from Moe's with a box of hamburgers, BLTs, donuts, and a large container of coffee. While I'm wasting time thinking negative thoughts, I feel Nan's eyes like a hot wind on the side of my face. If I don't give her another task soon, I'll have to fake an emergency and rush out of the office. Or if it comes to it, I can fake my death, again, and go to another country; start over. *What have I done?*

But to give the devil her due, Nan did find the murder-suicide of Caleb's parents. I'd like to have Ronnie get the actual police files. The event pings on my radar, but I don't know why. I could ask Clay to give me the case file on the parents since it happened in Port Orchard, but then he'd want to know why I needed it and it would become complicated. I decide not to interrupt Ronnie or Clay. My personal feelings should never get in the way of an actual case.

A voice speaks up only inches from my ear and I come out of my chair. Nan says, "Sorry, Detective Carpenter. I didn't mean to startle you."

My jaw is set and my fist is tightening, but I loosen up and try to play it off with a grin. "I was lost in thought, Nan. Do you have something else?" I hope she doesn't, but I can see excitement in her eyes.

"Detective Patterson faxed a copy of her follow-up reports. I made a copy for you and Detective Marsh. Should I make one for myself?"

Can I stop you? "Of course, Nan. I appreciate your willingness to help. This is a difficult one so I'd like you to see what you
can find on Riley Denton and Robert Spradley. Their info is in
Patterson's file." *The one you've already made a copy of no
doubt.*

"I'd be happy to."

"And can I ask a small favor?"

"Of course, Detective Carpenter."

"Sheriff Gray said you saluted him. I think that is a nice sign
of respect for his position and because we all admire him."

"That's what I thought too. We've gotten too sloppy
around here. We need some discipline. My nephew just
returned from the Marines and discipline didn't hurt him
any."

"I agree. But I think maybe saluting might be a little much."

She looks disappointed so I hurry and say, "Calling him sir
is a step in the right direction."

"Right you are. We all have to respect each other."

Nan gives me Patterson's fax of Dupont's personnel record
including several Internal Affairs complaints and subsequent
actions taken. Dupont was suspended twice in the last year for
excessive force complaints. She was currently being sued in
Federal Court for beating a handcuffed prisoner so badly he
had to be taken to the ER. Thirty-seven stitches across his scalp
and a broken nose. Dupont claimed he'd run into a wall. The
perfect shoe sole print on his chest was plain to see. There's no
doubt she had serious enemies as a police officer. From what
Patterson said, Dupont wasn't a good human being, much less a
good cop.

The clearance rate for homicides where a suspect is known
is only about sixty percent and that number has been steadily
declining for the last decade. When I was still Rylee, my clearance rate for murderers was one hundred percent. Much better
than the police. But, in their defense, the police have to obey the

law, and more and more roadblocks are being thrown in their paths.

And now there's Wallace. I can't shoot him for writing emails. I've changed. I'm not Rylee anymore. Is he the killer? Is he a threat to me? Why is he here? Why now? My suspicion the murders are related to Wallace, to something I've done in my past, might be nothing more than paranoia after finding out Wallace is in town and looking for me.

THIRTY-FOUR

I tell Ronnie I need to step out to run an errand. That's true, in a way, but I don't want her to know what the errand is. I need to get Caleb out of the picture for two good reasons: one, I'm concerned Wallace will target him. And two: I don't like the way he complicates things. I'm with Dan, and I don't need a ghost of boyfriends past running around my patch.

When I get out to my car, I call the number Caleb gave me at my apartment. He answers immediately.

"Rylee, what's up? Sorry, I mean Megan."

"You got time to talk?"

He does. I tell him to meet me at Moe's in ten minutes. When I get there, he's already seated at a booth with a coffee in front of him, studying the menu. He's wearing a plaid shirt and has a dusting of stubble. A goofy smile breaks out on his face when he sees me. I remind myself I'm spoken for and resist responding with my own smile.

"You hungry?" he asks as I slide into the booth.

I shake my head. "I don't have time to eat. We need to talk, and then I need to get back to work."

"That sounds ominous."

"It ought to," I say.

The smile drops and he takes on a serious air, folding his arms on the table and leaning forward. "Is this about this Walter guy?"

"Wallace," I correct. "And yes, it's about him. I think you need to leave."

"Why?"

"Because he's dangerous. He's been trying to intimidate me for months now, and he seems to be intensifying his efforts. You hear about those murders on the news?"

He nods. "You're working them, right?"

"Lots of us are working them." I lower my voice. "I'm trusting you not to say anything, but it's possible the murders are linked to Wallace. If I want to be able to do my job, I can't be wasting time worrying he's going to go after the people close to me."

He looks pleasantly surprised by the implication he's close to me but doesn't comment on it directly. "But why would he go after me?"

"I don't know." I hesitate, wondering how much to tell him, and then decide it's worth the risk. I tell him I think the postcard he got, the one with my address on it, could have been from Wallace. He protests that the signature on the back was an M. I remind him I didn't send it and tell him it's a W. We go back and forth on this before I lose my temper.

"Listen, I want you to go home, is that clear?"

"Perfectly clear," Caleb says. "Except for one thing."

"What?"

"If the postcard really was from this Wallace guy, he already knows where I live. Why do you think I'll be any safer at home?"

I open my mouth to shoot him down and then realize he has a point. My phone buzzes. It's Ronnie. I let it go to voicemail.

Caleb leans forward, tentatively putting a hand over mine.

"I'm not going anywhere," he says quietly. "If this guy is after you, I want you to know someone's watching your back."

*   *   *

When I get back to the station, Ronnie is tapping away at the keyboard and looks up.

"What is Nan working on?" Ronnie asks.

"Nothing. I just wanted to keep her out of our business for a while. Why?"

"She was very... I don't know... focused, quiet, this morning. The only time she's that quiet is when she's rummaging through your desk. She looks happy. Maybe we should really give her some things to help us out?"

I need to put a stop to this right here and now. I tell her a true story. "A while back Nan went to the news media with information on a triple murder that happened up in Snow Creek. She almost screwed the investigation. Not to mention putting the victim's families under a magnifying glass."

Ronnie, being kind, says, "But she might have learned her lesson? Maybe give her something real and she wouldn't go behind our backs?"

"I'll think about it." *Not going to happen.* "I need to clear my head. I'm going to see Clay."

"I'll get my things."

THIRTY-FIVE

We drive along Puget Sound, past Port Gamble, and on to the Kitsap County Sheriff substation in Kingston. Kingston is an unincorporated community of two thousand souls and sits along the shore of Appletree Cove. A major Washington State ferry terminal links it to Edmonds. Clay's office is in a one-story wood-sided building with a wood shingles roof facing the cove. There are three parking spaces marked, SHERIFF'S OFFICE ONLY. I take one of these.

Two guys, early twenties, are standing just around the corner of the station house. Both are smoking. I've never been a smoker, but the smell makes me want to start. Start retching. Both are dressed in T-shirts with logos on them. One has Hogwarts Castle silk-screened on the front. The other is of Harry Potter riding a broom and ducking one of those flying globes. On his shirt it reads, "NO ONE LIKES A SNITCH." Snitch guy comes toward me, scanning my entire body like an MRI. I should slap him, but I'm grateful I've still got it. Then I notice he's looking past me at Ronnie.

"You're Detective Marsh," Snitch says, and smiles showing teeth so badly stained I want to scrape them clean. He's wearing tattered jeans and flip-flops and I see he rolls his own smokes. It's not Mary Jane, but who knows what's on the drug market today.

The Hogwarts guy drops his smoke and crushes it with the toe of a flip-flop. He joins his buddy and they stand a respectful distance away. They were both smoking closer to the building than state law allows, but I don't care unless they give me some shit.

"Those things will kill you," I say to Harry Potter, and think if he keeps looking at my breasts, I might save the cigarettes the trouble. Hogwarts shuffles his feet and looks away. These are probably Clay's interns. They don't impress. Harry Potter opens the door for us and I can feel his eyes sizing us up from the rear. Or maybe he's checking Ronnie out. It doesn't matter. A douche is a douche.

The office has been reorganized. Where it once was a huge open space, it is now separated by free-standing partitions and several more desks have been added. Clay sees us and motions us over.

"Megan. I just got off the phone with your sheriff. Ronnie, you've done it again."

I say for the benefit of the geeks, "And she understands the meaning of Title 9 unlike your interns."

Clay chuckles. "Those two were working in Narcotics and they're here on loan. I was told they are the best we've got."

"God help us."

Clay smirks and says to the interns. "You can go back on smoke break."

The nerds leave, and I feel dirty. And smokey.

"How do you always get involved in this stuff, Megan?"

"Just lucky, I guess. Have your guys come up with anything Ronnie didn't pass on to us?"

Clay rolls his eyes.

"By the way. Where is your new partner? Cindy, right?"

A short, dark-haired woman comes out of the break room balancing three mugs of steaming coffee on a tray. She looks to be in her mid-thirties or she dyes her hair. "I saw you pull up. I take it you've met Beavis and Butthead?" I nod. "Clay said you take yours black. And Detective Marsh takes hers with cream and sugar."

I take one of the coffees and blow across the top. It smells strong and I take a tentative sip. I like it strong and this is perfect.

"I grind my own coffee beans. You like?"

We both say we love it.

"I'm Cindy," she says, and takes our hands in turn. "Pleased to meet you both at last." She's half Clay's size and age, but her grip is as strong as Clay's. She must be awful handy for opening jars.

"Clay said you've only been here a few months. Bad luck catching all this before you've settled in," I say to make conversation.

"Oh, please. Seattle was a cesspool of killings. Mostly drug related. This is like a vacation." Cindy looks toward the door. "Of course, we had better resources. Frick and Frack don't just work in Narcotics, I think they take them."

Clay says. "Not everyone is a fireball like you, Cindy. Give them a break."

"Smoke break is over." Cindy heads outside. "I'll find work for them."

After she goes outside Clay lets a breath out. "She's very passionate."

"I hadn't noticed." Clay would never have a thing for her. I shouldn't feel good about it, but I do. "Patterson tells us she has an IT person so we can share. Two heads are better than one, and all that."

Clay hands me a folder. "Everything we have on Riley

Denton so far." The file is pretty thin. "I'll wait for Cindy to fill you in when she's done chewing the interns out."

The two guys come in, one grinning and the other with his tail between his legs. They head to their cubicles and Cindy casts them a disparaging look. "Let's go to the interview room."

We follow her. I wasn't aware there was an interview room. In the past Clay just used the front area around his desk.

"We cleaned out a room. It was full of junk and supplies."

The interview room is a good size. An Army surplus table is set up with four folding chairs and a dozen more lean against a wall.

"We let AA use this room. The meetings are run by a retired officer so we don't have to worry about thefts."

I notice there are no cameras or recording equipment. What's said in an AA meeting stays in the room.

Cindy has a folder in front of her but doesn't open it. "Riley Denton, age eighty-four. Retired Chief of Police from St. Marie, Idaho. He was seventy-five when he retired. I called St. Marie PD and he wasn't well liked. One of the secretaries had worked for him for a year or two. She was hesitant to talk about him until I told her he was dead.

"She remembered he was very vindictive. He'd fired a couple of the officers and staff when she worked for him. The reason he gave was improper storage of narcotics. The story was he would find cocaine and other drugs in their police cars or in their lockers. He claimed he had confidential sources, but the truth was he hated these officers for personal reasons. She'd heard rumors that type of crap had been going on for years before she was hired, and she was always afraid she would be framed for something during his time as Chief.

"She said he had worked in the Narcotics Unit and made several big arrests and the suspects would claim there was money or weapons missing after the arrest. His people suspected he was stealing things when they searched the houses. They could never prove anything. When he made Chief the officers reported the goings on to the DEA, and they were looking at him. When he found out the Feds were interested in him, he retired and left town."

Ronnie fills them in on Detective Spradley, and David Ludwig. I tell them about Jason Lemmon.

Cindy says, "So we think Denton was killed because he was a dirty cop?"

I say, "A lot of people might have wanted to kill him."

Clay says, "Some of these deaths could be revenge killings."

Ronnie says, "But chances of this many murders defy the odds." We all agree. "There may be more that we haven't found yet. There's no way of telling how long this killer has been at work."

When she says this Caleb's father and stepmother's deaths come to mind. I haven't yet read the article Nan found about the murder-suicide, but it's like another ping on the radar. If I remember right, Caleb's father built sailboats. I have no idea what his real mother did, but according to Caleb, his stepmother worked hard at being a meddling bitch. Could our killer have gone after them? I dismiss the thought. Wallace has affected me in ways I don't care for.

The sun will be setting soon and my stomach is making noise like wild animals are loose in there. I don't want to go back to the office and be annoyed by Nan but I need to talk to Sheriff Gray. I call Tony's cell and ask him to meet up at Moe's.

THIRTY-SIX
WALLACE

The Uber driver is a young woman, twenty-three, good-looking, and best of all doesn't want to make small talk. The good-looking ones never meet your eye. He doesn't blame her. There are a lot of dangerous people out there.

"This is good here," he tells the driver, and hands her the fare plus a ten percent tip. Give them too much and they remember you. Give them too little and they remember you as yet another asshole.

He's on the street corner just down the block from the Tides. He's been here once before while Rylee was out of town with Ronnie. He's changed his appearance and is anxious to see if the waitress or bartender recognize him. He'd chatted them up last time, and he takes the same table as last time. The waitress comes and he orders the same meal with the same brand of Scotch. The same brand of Scotch Rylee drinks. The waitress smiles at him, but there's no recognition in her eyes. She catches a whiff of his cologne. Familiar. A dad brand.

She flirts, he feigns interest, eats his meal, pays his tab with a generous tip this time, and goes to the restroom. It gives him a chance to see the complete layout of the place. There's a side door leading to a parking area and a back door that leads to the trash receptacles inside a fenced area. He looks outside. There is a fence with a gate and no lock. Even locked it would be easy work for him.

The earlier disguise, the beard and dark glasses, worked like a charm. He doubts even the sheriff's secretary, Nan, would recognize him now. He used a deeper voice then, one that went with his getup and beard. Now he's clean-shaven, hair combed to one side, nice jeans, casual button-up shirt, and loafers.

He goes back inside and uses the restroom. The restaurant is busy this evening and there is a sign up by the door announcing live music after eight o'clock. He might come back depending on how things develop. Rylee is almost ready to meet him. He doesn't cherish the thought of the pain he may have to cause her, but she has to come to her senses.

THIRTY-SEVEN

Tony takes a rain check on my invitation to join us for a meal and instead calls us back to the office. Nan has gone home and Tony sits at his desk with his tie down, the top two buttons of his khaki shirt undone, and I can see he's wearing a black AC/DC band shirt. He motions for us to sit. "What have you got?"

I tell him about Denton's reputation among his officers and staff and that he was under investigation by the DEA for dealing narcotics.

Tony leans back in his chair and gives a tight smile. "Guess now you'll appreciate your old sheriff more."

We already appreciate him, but yes, he's a good guy so he won't be a target of this psycho.

He says, "Well, I guess DEA's investigation is dead. No pun intended."

* * *

Ronnie and I drive separately to the Tides. When I first took the job with the Jefferson County Sheriff Office, this was my hangout with my only friend, Mindy Newsom. I've grown a lot since then. I'm happier and I've learned to take deep breaths.

We sit at our usual table. The bartender nods at us. He'll make our drinks and hopefully the waitress will bring them and take our orders before we die. He does, she does, and we sit and look down in our drinks, lost in our own thoughts. As a unit, Tony, Mindy, Ronnie, Marley, and I have sat at this table, toasting to some victory or promotion, or just drinking on countless occasions.

I've sat here alone drowning my feelings after struggling with some case seemingly impossible to solve. When I was Rylee my job was simple. Catch the killer, kill them, move on. Not so easy now.

Suddenly, I'm thinking about Caleb. I've been doing that a lot, the last couple days, but for some reason he's fought the way to the top of my mind despite all of the competition.

And then Ronnie says the four words guaranteed to put Caleb—and anything else—right out of my mind.

"Tell me about Wallace." Ronnie is drinking Scotch. My brand. I've ruined her.

I don't pause long because that would infer there's something to tell. But it's long enough.

"Megan. You promised to tell me."

I've promised a lot of things and then broken the promises to protect myself. This time I feel I have to tell in order to protect myself.

"This has to stay between us," I say.

Ronnie holds up a pinky. "Pinky swear."

"Just tell me and I'll believe you." The pinky thing is something Hayden and I used to do many years ago. I feel a little pang in my heart.

"I'm your partner. I swear."

I almost pull a Ronnie and start with, *You'll never guess*, but she deserves the truth. Well, part of it anyway.

"A few years back I started receiving emails from someone signing the email as *Wallace*. The emails started by Wallace saying he knew where I was.

"Just a sec," I say, and take out my phone and open a file where I've saved all the mail from this psycho. "The first one just says he saw me on the news and asks how the weather is in Port Townsend. He said maybe he could come by and we could talk. I didn't think much of it," I lie. "But then the second one came soon after. I'll read it to you." And omit the part where he calls me Rylee.

"'I doubt you know what it's like to be hurt so deeply you've lost part of yourself. I know what it feels like. Soon, you will too.'"

"And here's one from the time you and I worked with Clallam and Kitsap on those killings that were done by Tony's cousin and his cop friend."

I read...

"'You are so busy these days. But then, you always were sticking your nose in places it didn't belong. I see you're on the hunt again. And this time you're interfering with Clallam and Kitsap County cases. Good for you. I'm sure you'll find your man. Just hope he doesn't find you first. You're not as clever as you think. I'm in Port Townsend. See you soon. Wallace.'"

It's ironic that we now have a cop killer. Ronnie's expression hasn't changed. She takes a tiny sip of her Scotch and then says, "That was over a year ago. Do you think that's the Wallace that talked to Nan?"

I'm sure of it. "He told Nan he was sorry he missed us at Drayton Harbor Oyster Company where we were eating with Rebecca. He knew I was with you and Rebecca. He told Nan he didn't want to interrupt our meal."

"He had to have followed you there. Does he mention me by name?"

"Not by name, but he's seen us together and I'm sure he

knows your name if he reads the newspapers." I don't tell her he has mentioned her in other emails. She doesn't need to know that yet.

"And you don't know this guy?"

"He told Nan I would know him, but I don't have any idea who he is." I'm depressed and anxious and murderous, thinking about how this guy has infused his psychotic fantasy into my life.

Our food comes, but I've lost my appetite for food. I am thirsty and down my Scotch and order another. Double. No ice.

"At least you still have the emails."

"I do."

"Megan, this is just too coincidental. Don't you think this Wallace character is involved in some of this?"

"I didn't delete the emails, but I don't think they'll do us any good."

Ronnie smiles and downs her Scotch. This time she does choke a little and I'm pleased to see I haven't totally corrupted her. "I think you'd be surprised. If you want my help, you know I'm here for you."

I feel a warmth inside and it's not just the Scotch. I just nod. She reaches across the table and puts a hand on mine. "You helped save my mother. If I can help you find this jerk, we'll do it, together."

Now I'm hungry. My phone rings.

THIRTY-EIGHT

We left Ronnie's Explorer at the Tides and are now back in Kingston at the Sheriff Substation. Patterson has brought one of her research people. Donna Kerwick is young, blond, ridiculously attractive, and is almost a duplicate of Ronnie, both in appearance and, annoyingly like Ronnie, she prefaces her sentences with, "You won't believe this" or "Guess what?"

Detective Cindy Brook had run the interns off earlier and made her special coffee while we pull some desks together. To me any strong black coffee nowadays is special.

Clay looks embarrassed. "Sorry about the interns. They were supposed to be the best, but I think they just wanted to get back to their unit. Narcotics guys are a different breed."

"Maybe they were intimidated," I say. "After all, they were working with the legendary Clay Osborne."

"Were you intimidated?" he asks.

"Of course," I lie.

Cindy sips her coffee and listens.

Patterson takes the floor. "Donna has something you should hear."

Donna Kerwick shyly begins. "Detective Dupont opened a

modest bank account in Port Angeles at Seattle Bank and Trust when she moved here from Cleveland. At the time she deposited just under ten thousand dollars. Right now, she has over three hundred thousand in the account and then there's her 401K, and she paid cash for her house: 2.5 million dollars according to tax records. From what I could find, she's been putting half of her police pay in a 401K and is still making monthly deposits of nine thousand dollars. All in cash."

Patterson interrupts. "I'll be looking into the bank. That should have raised a red flag unless she has an inside person at the bank."

Kerwick says, "Her Hummer is worth over one hundred thousand. Maybe as much as one hundred thirty."

I ask, "Did she pay cash for that as well?"

Kerwick is silent for a short pause and says, "She bought it outright with a Cashier's Check from her bank account."

Clay's eyes grow wide. "No way."

Kerwick says, "Way."

"Where is the money coming from?" I ask.

"That's the thing," Kerwick says. "I couldn't trace the source since it all seemed to be cash deposits. But I called the bank and told them Dupont was deceased and we were investigating the possibility her finances were involved. I had them put a hold on any accounts she has with them and asked if she has been depositing money from other banks."

Patterson looks at Ronnie and then at me and grins. The grin says, *I got me a Ronnie too.* She may be right.

"So, the bank manager told me most of her deposits were in cash. No checks except for her police pay. No transfers. She never withdrew any of it. The deposits were monthly and just under ten grand each. Anything over that amount and they would have had to report it to the Feds." We were all aware of the rule to help prevent money laundering. A lot of good it does for savvy criminals. I'll never have that problem.

Ronnie says, "I was getting around to doing financials."

"I'm sure you would have found it," Donna says.

Her smile irritates me, but Ronnie seems pleased to find another computer nerd.

Ronnie says, "I have something, too. You're going to like this."

She waits for someone to ask what we're going to like, but I'm not an enabler and I thought I had her house-trained. Evidently, she has picked up bad habits sitting close to another "guess what" addict.

"Okay. I checked tax records and found out Dupont worked with the Columbus police in Ohio for a year or two before going to Cleveland PD."

Patterson sits up straight. "That wasn't in her file. We would have known."

Ronnie continues as if Patterson had said nothing. "There were several unsolved robberies when Dupont worked there. All told the amounts taken were close to what Dupont deposited here and paid for the house."

Clay asks, "I didn't think she lived in Columbus."

Ronnie says, "She didn't report it on her Clallam application and I only found it by doing tax records."

"Was she working on the robberies in Columbus?" Patterson asks.

"I was just getting to that. She wasn't lead detective, but she would have access to all the information in the investigations. She was dating the lead investigator on each of the robberies."

Clay says, "Good job, Ronnie and Donna."

Cindy says, "I don't have anything new on ex-Chief Denton. Maybe one of you can profile him."

The computer geniuses look at each other and I see a bond being formed. Or an alliance. Or whatever. I'm not sure I like sharing my computer nerd freely, but it's good for the cases at hand.

"And one more thing," Ronnie says. "There was a suspect in two of the robberies in Columbus. Police suspected he was an accomplice, but before they could apprehend him, he died from a beating."

Everyone goes silent.

Clay says, "Well I'll be damned. Dupont again."

I ask, "Were you able to find anything more about Duncan's history?" Blank looks from Patterson and Donna. Clay says, "I thought he was eliminated?"

Ronnie speaks up. "I did a little workup on Duncan. We can rule him out as a suspect in Dupont's murder. I checked with the jeweler that sold him the engagement ring. It cost him four months' pay. The jeweler said Duncan told him it was going to be a surprise."

The surprise was on Duncan. "Ronnie, will you and Donna get together on the dates of the robberies and check them against Dupont's whereabouts? And I'd like copies of the robbery files. We need to nail that down solid."

Ronnie and Donna give each other a high five. How childish.

Patterson says, "We know that Dupont couldn't have killed Riley Denton. If the coroner is right about Denton's time of death, Dupont was missing and dead herself."

Clay says, "There go our two best suspects."

That leaves Wallace.

THIRTY-NINE
WALLACE

His name is Wallace now. Wallace is unafraid. Wallace is adventurous. He chews gum and kicks ass as the sports jocks like to say. His old track coach would be surprised to see how confident and decisive and powerful he's become. But Coach died in the parking lot of high school. Run over by a hit and run driver. Poor bastard. Coach's mistreatment of his team was legendary. Nothing he did was never good enough for Coach.

He'd taken enough of that crap at home. Home. What is home but a house, a bed, a meal sometimes, when the bitch deigned to cook. Most of the time it was frozen dinners or take-out. He'd learned nothing during his school years, except how to put up with the bullshit, keep his head down and his mouth shut.

Then he learned about real power. Control. He was an eager student. Plan, preparation, execution, escape. Those are the things he's learned over the years. The things that have kept him alive and out of prison. Some he learned from Rylee. Some from other killers who were quite talkative thinking he'd let them live.

It still bothers him that Rylee would leave her apartment so unsecured. She should know window locks are easy to slip. But then she's only had one killer come for her. Her real father doesn't count.

He was watching when the woman who had hunted Rylee down was prepared to end her life and he was prepared to intercede. But it was Megan's partner that had come to the rescue.

That little event ended in disappointment. Rylee hadn't disposed of her would-be killer. Ronnie had been the one to put the bitch down. Rylee has let her emotions cloud her judgment. She's become soft.

He's watched her career as a hunter since the beginning. She has committed atrocious crimes, conned, and lied to get next to her targets. She's like a chameleon when she's on the hunt. She can be a convincing reporter, a student, a lawyer, a Good Samaritan trying to find the owner of a missing cat to get intel on her target.

He wants to make Rylee revert to the ruthless killer barely hidden under her goody-goody façade. They would make a formidable killing team. But killing her while she's this weak version of Rylee is no accomplishment. He hopes it won't come down to that.

She has a boyfriend now. Thinks she's in love with Dan Anderson. He'll have to take him out of the picture to... motivate her. Not kill him. Just hurt him enough to let him linger to light a fire that will burn bright in her heart and mind. Rekindle the old passion of the hunt.

And then there's Hayden. The little brother. Her albatross. From what he's found out about him, he's like them and Rylee has no idea what he's done while in Afghanistan.

There's no hurry to do anything yet. Plan. Preparation. Execution. Escape. A creed to live by. A creed to kill by.

FORTY

The meeting at the Kingston Sheriff Substation broke up and Ronnie and I headed back to the Tides. Ronnie had exchanged contact info with Donna Kerwick, which I thought was unnecessary considering they can find just about anyone they want to.

As we approach the Hood Canal Floating Bridge, a caravan of news vehicles comes up behind us and more are ahead of us. Individual reporters and their cameramen are scattered around the area where the body parts were dumped. There's not much to film now. The bridge has been opened and the body parts taken away to the morgue. But then I see Ernie; the local Washington State Board of Public Works manager is lit up with floodlights from several news vans and cameramen and is being interviewed. The talking heads are spaced out ten feet from each other, holding microphones and looking somber. The newspaper reporters have notebooks out scribbling frantically to get every word. They will take the notes back to the newspaper office and twist them around to suit the editor who is all about sales. The truth is of no consequence.

One of the TV vans has the KOMO logo imprinted in over-large letters on the side. That's Seattle-Tacoma news and an

affiliate of NBC and CBS. I recognize the Port Townsend Television, PTTV, reporter from some earlier cases. She's young,
and eager, and pushy, and fearless, hence she's beautiful. There
are also newspaper reporters from the *Port Orchard Independent*, Bailey something or other, and Lacy Pittson from the Port
Townsend Jefferson County newspaper, *The Leader*, both gathered greedily around Ernie, who is eating the attention up. I
forgot to threaten him to keep quiet. As it is, we've gotten almost
a day ahead of this circus.

"I'll drop you at the Tides to get your car, but I'm not
hungry. I think I'll just have a sandwich and go to bed," I say.

"I can stay at your place tonight if it's okay. We'll be up and
at it early and I could use a sandwich."

"Sorry partner, but I haven't been sleeping very well and
might keep you awake." I don't want to take Ronnie to my place.
Not when there's a chance Caleb might decide to pay another
unannounced visit. I've told her about Wallace. She doesn't
need to know any more about my past.

"Understood. I'll see you at the office around five o'clock."

"Sounds good. Oh crap..." I duck my head, but it's too late.
Lacy Pittson of *The Leader* is waving both arms at me like she's
landing an aircraft. I speed up and fly by the vans and gaggle of
news-geese and don't care if any of them get sucked into the jet
wash from my engine.

Two Jefferson County cruisers pass us at warp speed,
bubblegum lights flashing, going in the direction of the bridge,
and wave at me.

Ronnie twists around. "Wow! Sometimes I wish I'd had
some more time working in patrol. What would it be like to
drive like that?"

I punch the gas and she is shoved back in her seat as my
Explorer rockets forward winding its way around several cars.
"It feels like that," I say with a grin. "Going supersonic is one of
the benefits of being the fuzz."

The radio comes to life and Bonnie, our dispatcher, calls my unit number. When I answer she says, "Megan, are you on your way into headquarters?"

"Affirmative."

"We have a report of a reckless driver on Highway 19 going northbound. County units were requested to, uh... direct traffic on the Hood Canal and said they couldn't pursue the Explorer." I swear I can hear her snicker. "They didn't get a license plate, but it was an Explorer. If you locate, the vehicle please advise."

Ronnie giggles and covers her mouth.

"Will do, Dispatch," I say, and I realize the deputy wasn't waving at me. He was motioning for me to slow it down. *Where's the fun in that?*

FORTY-ONE

When I get home the entry door to the house is shut and locked. Miracles do happen. I come in as quietly as possible and shut and lock my door behind me. Gun in hand I check the windows, closets, and under the bed. Dust bunnies but no monsters. All the windows are locked. But being locked hadn't stopped the last intruder.

The refrigerator is calling me and I get a plastic tumbler and fill it from the box of wine that lives in the fridge. There's sandwich meat, bologna, pimento and pickle loaf, Colby cheese slices, mayonnaise, and half a chicken hoagie. I sniff the hoagie and it goes in the trash. I make a sandwich with what's there, take my wine, and go to my desk.

The bottom drawer is locked and doesn't show signs of tampering. I've got the encrypted tapes on my phone, and my computer, and so there is no need to keep the old analog recordings. Not really. They are relics. Touchstones. Physical reminders.

Even if someone found them and played them, my current name is never mentioned. My voice isn't the same. The young

Rylee's voice is barely recognizable, even to me. I don't know anyone who likes the sound of their own recorded voice. I loathe mine.

The tapes are helter-skelter in the box. No specific order but all are marked with the date the session was taped. I've listened to them so many times I've memorized them. Like watching a movie over and over and saying the lines before the actors do. For now, I need to hear Dr. Albright's voice. Her questions were never judgmental. She didn't tell me what to do; she just helped me open up and understand what needed done.

I select a tape from among the scattered array and am still amazed I talked to this woman, this stranger really, and bared my soul. If I'd had her for a mother, maybe I wouldn't be so messed up.

Stripping out of my clothes and leaving them over the back of my desk chair, I find my Portland State University T-shirt and put it on. I haven't worn the shirt for quite a while and I wonder if my subconscious is working on the present stress. Wiped out doesn't begin to describe my condition, but I take the sandwich, the wine, and the tape recorder to bed. I'm too tired to sit at the desk or in the kitchen.

I feel naked, basically am naked, but I need the gun, retrieve it from my shoulder holster, put it under the pillow, and start the tape.

My voice, the younger version, comes from the tiny speaker of the mini-cassette player and it's no wonder I selected this one. It revealed the last of my relationship with Caleb.

Me: I had a boyfriend. Sort of. Caleb and I said our goodbyes in front of a church where we—where I—decided Angie would be safe.

I pause the tape. Angie was the little girl Ted Duggan had

kidnapped. Caleb and I saved the girl, but it wasn't enough for me. It was for Caleb. I hit the play button.

> *Me: It should have been a moment of joy, but it wasn't even close to that. Things had sputtered out of control at Ted Duggan's house. The house where he'd been imprisoning little girls, and when he was finished with them as a sex toy, he'd kill them. Angie was the last of those girls. She'd lived because of what Caleb and I had done.*

> *Dr. Albright: You saved the girl. It was a good thing, Rylee.*

> *Me: It should have been. We were going to take her to her mother's, but we knew there would never be a family reunion, a happy ending of the sort in fairy tales. She was traumatized. Barely able to speak. So, I took her to a church. People there would help her. Bring her home and look after her well-being. At least that's what I believed.*

The tape is silent. Karen isn't asking questions. She's patiently waiting for me to tell this my own way, in my own time.

> *Me: Angie was traumatized and maybe scarred for life, never to trust another man, allow them to touch her. There is a rage inside me that I don't understand. I wonder if it's the result of my father's DNA, the poisoned blood that travels through my veins. I'm confused. I'm mad at the world. Furious at the way evil people seem to exist only for the torment of others, as though their happiness is directly dependent on the suffering they inflict.*

> *Dr. Albright: You thought you were doing the right thing. Something good for others.*

Me: I don't regret doing what I had to do to stop him from harming other little girls. I wished I could have made him suffer like he did to Angie. But that's as evil as what these monsters do to their unsuspecting victims.

I could have taken Angie from her doll-house prison and returned her to her mother. She would have told the cops everything Duggan had done. He would have been arrested. I truly can't imagine a world in which he might not have been convicted. I'm as sure of that now as I was back then, though I didn't tell Caleb that. Going to prison wasn't enough of a punishment for the Duggans of this world. Prison was like a cruel catch-and-release program. As hideous as Duggan's crimes were, the clock would run and he'd be free someday. I stopped him from doing harm to anyone else ever again.

Dr. Albright: Tell me about your friend Caleb. He was with you at Ted Duggan's house.

Me: Seeing what Duggan had done, and then knowing what I'd done to Duggan traumatized Caleb as much as Angie. But I wasn't sorry. I didn't feel much of anything at all. At least not right then. Not in that second. Deep down I always knew I'd have to do things on my own. Caleb was disgusted with me. Confused at his feelings for me, a murderer. I wanted to kiss him goodbye, but all the things we'd said back at the Duggan place were the kinds of things that could not be made better with a kiss.

I had lied to him. Betrayed him. Put him at risk. I hadn't done those things for any reason other than the biggest one of all. I didn't trust Caleb. He had a conscience. I was right not to trust him to be in on the kill. He rejected me. I thought he loved me. Or he could have if I had let him.

Dr. Albright: How did that affect you, Rylee?

Me: I was wrecked. Caleb said, "We never really got started."
He said, "It's really over for us." His eyes were full of anger and
disappointment. It was a look that I'd never seen. Not from
him. I told him I knew it was over, and the words nearly choked
in my throat. It was evening, just when the lights get low, and
his eyes glistened. He asked if I was sure. I asked if he was. He
said these words. "I'm sure that I can't do this, Rylee. I can't be
judge and jury." I told him that I can and he said that was fine.
That it was fine for me but not for him.

The tape spools to the end and the machine shuts itself off.
The wine is gone. The sandwich is gone. My mind is gone. I
started tonight wanting to know how I'd left it with Caleb all
those years ago. Was he right? Or is he Wallace, and he's come
around to my original way of thinking? And now, do I share the
killer's beliefs that killing is for the greater good? That was the
old Rylee. Now I'm Megan. I'm not like this psycho.

I've pored through books, searched the Internet, and
watched countless YouTube videos about the psychology of
murder. When I accused my mother of being as sick as my serial
killer father, she claimed he had made her do it. When I didn't
buy that, she said, "It takes one to know one." I wonder now if it
applies to me in the darkest ways imaginable.

Caleb only remembers the girl who left him behind. He
only knows what he's seen in the news media. Why is he here
now? Going by the W on the card with my address, I believe
Wallace invited him for his own reasons, but Caleb didn't know
that, and he had to want to come to be here.

As I nod off, I hear the last thing he said to me. He asked me
how I would get home. I answered that I didn't have a home. He
told me to be careful and pressed something into my palm.

Angie's friendship bracelet.

She'd had it on the entire time of her captivity. Caleb told me Angie wanted me to have it. He said I deserved it because I'd saved her. The Caleb chapter of my life was over. We'd never had a chance anyway.

Now he's here and I'm not ready for a reboot.

FORTY-TWO

When I get to the Sheriff Office, it's well before five o'clock, but I'm not first to arrive. Donna Kerwick and Ronnie have their heads together, and when they see me they come over out of breath.

Donna chimes first. "Ronnie's a genius."

"You'll never guess what we've found," Ronnie jumps in.

This feels like an ambush by a mutual-appreciation society.

"I haven't had coffee and I might get violent," I say.

This day is going to suck, I think.

Ronnie looks at Donna. "You have to excuse my caffeine-deprived partner. She doesn't talk before she's swimming in the stuff, and she hates it when I start asking her to guess."

"Got it," Donna says. "Patterson is the same way. Those two are so much alike they could be sisters."

I make my way to the coffee bar, where I'm tempted to keep going out the back door with my coffee until I can be civil. But I don't. I burn my throat with the swill, force a smile on my face, and return to the Bobbsey Twins. They have something to tell me.

"Go," I say.

"Okay." Ronnie's eyes sparkle with excitement. "We were able to get into Dupont's email account. Guess..." She stops herself and corrects, "She'd deleted a bunch of emails but not completely."

Donna jumps in. "People think they've deleted things but everything you do stays on the Internet in some form. Ronnie is a genius at recovering stuff."

Ronnie gets an *aww shucks* look, and I swear to God, she says, "It wasn't anything."

"Don't be so modest. Even I couldn't have found them. And I mean *I'm good*."

"If you two can pry your hands from patting your own backs, can you please tell me what you're talking about. My coffee is getting cold."

Ronnie thrusts a sheet of paper into my hands. "It's an email from Wallace."

My heart skips a beat and is now fluttering in my chest and I haven't even had copious amounts of caffeine. I turn my back so I won't be distracted by these two vibrating with excitement. I read:

I know what you did in Columbus and soon everyone will know unless you pay my price. Advertising section of the Port Orchard Independent. Directions will be in plain sight. You're a detective. You can figure it out. If you bring anyone, I'll post all your dirty secrets everywhere. Prison is awaiting. Do it now. I'll be watching."

Wallace

Now I finally have proof he's behind all of this. I'm sure if these geniuses get into Spradley's and Denton's and Ludwig's email, they'll find similar emails.

Donna says, "We've got a copy of the *Independent* and we

think we've found the article Dupont was supposed to read. It's from the same date she disappeared." Ronnie hands me a photocopy of an article from what I assume is the *Independent*.

GEORGE WALLACE. DUPONT. PORT ORCHARD MARINA
SLIP 45.

The date on the newspaper is the day Dupont went missing. That was all it said, but we finally have a lead. "Can you pull up any surveillance from the marina and the surrounding area?"

"We've already looked. We see a woman matching Dupont's description, but I can't be one hundred percent sure it's her. This was about six in the morning the day she went missing. The woman walks around the slips searching for something then pulls something from the prow of one of the yachts and sticks it in her pocket. She leaves the marina and we couldn't pick her up again."

A dead end. Maybe. But not necessarily. Dan had placed ads in the Port Townsend newspaper in the past, and he paid with a credit card. "Maybe we can get the newspaper to give us the payment information for the person that placed the ad?"

"Working on it when you came in," Ronnie says. "Donna has a friend that works at the newspaper there and..."

I hold up a hand. "Don't involve any newspeople unless we have to. They ask too many questions. I don't want Wallace to know we're on to him. Yet."

Ronnie looks deflated and I can't blame her. I haven't received this news with the excitement she'd expected. I didn't even thank them. And I'd just told Ronnie about Wallace yesterday, and here she has found him and from what I can tell she hasn't let on to Donna of his connection to me.

"Sorry. Not enough caffeine yet." I take a sip. "This was a miraculous find. You two are just what this case needs." I slather on the compliments. Actually, it is a miracle of tech. I could never have done it and made the connection between Dupont and Wallace. We can't even prove what Dupont did in Columbus that Wallace is threatening to reveal. He's used the same or similar threats in his emails to me.

Donna looks a little let down too so I give her a lie sandwich. That's a truth with a lie filling. "Someone calling themselves Wallace came to my office while I was out of town. He said he was looking for me." Now for the lie. "I don't know any Wallace. I can't imagine why he would be looking for me, or that it's the same Wallace."

Donna perks up again and Ronnie gives me a sly look. I make people happy. It's a gift.

"You've given me a couple of ideas. Ronnie, why don't you see what you can find in the other victims' emails. Donna, there's a surveillance video from my office for the time this person calling themselves 'Wallace' came in. It's not very clear and the person is wearing a hoodie."

"Video is my specialty," Donna says.

"I'd like you to use your magic on it and see if you can get a better look at this guy."

"Didn't someone in here talk to him?" she asks. And so she should.

"Our secretary, Nan. She was so busy drooling and thinking of the rumors she could spread that she had only the most basic description. Male. Attractive. That's about all she knew for sure."

"I need to pass this on to Patterson. I'm sure she'll approve."

I say, "I'll call Patterson." It's so early I don't want Donna to get chewed out for waking her. "And I'll call Clay and Cindy in Kingston. This is big news. You guys did a great job here." I say that and mean it. These two are bloodhounds. I don't want them looking into my background. I'm not eager to run again. If I have to I want to go somewhere warm this time. Someplace I don't see monsters. I don't know where that is. Besides, I don't want to leave Hayden behind this time. Or any of my friends. Shit!

Someone, maybe the sheriff, said one time, "The past has a way of catching up to you." At the time I think they were referring to the killer we were after. They could as easily, and more accurately, have been referring to me.

FORTY-THREE

Ronnie's cell phone plays the intro music for *CSI*, which is the Who's classic, "Who Are You?" I can't help but grin, but she'd better stop. There's only room for one sarcastic and humorous person in this office.

While Ronnie listens to the caller, her head bobs up and down like those little plastic dogs on a car dash. "That's great! Let me put you on speaker phone. Megan and Donna are here. Donna? Donna is from Clallam. She's an IT like me. Hold on."

She puts the call on speaker. "Greetings from the crime lab," Marley Yang says.

"You're in early," I say. "What gives?"

"Ronnie asked me to put a rush on some of this. She said you were hitting a wall."

Ronnie gives me a sheepish look. At least her version of one. "We weren't getting much and I thought if anyone could find a clue it would be Mar."

Mar? What the hell kind of nickname is Mar?

"What have you got for us, Mar?"

"Well, you're never going to believe this."

He's been with Ronnie too long.

"Kitsap sent me some things found in Dupont's yard. Most of it was junk, but there was one thing."

"And?"

"The handle of a baseball bat. The club end is missing. At first it didn't seem to have anything on it, but I used some equipment I'm sure you don't want to know about."

I'm going to strangle him.

"I found traces of blood and hair . Some tissue too. I took the liberty of calling Sam—that's the coroner—and he said the wound on the back of Denton's head could have been made with a club."

I'm a little disappointed. By the way Ronnie was acting, he'd found the killer's name engraved on the wooden handle. "Thanks for calling, Marley. Good work. If you have anything else..."

"I'm not finished, Megan."

"Right. Sorry."

"I tested the meat cleaver Clallam sent me. The blood is from a dog. The hair on the blade is a dog's. Mindy said you think the cement block you found might have been what the killer used to cut the head off, but the blade on the cleaver isn't dulled or nicked. It's still razor sharp."

So, we made the right call releasing John Duncan.

Marley goes on. "I matched the hair and blood on the bat handle to Denton. I'll have to run DNA on the tissue. I assume it's from his scalp. But we have the weapon now." He pauses for so long I think we've been disconnected, but then he says, "I have blood, hair, and tissue from Dupont from the cement block. The hair was hers. I didn't find her blood on Denton's evidence or hers on Denton's, but that's not an issue since we think Denton was killed first. But Crime Scene had scraped under her fingernails."

Marley, as always, is saving best for last.

Ronnie can't wait for him to spit it out, so she says, "Come on, Mar. Repeat what you told me."

"Okay, babe."

Babe? Mar? When's the wedding?

"I was able to get a blood type from the scrapings and the blood doesn't match either Dupont or Denton. Probably your killer's. The scrapings also revealed a small amount of tissue and blood. She'd fought her attacker. I'm running DNA on the tissue. The blood is the kicker though. It's the same as the spots found on Dupont's clothing. You find a suspect and I'll do the rest."

"Thanks, Marley. You've made my day... morning. Keep at it."

Ronnie takes the phone off speaker and speaks to him in a hushed tone for a moment then disconnects. "Now we're getting somewhere. The blood and tissue will belong to Wallace."

I'm tempted to turn Donna loose on the emails I've received from Wallace, but I won't. Ronnie was the one that turned up the deleted emails from Wallace to Dupont. She can do this on the side, and if it becomes necessary, I'll reveal the emails. I won't be able to explain why I kept them from the others, but I can't worry about that now.

I gulp the last of my room-temp coffee.

"Here's what we need to do."

FORTY-FOUR

My first call goes to Sam Reed since that conversation would undoubtedly be the shortest. He isn't happy to be awakened, but he verified what Marley had just told us. He'd sent Marley some of the photos of the wounds before the autopsy and said he would send me a set after he had his coffee.

Next, I dial Patterson. She's already up and I hear her slurping coffee. She isn't too enthused to hear about the Wallace connection and my failure to report it to everyone.

"So why didn't you tell me or Clay about this Wallace character?"

"In my defense I wasn't sure Wallace was involved."

Patterson makes the equivalent sound of someone waving a comment away and asks, "Why didn't Donna call me?"

"Is that important now?" I ask.

"I'll let it pass this time. But she works for me. I don't want her and Ronnie getting too chummy. Loose lips sink ships. I'm thinking of future leaks."

"I don't want Ronnie getting too 'chummy' as you put it, but if separately they are really good, together they are like a nuclear reactor." That gets a chuckle from Patterson. "I'm going to call Clay and Cindy. Can you think of something we should be doing?"

"We can call Wallace PD and St. Marie. See if they have something else they didn't pass on. Maybe they still have the computers. I'd like our gals to have access to the computers."

"I'll call St. Marie," I say.

Patterson will reach out to Wallace PD. We disconnect and I find the home phone number Detective Thompson had provided. I know he'll enjoy being pulled out of bed. But before I call Clay, I punch in Sheriff Gray's number.

FORTY-FIVE

Dan Anderson had gone to Colorado Springs for another meeting with investors and then had driven all day and night back to Port Townsend. Megan had sounded tired and he knew she wouldn't rest or eat right until this case was solved.

He was beyond exhausted but excited and a little anxious when he arrived home. Luckily, the trip had been worth it. The days he'd spent arranging finances, talking to accountants, the lunches, dinners, drinks had been a whirlwind for him. He wasn't used to that kind of life. He wasn't sure he even wanted that kind of life. He was an artist, of sorts, and his passion was in woodworking, but his heart was taken by this wonderful woman who had such a strong personality, looks, and work ethics. They complemented each other perfectly.

Sure, if he franchised, he could make ten times what he's making at the moment, but he loved running his little shop downtown and selling some special and large items from his cabin in Snow Creek. Making tons of money had never been why he'd started doing this. It was art and he was good at it. It was an art form in which he could see a way from kitsch to classic. It had been an escape as well. He could put himself into his carvings and forget all the bad things the news media spat out to the public.

He'd heard on a Seattle radio station there had been two murders while he was gone. Both somewhat close to home – on the peninsula. One in Port Orchard and the other on the Hood Canal Bridge. They said a woman had been beheaded. What was the world coming to? He'd been about to turn the radio off when he heard Megan's name. She was always right in the middle of the action.

She is a good detective, and he had no doubt she'd sort it all out. Even so, he worried about her. On one of her cases he'd been kidnapped, his cabin and carvings burned down and he was drugged by one of her murderers. He'd ended up in the hospital for a few days. Megan had been drugged and roughed up, but she must be made of sterner stuff. She had come out on top of that one.

He was old school. And in a world in which roles were rapidly changing, fluid this, fluid that, in some eyes, he was archaic. He still believed men should take care of women. It was a man's job to protect and provide. He'd learned that from his father. Megan knew that. She didn't like it. They had a kind of truce about it.

The truth was, *her* job was dangerous. The only danger he was in was cutting himself and needing a Band-Aid, or maybe a few stitches, but she could be killed. Every time she went to work she might not make it home. Nevertheless, she wouldn't hear of quitting. She was smart. Could do almost anything. Maybe help him run his business. Make a life together?

All of that played into why he'd gone on this trip in the first place. He'd done everything but sign the contract and had asked for a day or two to think it over, which they gladly gave him. He wanted to talk to Megan first. Talk. That was a joke. He was going to ask her to marry him. He loved her and she loved him, and in his world that meant they were committed to

each other. He just hoped she would see reason and stop being
a detective.

It was early morning and still dark outside when he arrived
at Megan's place. Her Explorer was gone so she must be working. Probably working on the murders. He didn't know he'd
missed her by less than twenty minutes.

She would have known, of course. She'd have noticed the
dry rectangle where her car had parked and protected the pave-
ment from the light rain that had just passed by. Dan was tired.
He had a fold-out bed in the back of the shop downtown, but
the mattress was lumpy and smelled of mildew.

He'd broached the subject of he and Megan living together,
but she had reacted like a timid mouse. She wasn't ready for it,
but he could wait. If he had to. He'd thought about waiting to
ask her to marry him, but he had to sign the papers on the business deal by the next weekend. He had to see where he and
Megan stood. If he took the deal, it would mean spending
several months traveling between San Francisco and Colorado
Springs.

He parked on the street where Megan usually parked and
considered driving all the way to Snow Creek, sleeping on the
lumpy mattress at the shop, or going in and sleeping in a real
bed. He'd stayed overnight with Megan enough that she'd
finally given him a key. She'd acted like she'd given him the
nuclear codes. It was a big thing to her and he didn't want to
mess it up. He'd never just come over and let himself in. And
when she came home and found him in her bed, what then?

He was bathed in light as a panel van pulled slowly down
the street. He thought that it was very early for someone to be
making deliveries. Maybe a worker going home?

He took the ring out of his shirt pocket and tried to put it on
his pinky finger but his finger was as big as her thumb. He'd
agonized over getting the right ring, the right size, the right
price. Megan wouldn't care for something too expensive. She

still drank box wine and cheap Scotch. Her life must have been hard growing up. He didn't ask. It didn't matter. He loved her. This her. Not who she had been.

He couldn't wait to see her. He'd driven all night just to surprise her. She'd been so good about letting him take care of business and not expecting him to check in every five minutes like she didn't trust him.

Megan Carpenter was a keeper.

Dan shut off the engine and made his way to her front door. He reached for his key, but it was unlocked. Megan had complained about this for weeks. He wasn't too tired to not feel pissed off at the neighbor.

This is not right and he's gonna hear about it.

Then Dan opened the door.

FORTY-SIX

WALLACE

Even for a stalker, it always feels like a stroke of good luck being in the right place at the right time. Of course, luck is funny. Lucky for him. Not so much for the other guy.

He's rounding the corner onto the street where Rylee's place is when he sees an unfamiliar vehicle parked outside. There's a man walking toward the front door, which Wallace already knows he will find unlocked. He makes sure not to slow his speed as he passes by.

Wallace takes a good look at the man as he raises his hand to his eyes to shield the glare of the headlights. He's in his thirties, strong build.

He gets a good enough look to confirm his hunch. At last, the famous Dan Anderson is returning home to his beloved "Megan." Wallace allows a smile to cross his face as he glances into his side mirror.

Yeah, that's him. Should have been me. But him. It's him.

Wallace steers the van around the next corner and a little way down the street before parking at the curb. Taking his time, he opens the back of the van and selects the right tool for the job. This one will be delicate. He wants to accomplish a specific aim. He makes himself pause to think for a minute, plan out the next few steps. Failing to plan is planning to fail, after all. There's a pair of work boots in the back of the van. He doesn't know where they came from, but he's thought of a use for them now.

He slides a baseball cap on as he walks back to Megan's, lowering the brim so the streetlights cast his face into a black void. He slows as he reaches the house. There's no sign of Dan in the car or outside the house. He must have a key.

Without hesitation, he walks up to the main door and opens it, using his left hand, with his right behind his back. It's still unlocked, not that that would pose a problem for him.

Dan Anderson is standing in Megan's doorway. He spins around in surprise.

Before he can say anything, Wallace furrows his brow, affects a suspicious tone of voice, as though this other man is the one that doesn't belong here.

"Can I help you?"

Dan looks a little taken aback to see someone arrive at this hour, but he smiles unconvincingly. "My girlfriend lives here."

"Oh, okay," Wallace says. "I'm her neighbor."

"So you're the guy who keeps leaving the door unlocked, huh?"

Wallace smiles disarmingly. "Sorry. I really need to stop that. You never know who's going to wander in off the street, huh?"

"Yeah," Dan says. "Say, do you have any idea where she is?"

He affects a puzzled look. "She's right there, man," Wallace says, looking past him.

Instinctively, Dan turns to look and then, seeing nothing, turns back.

Wallace is already swinging the bat. He's going for his version of home run.

FORTY-SEVEN

The words of the paramedic echo in my mind as I double the speed limit on my way to the hospital: *He's in a bad way, you should get here as fast as you can.*

Why didn't Dan tell me he was coming home? I could have been there, I could have stopped this. Even as I think this, I'm wondering if it's the truth. I haven't been able to do jack to stop Wallace up until now, have I? And now he's reached out to hurt the person closest to me, maybe kill him, and in my own apartment.

The paramedic passed on other details in the call, but I barely heard them. A passerby disturbed the guy who attacked Dan, perhaps saved his life. I'll need to find him and thank him later, but for now I'm focused on getting to Dan's side.

I park in the first space I can find at the hospital and run to the entrance. It gets a little hazy after that as I babble something to the receptionist, and someone comes to get me.

A doctor meets us outside Dan's room. He wears glasses that fall from the bridge of his nose as he speaks. Indeed, I don't catch most of what he says because it sounds like he's underwater, but I catch the odd thing about brain bleeds and blunt trauma and "not out of the woods yet."

My feet carry me inside the room and I see Dan in the bed, eyes closed, head mostly encased in bandages. He's hooked up to all kinds of cables and tubes. The distinctive hum of hospital machines fill the space around me.

Around me.

Me and him.

I sit in the chair beside him and hold his hand. It feels cool. Tears tug at the corners of my eyes. This is my fucking fault. I know it is. I don't mean to be, but I am poison.

FORTY-EIGHT

Ronnie hurriedly plants herself in the chair beside me in the recovery waiting room. She assesses me like a stealth doctor. Medical? Psychiatrist? She knows the hurt and responsibility I carry. She knows what Dan means to me. I've been here at the hospital for what seems like an eternity.

Ronnie knows that I'm through wringing my hands and am up to wanting to wring someone's neck.

"What did the doctor say?" Ronnie asks. I shake my head and her hands go to her mouth. "Oh my god!"

"No. Ronnie, I mean the doctor hasn't come to see me yet. I had to threaten them to even give me the information since I'm not family."

"Has his family been called?"

The question startles me. I've never asked about his family. I realize I don't know much about his background. He's never asked about mine and I guess I was just satisfied with that.

The doors to the waiting room open and the surgeon comes through wearing scrubs, head cover, and mask. I look for blood but see none. That's good. Or maybe not. Ronnie and I stand

and the doctor lowers his mask. He looks like he's twelve years old and wearing a surgeon costume for Halloween.

"Is one of you the family for Mr. Anderson?" His voice is pleasant and much older than twelve, and I relax. A little. He's not smiling and I steel myself for bad news.

"I'm his fiancée," I say. It's a lie, but it will suffice.

"Your fiancé has suffered a severe head injury with a brain bleed. I had to relieve the pressure on his brain from the swelling. But I'm afraid it wasn't soon enough and I've had to medically induce a coma to keep the brain from swelling further."

"Did he regain consciousness?"

"He was unconscious when he came to me. I was told he was in and out when he arrived in the ER. He'll go to ICU."

That's just great. The control freak ER nurse that I had to threaten will now be the one to tell me if Dan said anything when he was brought in. I hope she'll see reason. Otherwise, I'm armed.

"How is he?" I ask.

The boy doctor gives his impression of cautiously optimistic.

"His vitals are good. He's been given propofol to keep him asleep. It's the same anesthetic that we use for general surgery. We will watch his vitals to see if he's waking up, and as soon as I know something, I'll find you. I'm on call but will be in the hospital to keep an eye on him. If you aren't going to stay, leave your phone number with the nurse. I'll tell the nurse one of you is allowed to stay in his room. I'm so sorry. I'll do my best."

Ronnie takes my hand. "You stay, Megan. Tony assigned this to me. I'll let you know what I find. I'm heading over to your place. I'll get you a change of clothes and something to eat. I'll keep in touch in case anything happens."

"Do you really expect me to sit this out?"

"Okay, but you have to keep your temper under control. Can you do that for me?"

I don't answer. I don't hold back for anyone.

"For Dan?"

"I can try," I finally say.

"I'll make a note of the date and time," Ronnie says, doing her best to lighten things that can't really be anything other than grim.

I give her a nod when she asks if I think Wallace has something to do with the attack on Dan.

"Who else? Dan was found in my apartment. Wallace must have thought it was me. It's all my fault." I break down in tears. I don't cry. I don't. But I do. "My fault," and I fall into Ronnie's arms. "I'm going to find Wallace and I'm going to..." I don't finish the thought and make Ronnie an accomplice. I know I can't help Dan here. I can only make sure this doesn't happen to anyone else.

"There's nothing I can do here. I can't just sit."

FORTY-NINE

The nurse wasn't such a bitch this time. Possibly because the young doctor had found some heretofore unknown way to charm her. Or possibly because I'm armed. I leave my contact information with ICU, and Ronnie and I drive to my apartment. The Crime Scene van is still there. Mindy Newsom greets me outside.

"Megan, are you okay?" Mindy hugs me. I let her. I've gotten over my aversion to being touched by people that I care about. I'm all business now. No time for emotion until I find Wallace and unleash the hounds of hell.

"What have you been told so far?" Mindy asks me.

"The paramedics called and told me Dan was on his way to the hospital from my address with a head injury. A passerby interrupted someone attacking him and found him on the floor in my front room bleeding from the head wound. The ER doc said he'd come around long enough to tell them my name. I haven't talked to the on-scene officers yet."

Mindy hands me a handwritten report from one of the responding officers. "Hajek was dispatched to another run, but he left this for you. He already talked to the other guy. Sounds like he was lucky to get out of it in one piece. I got here after Crime Scene and they've walked me through and... Oh, Megan, I'm so sorry."

I realize I haven't thought to ask about the Good Samaritan who saved Dan's life. It's blind luck somebody happened to be passing. "Who was the guy who found him?"

"His name was Hunter, I think," Mindy says.

"*Hunter?*" I repeat. A passerby randomly being on the scene at five a.m. suddenly makes sense.

"Yeah, it's in the report."

I look closely at the handwritten police report and a familiar name jumps out.

The report said Caleb Hunter had dropped by to see the homeowner when he heard a scuffle and then someone moaning. The door to the apartment was wide open and he could see someone's legs down on the floor. He went to see if they were injured and found the victim on the ground, bleeding from the head. He started to get to his knees to see how bad the person was hurt when he was struck from behind and went down. He heard someone running away and caught a glimpse of a man – big, tall, maybe burly, or heavy. He couldn't tell because they had on a puffy coat, like a parka with the hood up. Then he blacked out.

He said he didn't call the police right away and may have lain there for a few minutes. Then he checked the other guy for a pulse before going to his own apartment and calling 911.

The report went on to say Caleb didn't recognize his attacker. I put the report down and must have gone into a fugue because the next thing I hear is Mindy saying, "Earth to Megan." Mindy is snapping her fingers in front of my face and she and Ronnie are giving me concerned looks.

"Where is he?" I didn't want to go into more detail. Besides the article Nan gave me yesterday, I haven't told Ronnie about

Caleb. There was no need to. Now she'll have to interview him. It's her case after all.

"Who?"

I point at the report. "Hunter. The guy who found Dan."

She must be thinking the same thing and asks, "Mindy, have you talked to this guy..." She reaches for the report and I hand it back to her. I watch her eyes scan over it.

Mindy shakes her head. "Caleb Hunter? I haven't. I've been busy inside the scene, but I'll need his footprints and so on. I believe he's still at the ER, getting checked out."

"Ronnie," I say, "why don't you stay with Mindy and look through my place. I'll talk to this Hunter guy if he's still there. He might be more comfortable talking to me first." I don't want to sound like I'm pulling rank on her and add, "It's your investigation so you tell me what you want me to do."

I don't want Ronnie to meet Caleb before I can find out why he was coming to see me. Most certainly I don't want him to slip up and call me Rylee. He was never a good liar. He was this gentle vulnerable soul trapped in a house with no love. After what I'd put him through years ago, he had no reason to show loyalty. But I didn't think he would deliberately out me. Slip up. Maybe.

Mindy gives Ronnie some protective gear and they go into my apartment. I get in the car and drive back to the hospital, feeling the past wash over me and dreading the coming conversation. Is it possible I still have feelings for Caleb? Possibly but even if I do, they're not likely to be returned.

Stop it! Just stop it! Dan is in a coma; his head is bashed in because of me. I disgust myself even thinking of the Caleb I knew in the past.

I've been screwed up since returning from Cougar Point. I felt the real possibility of losing Ronnie as a partner. As a friend. And that has set in motion a string of emotions I never thought were possible given my screwed-up psyche. I've pushed my feelings away, stuffed the pain and fright and loss, and now Pandora's box is wide open and I can't put them back.

* * *

When I get to the hospital, I hesitate before going inside. I need to pull myself together. The threads are unraveling, twisting and turning.

Stupid, stupid, stupid! One more shallow breath, release it slowly, close my eyes, open them, and approach the entrance. My legs feel weak. And no wonder. I'm just on the other side of the door from ruination. Damnation on a nuclear scale.

I've made my mind up. I'm going to ask him to leave. To never come back. We can't possibly be friends. Not after all this time and the things that have changed in my life.

I go inside reception and ask the duty nurse for Caleb Hunter. She looks blank until I explain he's the witness from the assault. She points over to the seated area in reception. "He's right over... oh."

There's nobody there. Nobody who looks like Caleb, anyway.

"Dr. Lewis told him to drink some water and stick around for an hour before he went home. Precautionary, you know? In case he had a concussion."

I don't waste any more time talking to her. There's every chance Caleb is in danger. Perhaps Wallace only left him alive because he didn't realize who he was in the dark.

I push through the doors and run back outside to the parking lot, looking left and right.

Across the road there's an all-night coffee shop. It's the only place around he might have gone. I run across the road, praying he's okay. When I get in, the place is deserted, just a tired-looking waitress standing at the counter, crouched over her Instagram feed.

She lifts what must be an exhausted scrolling finger and looks up.

"Table for one?"

"No. I'm looking for a guy," I say. "About six feet, well-built, dark hair..."

"Join the club," she says.

I'm about to lose my shit when she points at something behind me.

"You mean like that guy?"

I turn around and Caleb is there, emerging from the restroom. There's a bandage on his head and some dried blood peeking out of the edge.

"Caleb, Jesus, I thought you were..."

"Rylee? What's up?"

My mouth works, but words won't come. I realize my mouth is hanging open and I snap it shut. I hope he doesn't notice, but the warm smile on his face tells me different. And then the asshole says, "I'm fine, just a bump on the noggin." I want to slap him, punch him, kiss him. I don't know what's going on with me. I know I love Dan. I should be across the road at the hospital. With him. Instead, I'm here, working a case, looking for Dan's attacker, looking for killers, talking to an old boy who's a friend.

Would Dan want me acting this way? Am I Dan's girl-friend? Or am I interested in Caleb just a teensy bit?

I don't want to do this in front of the waitress, who seems to be taking more of an interest in our drama than her Instagram. I push the door open and wait for Caleb to follow me out into the parking lot. When I turn Caleb is standing behind me. His arms come up and his hands take my shoulders and I'm looking up into those eyes. He's smiling and it's infectious, but I don't want to smile. We stand that way for what seems like forever, neither of us saying a word, but he doesn't release me and I make no attempt to pull away.

What the hell am I doing?

He's still wearing that damn smile. "You want to go back in there and get some coffee?"

I decline. "I'm only here to ask some questions."

His smile falters. I've hurt his feelings and maybe it's what I meant to do. Damn him anyway. He has no right coming back into my life. He couldn't have come at a worse time and I'm so torn in so many directions with all that's going on I'm not thinking straight. And I badly need to keep my wits about me.

"Look, Caleb, I know we were going to catch up, but my boyfriend is in a coma and he was hurt in my apartment. I need to know what happened. I need to know who did this."

"Of course. I understand." He sits on the trunk of a parked car. "Ask away."

FIFTY

"Shoot," Caleb says, and holds his hands up by his massive shoulders and looks at my shoulder holster. "Sorry. No pun intended."

I give him a sharp look. He's trying to be funny, but his timing couldn't be worse. "You have to focus, Caleb. This is serious. We aren't kids anymore."

"Sorry, Rylee." He sees me visibly jump and look around to make sure no one is around. "I mean, Detective Carpenter." He mouths at me, "Is that better?"

"Let's keep this simple." My heart is pounding. It feels like I've swallowed an ice cube. "What did you tell the police?"

"Well, I told them I came by to see you and..."

"You know what I mean. What did you tell them about us?"

He looks at me for a long time "Still the same old Ry... I mean, Megan. You were always intense. At first, I couldn't imagine you doing this kind of a job; a cop of all things, but I should have realized it's perfect for you. I mean with your father and all."

"What about my father?" I never told him about my real father. How does he know?

"Sorry. Your stepfather. That thing in Port Orchard. When he was murdered it changed you. You became this arrow of justice, knocked in the bow and ready to fly. I've read the news articles and in the past you've done some things I may not have approved of. But that was then. I can see why you felt compelled to right those wrongs. I still wonder what you feel when you've—in your own words—*ended* one of the monsters. That's what you said when you killed Ted Duggan."

My eyes mist up. His words punch me in the gut. When I get my wind back, I say, "I feel good. I always have. I'll feel great when I catch the asshole who attacked Dan." The rage that's my own monster is building in me and I have to force it down. Caleb's done nothing wrong, and he may have saved Dan's life.

"Thank you for checking on Dan. You might have kept him from being killed. I'm sorry you were hurt. Is it bad?"

He lightly touches the bandage. "It just glanced me. I'll have a knot, but I'm okay. And I don't know about saving anyone's life. When I heard the scuffle in your place, the first thing I felt was fear, but I didn't know it was your boyfriend. I was afraid it might be the someone who had broken into your apartment yesterday and that you were in danger. I'm ashamed to say it, but I just reacted. If I'd had time to think, I may have just turned around and run."

He hasn't changed one bit.

"So what did you tell them?" I ask again.

"Relax. I haven't said anything about us being old friends, if that's what you're afraid of. I guess you didn't want your boyfriend to find out about us."

There was never really an us. We were just friends.

"Let's keep it that way if you don't mind. I'm Megan Carpenter now. Is there somewhere you can go?"

"You mean like my hotel?"

"No. It's not safe. If Wal... if the attacker remembers you, he could come after you. But when I catch this fucker, I'll need you to testify in court."

Caleb shakes his head, wincing a little. "I'm afraid I won't be much of a witness. I never saw who it was. I only saw a figure running away. I gave the description to one of your officers. The guy must have been behind the door and cold-cocked me when I knelt by your boyfriend."

"His name is Dan. My boyfriend. Dan Anderson. Didn't you notice anything? When I left this morning, I made sure the doors were locked."

"No," he says. I can tell by the look on Caleb's face he's telling the truth, or at least thinks he is. He stepped through the door to my place and got clobbered. He might really have interrupted the attack and kept the killer from finishing the job. But that doesn't feel right. This killer has never left anyone alive so far.

Caleb won't give me away. I'm sure of that. That he seems a little jealous of Dan is weird, but maybe he'd really come to find me to rekindle what he thought was a romance.

"Did you touch anything? Move anything? Move Dan?" I add, "To see if he was breathing or something? If you did, I understand. You were just trying to help."

Caleb appears to be thinking. That's good. He says, "I don't think so." He cocks his head. "No. I'm sure I didn't. I did touch his neck to see if he had a pulse. But that's all. Can you get my fingerprints from his neck? Or my DNA?"

I can't believe he's that naïve. It seems put-on. Maybe he's a little tiffed I asked if he'd moved Dan. I had to ask. If I didn't, the officer should have. Or Mindy will ask.

"You understand I have to ask these questions, Caleb. I don't think you're stupid. I need to document that you hadn't touched anything. Including—Dan." I almost said "the body" out of habit.

"This is just like on Netflix. You do a good job, Megan. I really hope you find your man. You always do."

I decide to go for broke. "Caleb, look at me."

His smile fades when he sees how serious I am. "Okay."

"I'm going to ask you something. I don't want to make you mad, but if you ever cared about me, you'll tell me the truth. It will stay between us."

"What is it, Megan? You're worrying me."

"I've gotten emails from a guy calling himself Wallace." I don't say more. I watch him closely and he looks blank.

"You mean you don't know who this Wallace guy is?" he says after a minute. "I mean, are the emails bad?"

I watch him for a few moments. He's either become a good liar, or I'm off my game.

"Do you think *I'm* this person?"

"No." I don't know. Maybe. There's that ping again. I hate it when something niggles at me and this one raises the hair on the back of my neck. My thoughts are interrupted by my phone buzzing. It's Mindy.

FIFTY-ONE

If Mindy is surprised to find I'm with the very person she wanted to find, it doesn't reveal itself in her voice. She asks me to drive Caleb back to the apartment so she can go over the scene with him. She's waiting outside the front door as I pull up to the curb. Mindy is very thorough. She's a brilliant forensic investigator. What she doesn't know she intuits. She introduces herself to Caleb and I advise her he didn't see anything more than what was on the officer's preliminary report. She then surprises me.

It wasn't the first time. Mindy could be that way.

"Mr. Hunter, I'd like you to come into Detective Carpenter's apartment and show us exactly what you did."

"I told the officer..."

I interrupt. "It's procedure, Mr. Hunter. It helps us visualize the scene and it helps witnesses recall minor things."

My mind goes back to my first meeting with Caleb when he'd come inside to check out my apartment. He might have left fingerprints.

"Do I need to put on latex gloves and paper booties?" he asks, and Mindy chuckles.

"No, sir. Actually, I need to collect your shoes for a bit. And I'll need a set of fingerprints."

"Anything I can do to help, detective. I just want to help catch this guy."

"I'm not a detective, but I'm glad you want to help," Mindy says, and gives me a spicy wink.

Without stepping inside Caleb pointed out where he'd walked. "I saw paramedics go in there too. Do you need to get their shoes and fingerprints?"

Without missing a beat, Mindy says, "Already taken care of."

"I watch a lot of crime shows . It's fascinating the things you all do."

Mindy radiates a smile in his direction, then sweeps her eyes over me.

"Sometimes I fascinate myself."

Caleb turns those afterburner eyes on her, and she blushes.

"Let's go back to your apartment and I'll get your prints there. Detective Carpenter can come with us."

I can see she's smitten. She doesn't need me for this part, but she might need a chaperone.

At the kitchen table she and Caleb sit and I stand and watch like I'm supposed to witness this. After she gets his fingerprints she asks, "Were those the shoes you were wearing when you found the victim?"

Caleb says, "I only have one pair. I have some flip-flops if you need to take the shoes."

"Won't be necessary," Mindy says. "I need to borrow them for a few minutes while I take them to my van and make casts. Nothing to worry about. Detective Carpenter will keep you company."

She gets up to leave and gives me another of those conspiratorial winks. I'm wondering if it means something other than she thinks he's a hunk. I've never seen her like this around a witness. And she's married.

While she's gone I take a seat.

"Do you want another cup of coffee?"

I shake my head.

"I have a couple of soft drinks and some orange juice. I haven't got anything else right now. Shopping really isn't my thing."

"I'm fine," I say. "If I drink any more coffee, I'll overdose."

He takes a seat. "That Detective Newsom is quite a looker. I mean, WOW!"

Was that a twinge of jealousy I just felt?

"She's married," I say.

"Sorry," Caleb says. "Don't tell her I said that."

"It's our secret."

Mindy comes back in and hands Caleb his shoes. "Thanks for your cooperation, Mr. Hunter."

"Call me Caleb. I just told Detective Carpenter to do the same. After all, we share this experience." He gives a shudder and then smiles at her.

"Thanks again... Caleb."

"Yeah, thanks, Caleb," I say, and follow Mindy outside.

Mindy leans in my direction. "We're done in your place."

I nod back at the door. Caleb is still inside. I don't want him to hear me, and I don't want Mindy to suspect I have a personal investment in the answer to my next question. "What do you think?"

"In the absence of any other evidence to the contrary, I think it happened the way he said it did."

"Yeah?"

She nods. "There were three sets of footprints in the blood. Your boyfriend's, Mr. Hunter's"—I ignore the slightly dreamy way she says his name—"and a third print. Larger than either of the other two, a size thirteen."

Relief washes over me just then. "Okay. Maybe we need to try the Cinderella routine, huh? Check the feet of every man in the kingdom."

Mindy chuckles at that. "I'll help you clean up if you want?"

Fingerprint powder is on the door, the door frame, my tables and countertop, window frames, windows, refrigerator door and handle, the top of my desk, closet doors, and I don't want to look at the bathroom. But nothing was turned over or dumped like burglaries – staged or real.

No one died so I won't have to put crime scene tape up or seal the door like a homicide scene. Although it could be if Dan doesn't come out of the coma. I'd asked Siri about brain injuries while Ronnie and I were on our way here. She said that coma due to brain injury had a fifteen percent recovery rate. If Siri says it, then it must be true. Right? Wrong. Siri doesn't know Dan Anderson.

Oh, Dan. I'll be there as soon as I leave here. Promise. "I'll clean later. I'm a slob. What can I say?"

"Megan, I need your fingerprints as well. I guess I can get them from personnel, but this will be faster."

Ronnie says, "I'll lock up for you."

Emotion overwhelms me and I feel so goddamn helpless. I break down in hard sobs and try to hide my face, but Ronnie and Mindy both hug me and say soothing things that make me even more embarrassed. I take a deep breath and disentangle myself. "I'm okay. Really. It's just a little much."

"Of course it is," Mindy says.

At the van I start to take my boots off and Mindy says, "I don't need yours. You're what—a size seven?" I nod. "Your shoe soles are waffled. You don't by any chance have any clown shoes in your closet?"

I try to smile, but it's a complete fail.

"Sorry, Megan. There's nothing here."

"Complete transparency," I say. "I already know Caleb Hunter. He was in my place yesterday when I came home. He said my door was standing open. He called out and came in to see if I was okay. He checked the rooms for me and he opened the window over my desk."

Ronnie had come back and she and Mindy look at me like I'm a sign that reads: I LIED. "When I talked to him alone, I asked him not to mention it to anyone. It wasn't in the police report so I thought I would just tell you two. I don't want Dan to hear rumors and think I'm cheating on him."

That's a very believable lie and it appears to satisfy both of them.

"Got it," Ronnie says. "Officers are checking with your neighbors. So far all I've heard about is a white delivery van, kind of like Mindy's. It has been parked in the neighborhood a couple of times and no one thought it belonged. The neighbors also pointed out Dan's car. I had Dan's car towed to the garage where Crime Scene can have a go at it. One of your neighbors asked if you were living with two men."

"Screw them."

"They're just jealous," Mindy says. "Dan's a hunk. And speaking of hunks. That Caleb. Yowzah!"

"I hadn't noticed."

She gives me a wicked grin. "Sure you didn't."

"Can one of you give me a lift to the hospital?"

FIFTY-TWO

The nurse takes me to Dan's ICU cubicle. IV drips and wires lead from under the covers to machines that beep and screens that scroll and God knows what else. This is the second time Dan's been in the hospital because of me. I don't want to think about that. I just need to be here for him.

"If you need anything, hon, just push the button."

If I need anything, I'll scream for help. "Thank you so very much."

The nurse turns to leave and I take her arm. "Give me the honest truth. I'm not some starry-eyed civilian. Tell me what his chances are. I can take it and I won't say you told me."

The nurse looks at my face a long moment deciding if she will violate hospital policy and I can see her expression soften. "Doctor says he's doing as well as can be expected but the swelling in his brain is our main concern. That's why the jumble of equipment. I'm closely monitoring him from the nurses' station and there are alarms on the equipment." She sees tears standing in my eyes and says, "I've seen worse. I'm sure you have too."

Her eyes tell me she's seen better too, but I don't press.

"Take care of him." I can feel a tear run down my cheek, and this big old mountain of a nurse hugs me and pats my back and I break down. I don't know what has happened to me, but I don't care if I let it all out. I'm lost in my grief and my cynicism that everything won't be okay. It's an occupational hazard. Being me sucks. I feel my arms go around the nurse and I know I'm making the front of her spotless scrub top wet, but I don't care and she doesn't seem to mind either.

I release her before I'm ready. She has things to do. And so do I. She's making people well. I'm going to make someone dead. I promise myself to find them. The rage is just under the surface, but it does its job and the tears cease. The nurse hands me a couple of tissues she keeps in her pockets. I don't wear much makeup, but I do wear eyeliner and I see some has gotten on her top. "I'm so sorry. I'll have it cleaned," I say, and dab at the mess, only making it worse, and another wave of tears overcomes me.

"I'm not usually like this," I hear myself saying through the waterfall that blurs my vision.

"None of us are, hon. You love him. Stay by his side and talk to him. That helps. I've seen it work wonders. You'll be okay. And I'm here."

I tell her I'll be fine and thank her for the umpteenth time. When she goes back to the nurses' station, I take Dan's hand.

"Why did you pick this morning to come home, you big idiot? Why didn't you call me? I would have..." I don't know what I would have done differently. If I'd gone inside my apartment, I'd be the one lying here. Dan wouldn't know where to begin. But I do.

"I hope you know I love you and that you're scaring me to death. I just want you to wake up. I want you to fight this. You're a fighter. I know you are. And if you don't think you can do it, just imagine I'm there with you. I'll kick its ass and bring you home. We'll kick its ass together. Just get better. I need you. I really need you."

I hear a beeping and look down. I've lain on him, hugging him in a death grip, and pulled something loose. The nurse appears and plugs a wire back in. "It's okay. Look how quick I got here. Better than the police, ain't it, hon?"

I smile at her little joke. She's right.

"You'll never get a ticket again," I say. "I promise."

FIFTY-THREE

The days are drawn out, and in the windowless ICU it's impossible to tell if it's sunny or raining or sleeting. I know I've dozed several times, but I don't want to look at the clock. That will be like a count down. The promise I made to myself is like a siren song. I can't sit here any longer. I know it's terrible and I should stay, but I just can't watch him. Waiting for the damn machine to beep, or stop beeping. I have no control. I'm not sure anyone here has control and that's the scariest thing. The doctors and nurses can only do what they can. The rest is up to Dan, and I hope he's heard me and is fighting his way back.

To me.

The nurse has come in and checked his vitals and left me sitting in a big chair on the other side of the bed holding his cool hand.

It will be at least twenty minutes before she comes back, and so I go to the nurses' station and tell her I'm going to make a call. I exit ICU and check the hallway. It's empty. I find the stairwell and I go down three flights. With each step my heart hurts and wonder if I should go back. Tony has called and told me he's taking me off the case. I won't say what I told him, but I made it plain I'm still on the case.

One of the uniformed officers brought my SUV to the hospital and parked it near the ER entrance. It's dark outside. I'm pulling out of the hospital parking lot when Ronnie drives up beside me and we roll our windows down.

"How is he?"

There are no more tears to shed. I park and Ronnie climbs into the passenger seat. I tell her what the nurse told me.

"I'm so sorry," Ronnie says. "But at least there's hope."

"Yes. There's that."

"Sheriff said he told you to go home."

"How can I?" I don't know if I'll ever be able to step foot in that place again.

"You'll come home with me until this is over." Ronnie puts her hand on mine and squeezes. "I won't take no for an answer."

And I won't argue because it's not going to happen. "First, we need to go to the office and call Clay and Patterson."

"Already done."

"Well, then we need to get cracking on the emails. The newspaper ad. The surveillance footage."

"It's underway. There's nothing else we can do for now, Megan. I'll drive. You need to sleep or you won't be good to anyone."

"I'll stay with Dan then. Thanks for the offer."

"I'll stay too," she says.

"Ronnie, I appreciate what you're doing. You don't know how much I'm glad it's you. I need to be alone to deal with this in my head. You get some sleep. You need it as bad as I do, and now I won't take no for an answer. I outrank you."

She squeezes my hand and I see compassion in her eyes. With Ronnie, it's real. It always has been. I don't want to lie to her.

"Okay. You're sure you don't want to come with me."

"I'm sure."

"I don't feel good about leaving you here, but if it's what you want. I'm going to get some rest. I'll be back in the office around five. Donna will be there. If you feel the need to come in, at least sleep for a few hours first."

"Will do, Mom."

She gives my hand one more squeeze and gets out. When she drives away I start the engine. I don't know where I'm going. I don't have a plan. At least not much of one. I just know that Wallace was in my apartment. He's making good on his threats. Even Caleb won't be safe until I catch this psycho.

I call Tony.

"Megan," he says in a sleepy voice. "Did you go home like I said?"

"I'm staying with Dan. The nurse has pulled in another bed so I can sleep beside him." It's a good lie. "I just want to ask you to have someone guard Dan's room. The killer was interrupted before he was finished."

I'm sure he's wondering why I want a guard if I'm staying in the room, but he doesn't ask.

"If you're certain."

"I am. I just need some sleep. Sorry for waking you."

"Not a problem, Megan. Get some sleep."

I pull out of the lot and head north. It's random. No destination. I need to think. I can't do it at the hospital. Every time those machines beep, I feel like it's started the clock and Dan's time is running out.

I get four blocks away and Ronnie pulls up alongside me.

* * *

Ronnie escorts me back to Dan's bedside. We stop by the desk and the nurse gives us both coffee and a pastry. A smile too. A knowing smile. A warm smile. The nurse had ratted me out. I'm sure of it. Even so, I can't be mad at her.

"Should we be in the room with him while we talk?" Ronnie asks.

"Nurse Nightingale said it was good for him to hear voices. I've been talking to him. Now I'll talk to you." The nurse wheels another padded chair into the room, checks Dan's vitals, writes something on a clipboard, and leaves. I pull my chair closer to Dan's bed and hold his hand.

Is it warmer?

Ronnie sips her coffee. She's stalling. She knows something.

"What aren't you telling me?"

Ronnie takes out her tablet and finds a page. "Donna traced the service that the texts were sent to the victims from. It's in Portland. We convinced the person there to give us the subscriber name and address."

She stops and looks at me.

"And?"

"It's yours."

"What do you mean?"

"It's in your name. The service was prepaid."

Wallace had been thinking of me long before he sent the first email. Maybe as much as seven years ago. I tried to think of who I'd pissed off back then. The list would be endless. But I didn't think there was anyone that would go to these lengths to get to me. Why not just kill me? Why kill all these others? Were they copycatting me and waiting to save the best for last? One-up me? That's sick.

"We traced the general location where the emails were sent from and it matches the dates of the murders. Portland, St. Marie, Port Townsend. The ads, and there were others placed by phone—a burner would be my guess—and paid by stolen credit cards. Different cards. We called the cardholders and they said they canceled the card and didn't call the police to report it because the usage was so small and the bank ate the loss."

I didn't ask how she knew the cards were stolen. I'm sure it's so tech-y that I'd go to sleep. "Did someone attempt to use the cards after that?"

"No such luck. No bank attempts. Whoever this is has got some smarts."

"Good work, Ronnie. You don't have to sit with me. I'll stay put. I've got nowhere to go, even if I didn't want to stay here with Dan." His hand *is* warm in mine and gives me some hope.

"Well, I'm in charge of the case like you said, so I had Donna contact her friend with the Port Orchard newspaper. He's a stringer so he has lots of friends at other newspapers."

I wouldn't have done that. Too late now.

"That's how we found out about the credit cards. Simple. And we were told the same person placed an ad for tomorrow's paper. We think it's for you."

Ronnie's revelation takes the breath out of me for a second. After all this time, all this death, maybe Wallace is ready to bring this to an end.

"What does it say?"

"Pretty much the same as the one for Dupont." She shows me the ad on her phone.

Megan, meet me at your first prison.

Wallace didn't give me away. At least not yet. Ronnie looks at me for recognition of what the ad means. I shake my head and lie. "Maybe he's just trying to tie us up looking for the wrong things. The last place I lived was in Portland."

He's given me an idea. They say the pen is mightier than the sword. I'll use his method to contact him.

I hand Ronnie my phone. My hands are shaking too much

to punch the right numbers. "Call Donna." She does and puts it on speaker.

Donna picks up right away.

Eveready Donna.

"Detective Carpenter. I guess Ronnie found you."

"I've got something I want your friend at the newspaper to do."

"What?"

"Discretion is warranted. Will he do what I need with no questions asked?"

Donna lets out a little laugh. "I own the guy."

I don't know what she means, and I don't want to know.

I tell her what I need done and she giggles like Ronnie. I'm surrounded.

FIFTY-FOUR

"Do you think it will work?" Ronnie asks.

The article I had Donna's friend post in the *Independent*'s website is simple, but I don't expect Wallace to agree. It will read:

> Wallace, if you've really been following my career, meet me on Marrowstone. You'll know the place. Seven. Be there.

I don't have to sign it. I'm counting on his not coming there. He'd be a fool to do that and he's proven he's not a fool. He knows I've gotten his message and I'll meet him where he said.

My own message isn't for him, it's for my friends. I want them miles away from the two of us when this goes down.

"Why Marrowstone?" Ronnie asks. "Mystery Bay?"

We had worked a series of murders and one of the bodies was found in Mystery Bay. It was all over the news. But I lie to my partner one more time. "It's a test to see if he really knows any of our cases. An island makes sense. There's nowhere for him to run. He thinks I'll come alone. And we don't have to put up surveillance. Just post some plainclothes on the on the bridge."

Ronnie nods her head. "It'll go live tonight. Print paper will come out in the morning."

I hope I'm not defending my decision too much. "We know Wallace is using that newspaper, and he likes Port Orchard for some reason. It's not far from Port Orchard to Marrowstone."

"You switched things around on him. His ad will come out, and when he checks it, he'll see yours. He won't be expecting you to come after him like that."

My phone dings with an email. My blood turns cold when I see the familiar address. It's from Wallace. I put my phone back in my pocket quickly.

"Who was that?" Ronnie asks, and of course I must tell yet another fib. Not a lie. I hate lying to her.

"Just an old friend sending sympathy. I guess word travels fast."

I want to read the email, but I'm trapped. Unless...

I reach over and push the call button by the bed. The nurse is there in a flash and I tell her I thought Dan had squeezed my hand. Ronnie looks hopeful, excited, but it's just a distraction.

The nurse does a quick visual and checks vitals. "It's common for someone in a coma to still have some unconscious muscle twitches. He's okay. Can I get you two something else?"

I stand and dab at my dry eyes. "I've got to go into the hall and collect myself. I'll get something for us from the machine downstairs."

Before Ronnie sputter out another word, I head out the door and down the hallway and step into the stairway to read Wallace's message.

Rylee, I want to give you a chance to keep this from your people. I don't want anyone else to get hurt. I could have killed him if I had wanted. No one could have stopped it, not even the Boy Scout who happened by. Who was he, by the way? Have you been two-timing your beloved Dan, perhaps?

I want to meet you and see if you've still got what it takes. I'm beginning to think you've lost your mojo. It wasn't fair of me to hurt your guy, but I had to get your attention. I want to see the old you, and not this pitiful thing you've become. You owe me that. I've put a post in the Port Orchard paper's website. Read it. Come alone. If you try to trick me, I'll finish him off. You believe me, don't you? I can do anything I like. I have for years and no one seems up to the challenge.

P.S. Don't bother trying to track this email. I've used someone close to you as a subscriber. Sorry about that.

See you real soon. If not, Dan dies. Then Ronnie. Then your sheriff. Then you. Then it will finally be over.

Wallace

The article he'd put in the *Independent* was cryptic and only I would be able to decipher it. He was talking about the house on Salmonberry where I had lived with my mother, stepfather and Hayden when I was in high school. I knew the address but had never been back after what happened there. The anniversary of that horrible day is tomorrow. September is a clue to all the murders. I should have remembered my stepfather, Rolland, was murdered in September. September was also the month I'd fled to Portland for college. It was also the month I tracked down my professor, and his son, who had killed three young women from the campus.

Wallace won't take my bait. But it will keep the police out of my way. Tomorrow I will meet him but not at my old house. I know where he'll be and I'll be waiting.

* * *

Ronnie pipes up. "I still don't get why he would send you a message to meet him in Portland. Are you sure that's where he meant?"

I tell her I can't know for sure.

"Honestly, it's gibberish to me. He's got a screw loose and imagining things. I think he only fixated on me because of the news articles. That's when his emails started.

"What I had posted in the *Independent* will give him his answer. I don't know what that crap he wrote means, but mine is very clear."

Ronnie takes it all in and pounces. "Great! Sheriff will have the place on Marrowstone surrounded. We can set up the plain-clothes officers tonight. I'll go there myself and make sure no one—"

I cut her off.

"No, Ronnie," I say. "I know it's your case, but it's my ass on the line. You set up the surveillance teams, but I want to face him alone."

I'm resisting like she would expect.

She gives me a look. "You're kidding, I hope," she says, still pushing back. "You can't, Megan. He's killed five people. Maybe six. Others too maybe. He tried to kill Dan. Let me do this. Or at least I can be your backup."

"I've got an idea." I say this with feigned excitement. "You can wear my clothes and a wig that looks like my hair. I'll put on a ghillie suit and hide in the trees with a sniper rifle."

The minute the scenario came from my mouth, I knew it sounded utterly ridiculous. It was meant to, of course.

A wig?

"Be serious, Megan. This isn't anything to joke about. What if he—" She stops short.

"What if he kills me? We'll cross that bridge when we come to it. I'll go to the island alone. He won't expect me to fight back."

"Okay," she says. Too easily. I know right away that she's lying. Learned it from me.

There is only one way to make her listen to me. It is mean. Hurtful. Because I know how much she cares about me. Admires me. How fucking honored she's been to be my partner.

So I say it. And I say with utter conviction.

"I'm dead serious, Ronnie. If you do anything, we won't be partners anymore. We won't be friends. I won't work anywhere near you. Do you get it? You can take the job in Whatcom."

It was shooting someone point-blank while they beg for their life.

Ronnie looks at me with such disbelief. Hurt. Betrayal even.

I watch her turn away. I can see her struggling as she says my name. I feel shame that I've hurt her. But I'm not planning on taking Wallace alive. He thinks he's unstoppable. He may be right. But he's not immune to dead.

I wish I could take it all back. Not really. Not if it gets me what I need. If I could have found another way, I would have.

I feel sick inside.

"Ronnie, you are my best friend. I need to do this my way."

Ronnie doesn't answer or look at me. I try again. "Listen. Look at me."

Her eyes meet mine. My heart breaks seeing the tears in her eyes. I hate myself just then. I hate Wallace even more. And while I'm not sure I can do this it's the only way for this to come out right. For the life I've built to continue Wallace must be eliminated.

* * *

Ronnie leaves to coordinate the stakeout with the sheriff while I settle in to plan my next move. Dan is still in a coma. I watch his chest rise and fall and that's a good thing, but his color isn't right and I don't see his eyes moving behind their lids like he's dreaming or in REM sleep or whatever. His nurse has been great and came in early tonight. I didn't want to keep calling her "Nurse" so I asked for her name. Betty. Nurse Betty.

I wanted to ask Nurse Betty about Dan's stillness, his color. She'd give me her honest opinion, but I don't want to know the answers. She'd said earlier it was early days and he was doing fine. What does fine mean in nurse language? Does it mean his limbs aren't falling off? Or he's not lying in a pool of blood?

My chair is a recliner. It's not uncomfortable, but I won't rest in it. I've got too much to think about. The past is interspersed with the sights on the bridge, the autopsies, Caleb's smile, the blood on the floor of my apartment, the emails from Wallace. Something is still bugging me as I fall asleep.

FIFTY-FIVE

My phone buzzes waking me with a start. The screen shows I've been asleep for several hours and I've missed five calls. *Shit!*

I scroll down the list. Clay, Patterson, Clay, Clay, Ronnie. The number the call is currently coming from, though, takes my breath away and I come to my feet.

It's Dan's.

"Hello," I say, and try to keep the shock from my voice.

"Hello, Rylee."

The voice is distorted, some kind of electronic masking. He shouldn't have bothered. I know exactly who it is.

"Wallace."

"Aren't you glad to hear from me? That hurts."

Not as hurt as you're going to be if you don't answer me. With some effort, I keep my voice strong and steady. "I don't have time for games."

He makes a tsk-tsk sound before speaking. "Your boyfriend left his phone at your place. I guess it's understandable. You tend to get forgetful when you've sustained a serious head injury. How is, Dan, by the way?"

The phone buzzes in my hand and Ronnie's number comes up.

"Fuck you," I say, not giving him the satisfaction of hearing the hurt in my voice. "Just tell me what you want to tell me and get off the line, I have someone on call waiting."

"Five o'clock. Where I told you. If you come alone, we'll talk. If you don't, I'll finish what I started. Maybe I'll kill your partner next. Or your boss, Sheriff Gray." Then he chuckles, as though he only just thought of it. "Or perhaps I'll do your side-piece. Now what was his name? Caleb, wasn't it?"

Before I can tell him to go fuck himself again, the line goes dead. My mind is reeling from what he just said. How did Wallace find out who he is? And then I remember the card Caleb showed me, the one that brought him to Jefferson County. This has been part of Wallace's game all along.

I answer Ronnie's call. She's out of breath. "Megan. Thank God you're okay."

I'm still rattled and need to get off the phone so I can make plans, but she's in a state and sounds scared.

"Why wouldn't I be?"

"We went to speak to the witness again, Caleb Hunter. His hotel room is trashed and there's no sign of him anywhere. He's vanished."

FIFTY-SIX
WALLACE

After he hangs up on Rylee, he peers down at Dan Anderson's phone. Watching and waiting. He wonders if she'll try to call him back. Doubtful. Everything that needed to be said was said. She knows when and where he wants to meet her.

And they both know that she'll do something different, zig instead of zag, try to arrange the meeting on her own terms.

It's no good though. He's two steps ahead of her, has been this whole time.

That's why he was able to take out her boyfriend so easily, before she even knew he was back in town.

As pleasurable as it was to put her boyfriend in a coma, he knows it will be even more satisfying when Rylee finds out about Caleb.

Caleb is already dead and gone.

FIFTY-SEVEN

All of a sudden, I know where Wallace is going to be. Whether Caleb is alive or dead, I know where Wallace is holed up.

Before I go, I take a moment to say goodbye to Dan. His forehead is cool and dry against my lips. A tear splashes on his cheek as I look into his frozen face and I wipe it away gently.

There's been no change and Nurse Betty, true to her word, has kept a close eye on him. I squeeze his hand and brush his cheek. Even if everything goes well, I don't know if I'll ever gaze in those eyes again.

"I love you, Dan. I always will. No matter what happens just hang on to that. When this is over I'll move into your cabin or we can find a place together. I'm sorry I've been so slow to accept that we should be together. I'll change. I promise. Just wake up."

His words from the phone call the other day come back to me. *You still wearing that gift I got you?*

"I'll wear it, Dan," I say out loud. "I need all the luck I can get."

My determination says I'll win this battle, but there's always a chance I won't. For one thing, Wallace might not show. For another I'm distracted just like Ronnie said. I haven't been thinking straight since this began. The revelation that Caleb is missing, maybe dead, has disturbed my focus even more. I hadn't listened enough when we were friends. Maybe his life was more messed up than I could have known. Maybe he had no one else to talk to. Neither did I and he was always a good listener. Someone I could lean on. I should have been there for him.

Port Orchard isn't all that far and I have time to find the old place again before Ronnie will arrive at my place in Port Townsend. It won't take her long to figure out what I've done. I just hope she won't find me too quickly. If Wallace hurt her I'll want to die. I've had it with this life of running, hiding who I am, dealing in death.

My soul is as black as a smoker's lungs. Maybe this is my last rodeo. I've wanted to turn in my badge for a while. Live a life like everyone else. A husband, a house, two-point-five kids, get my hair done, learn how to cook, go to PTA meetings. But I can't see myself in the Betty Crocker role. For one thing I can't cook unless it's a frozen dinner or goes in a microwave. A gourmet meal is box wine and pizza. I don't like to clean. And I wouldn't do that to a kid. Having me for a mother would stunt their mental growth. I've got too much of my own mother in me. Not to mention the poison that is a part of my DNA.

The alarm on my phone startles me out of my thoughts. I gather my things, slip my boots on, tie them, check my gun is loaded. I'm about to leave when I remember about Dan's gift— the backup gun I can strap to my ankle; for once, I put it on. My kind of lucky charm. I go to the stairwell. Then I change my mind. Nurse Betty deserves to know that I'm leaving and so I go to the nurses' station.

She looks up and smiles. "How are you doing, Detective?"

"It's just Megan," I say. It may just be Megan after I commit murder. "I want you to know how much I've appreciated your kindness, Betty."

"It's what I'm here for," she says with a smile.

Once again, I'm reminded there are those who bring healing and there are those who bring death. I want to do something nice for her, but it's too late for now. If I come back from this, I'll take her to a nice expensive dinner. "I'm going to get something from the machine."

I go down the back stairs and stand outside where I can see one very bright star, or maybe Venus or Jupiter, I was never good at remembering that stuff. That was Hayden's gift. I'd make popcorn and we'd climb out of an upstairs window onto the roof of the house in Port Orchard. Hayden, all of eight years old, would point out the constellations and tell me stories about each of the stars. Stories he'd made up. For someone who couldn't pee without making a mess and not flushing, he was smart and talented in ways I knew I'd never be.

I scuttle Hayden from my thoughts. My focus should be on the task at hand and nothing else. I can be single-minded if I try and I give it all my effort as I start the engine and head south. In another half hour dawn will paint the sky with bronze and orange and yellow clouds. I can smell the unique and wonderful smell of Puget Sound. It's slightly stale and sulphury but familiar and pleasant to someone who lives near the water. When we were kids Hayden and I would go to the harbor where he would dig for clams like a pirate digging for treasure. He was book-smart and would tell me the smell I was enjoying so much was dimethyl something or other and it was made by bacteria digesting dead phytoplankton. He talked about sex pheromones at low tide and I quit listening. He was a brat, but I find myself thinking about him again.

Stop it. Concentrate.

Finally, I clear my head and picture the house on

Salmonberry in Port Orchard where I had lived with my mom and stepdad and Hayden. I'm sure Wallace isn't going to meet me there, though. He'll be at the house Caleb inherited from his dad. If Wallace has killed Caleb, I think that's where he's waiting.

And it's where I'll surprise him and end this game.

FIFTY-EIGHT

Sheriff Tony Gray rolls over and snatches the phone from the bedside table.

"What's the problem, Ronnie?"

His wife raises one elbow, wondering what emergency her husband will be rushing out of the house for now.

"It's about Megan, Sheriff."

The hair bristles on his arms and he breaks out in goose bumps. He shutters his eyes, imagining the worst.

"Is she okay? What happened? Where are you?"

"The hospital. Don't worry, she's not hurt. Not that I know of. She just isn't here. I was supposed to meet her this morning at her place. And then I started thinking that it was odd because she didn't want to go home last night. So, I came to the hospital to check on her and Dan. The nurse said she left an hour ago."

"Well, maybe she went home and you just missed each other? Maybe she had to get something to eat. Did you try her phone?"

"Yes, sir. She has it turned off."

"She might have turned it off while she was in the hospital

and forgot to turn the dang thing back on. You know how she is."

"Yeah. That's why I'm worried."

FIFTY-NINE

The short walk to my old house helps tamp down my anxiety. My Explorer is three blocks away in the back lot of a home business with a sign out front that reads:

MADAM ZYRTOC
PALMS READ

Sounds like a cold medicine. What would she tell me about my future? Wallace's? Maybe neither of us has a future.

I've never been to Caleb's old house, but I have a good idea where it is. He'd told me once that he lived on a corner lot with the back facing the bay. It's maybe a quarter of a mile away. He'd given me a detailed description right down to the crushed-shell path leading to the bay and I'd thought he was inviting me over. He'd looked horrified and said he never wanted me to go there. He thought the place was evil. Now I'm ashamed I'd blown off that comment and told him about me spending time with Hayden on the beach, collecting shells and skipping stones across the water. I'm back deep in my past, right where I never wanted to be, and about to do something Caleb had warned me against. Maybe he was right. Maybe the place is evil.

Behind the palm reader's house is a path and I walk slowly, looking out at the bay like a tourist until I come to a cut where the path turns to gravel and leads upwards to a lone house perched on a hill.

Caleb's house is a two-story brick with white vinyl siding and windows looking out over the bay. I reach the top in a crouch, partially hidden behind a mature monkey puzzle tree whose branches sweep the ground. A paved driveway leads from the main level garage to the lower-level garage where one of the doors is open. Inside is the tail end of a white box van. Ronnie had said my neighbors reported seeing a dark van that didn't belong in the area at my place a couple of times. There are no windows in the back doors of the van.

In a crouch I make my way across the short lawn of scrub grass to the concrete apron behind the garage and get a better look inside. The van has a FedEx logo on the side.

I hold my breath and listen, but the sounds of a horn blowing across the water make it impossible to hear much. If his van is here, he's here. Of that I have no doubt. The van is probably stolen. Plates too. But that's the least of his sins and I'm not here to write a ticket or arrest him for theft.

The inside of the garage is spic and span with lengths of empty tool racks on two of the walls. When I get closer my shoe slides on something and I look down to see I've stepped in fresh blood and there's a streak of it running down the rear bumper. There's probably a ton of physical evidence in the back of the van that will tie Wallace to the killings here. People will have no sympathy for a rabid Ted Bundy–like killer.

The garage is quiet, empty; the smell of engine heat fills my nostrils. I put a hand on the rear bumper and feel heat near the exhaust pipe. It hasn't been here long. Wallace has been busy. If

I open the rear doors am I going to find another victim? Is Caleb in there?

The handle pulls quietly and the door clicks open. I have to see what's inside before I go in the house to search for Caleb. The back door of the van opens quietly, six inches, eight, ten, and then swings wide with the hinges giving a screech that makes the hair on the back of my neck stand on end, and I look around like a criminal caught in the act.

The inside of the van floor is covered in moving blankets with dark stains on them.

Blood.

Near the back door is the carcass of a dog. Headless. The source of the blood. In the back by the driver's side is a roll of what looks like heavy black plastic landscape film and a spade.

Too late I sense movement, and from the corner of my eye, a dark shape is dropping from the ceiling rafters. I reach for my gun and a swarm of pink stars explode behind my eyes.

SIXTY

WALLACE

He stands over Rylee's motionless body and watches for a minute, cautious that she could be faking unconsciousness. But no, after careful observation, he's satisfied that she's really out. She's breathing too, which is good. He'd hate to bring their long relationship to an end in such a sudden way.

There's a line of blood dripping down her face from where he hit her. He wipes it away with his thumb, almost tenderly, before he checks her pulse. It's strong and regular.

He moves his hand down from her neck, opens her jacket, and finds her holster.

As he reaches for the gun, the sound of an engine outside makes him spin around. A car is coming this way. He moves to the door of the garage and peers out at the street as the head-lights approach. He breathes a sigh of relief when the car, a blue Ford Taurus, does not slow down, continuing to the end of the block and turning right.

The false alarm has focused his mind. There is absolutely no time to waste. He can't take the chance that Rylee's associates in the police aren't on their way.

Hurrying, he slips the gun out of its holster and pockets it, then rolls Rylee over onto her back and, with practiced ease, binds her hands with a cable tie. He wonders about gagging her. She always did have a big mouth. On reflection, it might be the safest option. If she happens to regain consciousness while they're stopped for gas or at a red light, it would be better not to have her screaming for help and head-butting the sides of the van.

He pinches her nose until her mouth opens and then slips a rag into her mouth. She winces reflexively but doesn't wake up.

He rolls her onto her back again and bends to lift her up, supporting her under her shoulder blades and behind her knees. She's surprisingly light. He lays her down on the floor of the van and drapes one of the blankets over her.

It looks like a burial shroud.

SIXTY-ONE

I come to in complete darkness wrapped in something scratchy. *Moving blankets. We're moving.* I'm on my side with my wrists bound behind my back. My hands are numb and my shoulders ache. The cloth stuffed in my mouth makes me gag and I'm glad I skipped breakfast. He hasn't bound my legs.

Mistake number one.

I struggle enough to be able to tell the shoulder holster is there but the gun is gone. Of course it is. The engine is loud and the smell of exhaust is leaking into the cargo area, but the blankets filter the worst of it.

Time is a slippery thing and there's no telling how long I was out. The van is moving at a good pace, and the wheels make a constant sound on a semi-smooth surface. I'm on a paved road. Maybe State Road 19 but I only guess that because it's the nearest road to Caleb's house.

The van slows and turns onto a grating surface. Gravel. Hardpack. And I smell something besides exhaust. Sulfurous. Briny. We're near the water.

If I wasn't unconscious long. The van comes to a stop and a moment later I hear a door open, then close, and I take advantage of Wallace's absence to try and work the gag loose to scream for help. It's useless so I start squirming to loosen the bindings on my wrists. Each movement causes them to cut even deeper into the flesh and shoot pain into my fingers. I can feel it loosening, but I have to stop before my hands go completely numb and become useless.

I crawl like a caterpillar toward the doors and stop when I feel them against my feet. If he opens these doors, I'll kick him in the face and take my chance to run.

A door opens, but it's up front, and I feel the slight sinking of someone getting in. The door closes. I hear a sliding sound and, at long last, Wallace is standing over me. I can't see his face in the shadow of the brim of his hat.

And then I catch that familiar scent. The scent I detected in Tides, not that I realized at the time. The olfactory cue that had me thinking of him for no conscious reason. The scent when I walked into my house the other day. And it all falls into place.

Caleb.

Caleb is Wallace.

He leans forward and his features become clearer, confirming what I already knew.

"Comfortable?"

SIXTY-TWO

"Holy shit," Ronnie says.

Sheriff Gray moves over to her desk, where she's staring at a document on the screen.

"What is it?"

"Megan's friend Caleb, the guy who found Dan?"

"The guy who's missing?"

Ronnie nodded. "I thought I'd dig into his background, see if there's any reason Megan's stalker might want to target him. Turns out there's a file on him."

The sheriff motions for her to spill, and she obliges.

"He was a suspect in his father's and stepmother's deaths, but they didn't have enough to arrest him. Two weeks before their deaths, Caleb's father had bought the gun that was used.

"Several people told police the parents had loud fights constantly. The father had remarried and the stepmother was threatening to leave her husband unless Caleb moved out. The stepmother had told Caleb to get a job and find a place to live. The neighbor said the stepmother was pressing her husband to change the will and leave the boy nothing. They were going to cut him off.

"After their deaths Caleb had no one to take him in. According to the police report, they found his real mother, but she didn't want Caleb. He was nineteen and they couldn't make her take him. The police said he didn't attend the funerals and just took off."

"Wait a minute," the sheriff begins. "Do you think...?"

Ronnie keeps talking, like she hasn't heard him. "The will hadn't been changed yet and he'd been left the house, two cars, and a substantial amount of money. Two hundred thousand and change. He kept the house and his father's car and sold everything else. Police said just before his father died, he had made an appointment with a lawyer to revise the will. When the police questioned him, Caleb told them he didn't know anything about the will. He claimed he didn't know his father even had a gun."

Ronnie took a breath. She had more. She always had more.

"I called the investigator," she went on. "He'd retired a year after the deaths. He said he asked for an inquest and the ruling was murder-suicide. Dad shot the wife then shot himself."

"So where has Caleb has been since then?"

"The detective said he just took off. The house has been vacant since then; as far as he knows, it has been sold. I looked for credit cards, bank accounts, email accounts, and everything I could think of that might belong to Caleb. I even called a friend at the Social Security Administration, and Caleb has never paid Social Security and doesn't have a card. He doesn't have a driver's license.

"The car he'd kept was found lodged on a sandbar in the Columbia. Plates were missing, but they were able to get the owner information from the VIN. Of course, the owner was the deceased father. The detective in Port Orchard figured Caleb had killed himself and been swept downriver. He said he knew in his gut Caleb had killed them, but there was no solid evidence."

"Do you think the detective was competent?"

"I called Clay. He said the guy was a good investigator, but he was close to retirement and maybe wanted Caleb to be guilty so he could retire with a big win under his belt."

"Did you tell Clay why you were interested?"

Ronnie shakes her head. "Said Caleb was a witness in Dan's attack and I was doing background. He was worried about Megan and wanted to come to the hospital, but I told him she needed some time to recover."

For a moment, they're both quiet. The sheriff finally spoke. "You told Megan Caleb was missing. You think she'd go looking for him without telling us?"

Ronnie shot him a knowing look.

"Yeah, this is Megan we're talking about."

SIXTY-THREE

I lie completely still as Caleb, as *Wallace*, stands over me.

"Rylee, I'm glad I didn't hurt you too badly. I saw the van rocking and you know what we said in high school. *If the van is a rockin', don't bother knockin'.*" He laughs, but it's high-pitched. Over the top. Like a mad scientist or attention-seeking Marvel villain. He's completely off his nut.

I mumble around the gag. He reaches over and removes it, carefully, like he's concerned I'm going to bite his fingers off. He's right to be worried.

"Why?" is the first thing I say.

He looks a little disappointed. "I thought you would be more surprised. What gave me away?"

"Old Spice," I say. "No two men wear that shit in today's world, Caleb."

He laughs uproariously, like I've told the greatest joke of the year. The greatest joke of the year is how long it took me to see what was in front of my nose. Even the ice-cold Megan Carpenter can be swayed by an emotional attachment. Who knew?

"Caleb is dead, Rylee. I was telling the truth on the phone: I killed Caleb a long time ago. I'm Wallace now."

"Why did you do it? Why did you kill all those people? You owe me the truth."

"I don't owe you a thing, Rylee." His voice has changed from playful to menacing. "You've never done anything for me. Nothing. You pretended to be my friend, to care about me, but you're like my father and that bitch of his. And then you abandoned me just like my real mother."

"Caleb I—"

"Shut up! You put me in a spot. When you killed Ted Duggan, you made me an accomplice to murder by me keeping quiet about what you had done. When I didn't want to live a life of killing like you did, you dumped me and disappeared. Do you have any idea how much that hurt? How much I struggled? I had nothing to live for. You knew I wanted to get away from home, but you never asked why. You never think of anyone but yourself."

"Caleb, I was seventeen. You know what kind of life I was living. I'm sorry for not asking how you felt back then. You treated me good and I always appreciated it. You were my only friend."

"Friend? Some friend. You move away, change your name, change how you look, but you keep hunting. That was more important to you than friendship. Than love."

Tension speeds his breathing.

"I never forgot you. I worried about you. Couldn't sleep without something to knock me out because I always thought you'd gotten in over your head. The Rylee I knew was a smart girl. A *nice* girl. One who loved her brother and I thought you were starting to love me. Finally, I realized you didn't give a shit about me or anyone else. So, I started looking for you. Studying you. Learning how to be like you. You had a purpose in life, and you even believed it benefited society. I realized you weren't so wrong. Not evil. *Committed*."

He stops for a beat.

"How do you like me now?"

"Caleb, what do you want?"

"It took a while to find you."

My heart is beating hard. I want to yell, but I know I need to calm him. Keep him talking. This isn't Caleb. This person is crazy.

"What happened to you, Caleb? I'm still your friend. Talk to me."

His eyes cast downward. "You would never understand."

"Try me. I've changed too. Maybe I can help you."

Wrong thing to say.

"Help me! You've already helped me in ways you'll never guess. You've been busy and so have I."

"What do you mean?" I know what he means, but I want to hear him admit to the killings.

In answer, he just slams the door shut. The sliding noise again. The passthrough has been closed. The engine starts and we begin moving again.

Maybe I was too quick to fake Ronnie and the others out. I should know better, but, like Ronnie said, this is personal. My anger and cockiness might have gotten me killed.

SIXTY-FOUR

Ronnie called Clay and Patterson to advise them of the plan. Megan will be pissed, but so what. They are in this together. A task force. Not a hunting trip for revenge. This may be their best and only bet to catch Caleb.

Now they are all gathered in the office. Clay, Patterson, Donna, Ronnie and Sheriff Gray.

Sheriff Gray says, "She's pulled one stunt too many. I won't put up with this. I'll... I'll..." His voice trails off.

"Sheriff Gray," Patterson says, "we'll find her. And then you can fire her if you want. Hell, I'm angry enough for all of us and look where it's gotten me."

Tony gives Ronnie a hard look. "And you're positive she didn't give you a clue as to where she was really going."

It's not a question. It's an accusation, and Ronnie resents it but understands his concern. They've already given pictures of Megan and Caleb to state troopers with instructions to treat the male subject as armed and dangerous. They've shown the photos to the ferry operators and asked if she or anyone matching Caleb's description had gone to Indian Island or to Marrowstone Island. Nothing. State troopers have checked the

islands and parks and scenic pull-outs and abandoned struc-
tures with zero success.

The state police superintendent gave Tony a piece of his
mind for keeping this from them for so long. Tony shot back that
anyone with half a mind should have assumed what was going
on from the news media accounts. The two wouldn't be on
speaking terms for a while, but state troopers would still be looking. How could they not?

Donna raises her hand and Patterson gives his head a shake,

"This isn't grade school. If you have something to say,
say it."

"You just all looked so mad about her going off on her own,
you haven't asked Ronnie or me how we can find her."

Clay says, "So how can you do that?"

Donna chews on the end of a pen. "We can track her phone
for one thing and—"

Ronnie cuts in. "I've tried that. She's got it turned off."

Donna smiles and gives a little shoulder shrug before
launching a complicated diatribe of how she can find the phone
and everyone, except Ronnie, looks at her as if she's speaking
Tagalog.

Patterson says, "So in brief, you can find the phone," and
Donna just smiles.

You're a genius, Donna," Ronnie says.

"You would have thought of it, Ronnie, if your partner
wasn't in danger."

Tony holds his hands up. "Instead of talking, get to looking."

The two computer geniuses scurry over to Ronnie's desk
and get started. Tony gets more coffee. Clay and Patterson sit at
the extra desks and talk in voices so low only they can hear.

A minute later Donna sits back in the chair and says, "Oh,
shit fire and save the matches." She looks around and sees every
face turned toward her. "Sorry."

Ronnie says, "Megan's phone isn't anywhere to be tracked.

The last time it was active is in Port Orchard. There are a couple of towers around the marina, but no way of telling which one it was near. We'll just have to search around each tower and hope to find her Explorer."

Clay says, "Give me the tower locations and I'll get my guys out there looking."

Tony rubs the back of his neck. "I swear I'm going to have a tracker surgically implanted in that woman."

"That gives me an idea." Ronnie starts tapping away at keys and after a few seconds says, "Wallace's ad in the paper said Dupont should go to Port Orchard Marina. Slip 45. We checked the surveillance footage and thought we saw Dupont there, but we couldn't tell for sure. I've got the surveillance pulled up live."

They all gather around the computer as Ronnie searches backward from the last time Megan's phone was active. Ronnie stops the video. "There," she says. On the screen a man can be seen standing on the dock at the marina. She backs up the video slowly, stops, and goes forward a frame at a time.

"He's throwing something in the water," Patterson says. "Can you zoom in?"

Ronnie taps some keys and blows the picture up. One of the items he slings into the bay is a gun. The other item is small and square and thin.

"Megan's phone?" Donna asks.

"I think so," Ronnie says. "But if I'm right, there's another phone he's still got."

SIXTY-FIVE

The van slows and for a moment the engine grows louder before shutting down. We're in a building, a garage, a warehouse, something enclosed for sure. The front door opens and the van lifts slightly. The door shuts and I wait. I don't have to wait long before the back doors open. "We're here, Rylee," Caleb says. "There's no place like home. Well, except for my home. Too many bad memories."

I lie completely still. Maybe he'll think I've been killed by the exhaust fumes. No such luck. Something slams down inches from my legs hard enough to make me jump and let out a muffled scream.

"No games. Scoot down and I'll help you out. If you try to kick me I'll break your legs. Understand?"

I say as clearly as I can with a gag, "I can't move."

"Don't bullshit a bullshitter, Rylee. I heard you kicking the doors a mile ago. Now scoot down, and if you do anything else, I'm afraid I'll have to knock you out again. We need to talk. What you say will make the difference between life and death."

I don't have much choice but to wait for an opportunity. I

mumble some unflattering words around the gag and begin to scoot toward his voice like a worm.

When my legs are hanging over the end, strong hands grab the blanket and pull me forward until my feet hit the ground. He flips the moving blankets back over my head and slings them into the van. He prudently steps back several feet. Darn. I'd wanted to put him in the lead role of *The Nutcracker Suite*.

The garage door goes down and I can see we're in a one-car garage. It's my old house. I recognize it because Hayden had drawn on the walls with crayons, and the green-and-red wide-eyed monsters are still there. Tears collect in the corners of my eyes, and Caleb must have mistaken my sadness as pain.

He says, "I hope I didn't hurt you?"

I mumble and this time it's obvious I'm really and seriously pissed. My anger has reached DEFCON 1.

"Sorry about the gag. I'm going to take it off. You can scream as much as you like, but I hope you don't." He slaps a cut-off baseball bat into one big palm. I nod since I can't speak. He stands to one side of me—he's that smart anyway—and pulls the gag down around my neck. "How about a tour of your old home?"

I work my jaws and the corners of my mouth are painfully stretched and raw. My first word is, "Bastard!" Well, that's the third or fourth word. The others are rated R-plus.

"Now, is that any way to talk to your new partner?"

Phlegm has built up in my throat and I spit at him. My aim is good and it hits him in the crotch. Where my foot would have gone if he'd been careless.

"I can see you're a little angry, Rylee."

I take a deep breath and hold it, hoping not to let loose on him verbally and cause him to let loose on me with that club. I've seen what it can do.

"Not ready to talk? No? Well, I'll talk and you can listen."

"Please don't." The words slipped out. Sometimes I'm my own worst enemy, but he just laughs.

He puts his hands in front like he's wearing handcuffs and says in an authoritative voice, "I have the right to remain silent. Is that it?"

"Something like that. Listen, Caleb. I don't know what's happened to you, but I want to understand why you killed all these people." I'm sitting on the edge of the van's bed and it's cutting into my backside. I squirm a little to get better purchase, and he takes hold of my shoulder and easily pulls me to my feet.

He steps back farther and lays a thoughtful finger alongside his cheek and cocks his head to one side. "Let's see. Where did I go wrong? Hmmm. That's hard to pinpoint because I don't think I was the one that went wrong. My dad ran my mother away and married the bitch from hell."

"You paid him back for that. Didn't you? And your step-mother too."

"You're one to cast stones Miss I'm-So-Perfect. You killed your real father. You put your mother in prison. I won't honor Dad's piece of trash with the title of *mother*. At least I was kind enough to put her out of my misery." He laughs at his sick joke. It is kind of funny, but I'm not that way any longer.

"The detective said he knows you killed them. He's going to prove it and you'll be in prison for a very long time. You weren't careful."

Caleb shrugs off my words.

"That old fool," he says. "He couldn't find his ass with both hands. It was my first kill. I may have left some clues. But I learned a lot from you when you killed Ted Duggan. Remember that?"

"He deserved it."

"So did they."

"I didn't teach you to kill cops."

"Forgive me if I'm wrong, but wasn't your first kill a cop?

And his brother? Also a cop? And that other cop on the boat? That's three. I'm ahead of you by, well, let's just say by quite a few."

I don't defend myself. He's right about much of what he said. But he's not me. He's just another monster to be dealt with.

What he said was the truth.

The Caleb I knew *is* dead.

SIXTY-SIX

"Hey. I've got something." Donna spins her computer around for all to see. "This is from the Port Orchard Marina yesterday morning before sunup."

The video plays frame by frame, showing a large figure in a heavy jacket and hooded sweatshirt. He goes past the office and down the docks where he goes off-screen for just a moment. Donna hits a button and they have a split screen. In one he's shown going down the dock to the last boat. He leans out to the hull and puts his hand on it. He then walks back toward the camera, keeping his head down.

Tony says, "He knows where the cameras are."

The figure comes back toward the office and goes around the corner of the building. There are no cameras on the parking lot.

"How long ago was that, Donna?"

"Yesterday morning at 5:13. He doesn't come back as far as I've checked the video. I tried to zoom in, but what you see is what you get. A man in a heavy dark coat and gray hooded shirt. No face. No hair color. He's big. Sound like anyone we know?"

Patterson lets out a breath. "Caleb Hunter, aka Wallace. He's taken Megan."

"Got it. I located Dan's phone."

Everyone looks to the source of Ronnie's triumphant cry.

"Where?" Tony asks.

SIXTY-SEVEN

I'm prodded in the back with the rough end of the shortened baseball bat like cattle along a chute to the kill floor. Caleb is not going to let me live. He hasn't made a misstep so far. He anticipated I would look for him at his old house. But even with the club pushing painfully into my spine, I don't feel any anger or manic excitement from him. He's stone cold.

We enter the kitchen and long dormant memories surge. The smell of Hayden's favorite cookies, the spaghetti I could manage without burning it. I hear ghost echoes of laughter and I see Hayden making faces and pulling his underwear up under his armpits pretending to be an old man. I look at the wall where the word RUN was scrawled in our stepfather's blood, and I can almost see Rolland on his back, the big hunting knife seeming to pin him to the floor like a butterfly. And there's Hayden on his knees looking at the bloody mess. I can hear the sharp intake of Hayden's breath into his skinny chest. I see the disbelieving stare in his eyes.

I'd never wanted to come back here. I even had a problem coming back to Port Orchard period. My chest tightens and I hear a keening whine. It's coming from me. Caleb is standing a few feet to my side, examining me like some behavioral experiment. *Okay, class, Let's see how far we can push her. Then we'll watch as she implodes.* I didn't think I could hate this man any more than I did after he hurt Dan, but anything is possible from this point on.

Caleb prods me with the bat.

"How does it feel to be home, Rylee?"

How do you think, asshole?

"This was never my home," I say. "It was my prison."

He smiles. A mean smile. "Brings back bad feelings, doesn't it? I thought it would be good for you to experience where you came from. You may have been born somewhere else, but this is what made you. Am I wrong?"

He's not. He's cruel. He's talking when he should be killing. Is this his plan? To make me beg for mercy. Or death. It won't work. I'll never beg. My anger transcends any other feeling. Fear. Even hatred.

"Gotta say it's roomier than your new place," Caleb says. "Of course, the apartment next door was a little bigger."

I hate the look of satisfaction in his eyes as my mouth drops open. All along, *he* was the asshole next door. The one who kept leaving the door open. He didn't just happen on Dan the other night, he was coming home.

He grins. "Howdy, neighbor."

Determined not to let him see how rattled I am that he was living next to me all those weeks, I go on the offensive. "So, Caleb, or Wallace if you prefer, what was it like coming back to *your* old home? Bad memories inside that place? Or did you enjoy reliving the murders of your parents?"

"They were not my parents," he spits the words out, and his face becomes a homicidal Halloween mask. "Parents?" He paces like a caged animal, breathing deep, jaws clenched. I've pushed a button, but I'm not afraid or one bit sorry. Screw him.

He suddenly looks at me and smiles.

That mean smile.

"I see what you're doing, Rylee. You were always good at these things. No. I didn't go inside." He makes a theatrical gesture with a sweeping of one arm and says, "'The house is evil. Possessed of dark imaginings'. I read that in a book. Cool, huh?"

Now he's smiling. Pleased with his witty reply. Like Jekyll and Hyde. He should run for political office.

"Yeah, cool, Caleb. You should have become a writer instead of a masked avenger. Or maybe a sicko killer."

He laughs. "It takes one to know one."

Goose bumps play at the hair on my arms. My mother had said these exact words to me, in this very room, not long before she and my biological father killed my stepfather. Ironic. I was in as much danger then as now. Only now I know who my killer will be.

"They painted in here shortly after I bought it."

Bought it?

"What did you say?" I ask.

Caleb nods. "My dad left me a bunch of money and some stocks. I'm rich. The first thing I did was buy this place. I got it cheap because of the murder. I'd never sell my old house. Too many ghosts and I don't want them to get out."

Now I know he's crazy. Does that help me? I think of one way. "Caleb, this house is full of ghosts too."

"There's only one here and I don't have to be afraid of him. Rolland and I have spoken often and he knows how I feel about you. He's the one that gave me the idea of taking you on as a partner."

"He did?"

"Of course. I see them. The ghosts. I know you do too. The ghosts in Ted Duggan's house told you to kill him. Duggan was a monster who raped, tortured, and killed little girls. There were many of his victims' ghosts in that house and would have been many more if you hadn't stopped him. You said so yourself."

"Caleb, if I remember correctly, my killing him was the reason we stopped seeing each other. It disgusted you. *I* disgusted you."

Caleb is on a roll. There's excitement in his eyes and his tone of voice. "You wanted me to be part of your mission back then. Why not now? We have the skill. I have the money. We can do anything we want. Go anywhere we want. Hunt monsters. Together. Think of the good we'll be doing. Think of all the people we will save."

I act like I'm thinking about his offer, when in fact, I'm thinking I have one of those monsters right in front of me. I wanted to end him before I realized just how crazy he was. Now I pity him. He needs to be stopped. But killing him? He was good back then. Maybe I am to blame for his becoming this. At least partly to blame. He hated his parents, but maybe he would have just run off to California like he dreamed of if I hadn't taught him about killing evil. I own that much.

"Caleb, I'm sorry for what I've done to you. I'm sorry for what your parents did to you. But you didn't have to be like me. You're smarter than I am. You could have done anything with your life. You didn't need your parents. You didn't need me. You were stronger back then."

"Stronger? Seriously?" He paces, all the time thumping the club into his palm. "I was weak. I threw up every time I thought about you stabbing that guy. But my dad and the bitch were stabbing me in the heart every day, all day. The only place I could escape was to school and that was just another prison. I tried really hard not to change. But why be a good boy and take the shit my family was shoveling? I knew I'd never see you again, and pretty soon I started seeing things your way.

"You were ridding the world of this plague of sexual preda-tors, thieves, scam artists, child abusers, and hundreds of others with sickness eating their souls. Like my parents. Most of them die, and their ghosts possess and spread their malevolent disease. The worst of these are the people sworn to protect us from people just like them.

"But that detective harassed me, followed me, talked to everyone about me until I had nowhere to go. The few friends I had avoided me like the plague. I could see in their eyes they thought I was crazy. I'm not crazy. The dirty cops are the crazy ones. Evil. They are especially cursed and must be eradicated."

"Who are you talking about? The detective that investigated your parents' deaths was just doing his job, Caleb. He wasn't dirty."

"He was as dirty as they come, Rylee. You don't know, do you?"

"Know what?"

"You didn't know what he was doing." Caleb stops pacing and his eyes burn into mine. "You really don't know. Well, how about that. Rylee the monster slayer doesn't know something." He turns a full circle and gives a whoop. "How about that."

"Enlighten me, Caleb." I need to keep him talking long enough to find a way out of this.

"Do you remember Caradee?"

I didn't think I could be shocked any further, but that name is a blast from the past. "Caradee Hagen?" I remember her like it was yesterday. She was a sophomore at Kitsap High School and one of the girls on the cheerleading squad. They are so over-the-top in their self-esteem that if you weren't a mirror, they'd never look at you. They never looked at me or talked to me. I remember something else too.

"You said I was prettier than the six girls that considered South Kitsap High their personal turf. You said they treated the rest of us like servants."

Caleb's eyes soften. The mania is lessened at least for now.

"You hated them. All of them. I hated them for you. They treated you like dirt they could wipe off their feet."

He's right. I did hate them with all my heart. Every second of the day, the gang of six demonstrated their power. They were interchangeable—slender, larger on top, and teeth as white as ascending wedding doves. They could snare a boy with just a look.

Yet I also felt sorry for them. Their existence was tied up in their prettiness. They had no personality. What you saw was what you got. And the football team got plenty.

He opens a cabinet drawer and retrieves a newspaper.

"I saved an article. Let me read it to you." He unfolds the yellowed newsprint and starts reading.

"'Caradee Hagen, a close friend of Rylee Cassidy, told this reporter that Rylee Cassidy was a strange loner. She never had anything to say. She kind of just clung to the background. Probably waiting and plotting.

"'Another close friend, Marilee Watson, told us Cassidy was often seen in the school bathroom. She was always in there, sulking around. I hope they find her soon because, well, I don't know that she's a killer, but I do know that she never, ever talked about her family. She must have really hated them.'"

When my stepfather was murdered and Hayden and I had to go on the run, I came across a Seattle newspaper story that hinted at patricide. They thought I had killed him.

"I remember all of them," I say.

He tosses the paper on the floor. "Well, you'll appreciate this then." He says this with a smile that looks like one on a television villain. "Right after you disappeared the detective that started hassling me was under suspension for, and get this, providing underage girls with liquor and illegal substances in exchange for sexual favors. Caradee was one of the girls. Marilee was interviewed but wouldn't admit the detective had molested her. She quit school and the family moved away. The

detective beat the charge somehow, but Caradee was so humiliated she committed suicide. She overdosed in a bathroom on
campus. The bastard got away with what he did. So, yeah, he
was a dirty cop."

"He's alive," I say.

Caleb refolds the brittle paper.

"Why would I go after him?" he asks in response to a question I didn't pose. "He did us a favor, wouldn't you say? He took
care of your tormentors. Showed them they weren't so high and
mighty. But don't worry, the asshole is still on my list if you
want him."

Caleb is not the boy I left behind. Not the love that I once
imagined. That boy is long gone.

"What about the others?" I ask, keeping him talking. "It
looks like you were enjoying the killing. I never enjoyed it,
Caleb. I was glad they were dead, but I never enjoyed the
killing."

He throws a dismissive look at me.

"You did, Rylee. You just can't admit it because you think
you've changed. That you're a better person somehow. But
you'll always be Rylee at the core. A hunter. A killer. A
predator."

That doesn't deserve a response. It's too close to the truth
for me to say anything that doesn't sound like justification.

"As for the others. The detective that called herself Susan
Dupont, was Susan Whitman. A nobody from Indiana. I met
her at the Indiana Women's Prison. After I killed my parents, I
rambled around a bit and found myself in this little Indiana
town called Santa Claus where I worked on a pumpkin farm.
Then I worked at Christmas Lake Village as a groundskeeper.
The St. Meinrad Archabbey was nearby and I thought I would
become a priest to make amends. But I guess you have to believe
in God to be a priest. If I believed in God, I'd have to believe He

let all this evil prey on us. Let my father run my mother off. Let him molest me."

This shocks me to the core, and there's no hiding it on my face.

"Didn't tell you about that, did I? Yeah. He was a child molester, the sick bastard. I always thought it was my fault. That something I had done made him do those things to me. When you killed Ted Duggan, I secretly cheered, but I didn't believe in doing what you did. Not yet."

In a weak voice I ask, "You were going to be a priest?"

"Yeah. Can you dig it? Father Caleb Hunter. Has a nice ring but it wasn't going to happen. I'd accompanied one of the priests when he went to Indiana Women's Prison to preach to the baby killers and scum of the earth. On one of those trips, I met Susan Whitman. Now Susan Dupont. Or the deceased or whatever. The priest had an in with the administration at the prison and he got me a job working there as a janitor and handyman. Since I had come to the prison visit with the Archabbey Prior, the prison asked me to assist with church services and help pass out the library books to the inmates. Susan was a voracious reader. The prisoners are not supposed to have books pertaining to crimes, but what book doesn't have a little of that in it? I got her whatever she asked for. She was interesting.

"She was in prison for white collar crimes, and boy, did she have some stories. We talked a lot. There wasn't much else to do and she liked me. She opened up to me and told me what she'd really done and it wasn't white collar. The authorities only knew the tip of the iceberg. She had preyed on wealthy widowers with teenage children. She would pretend to be a nanny, a teacher, housekeeper, or companion and gain the trust of the family and then slowly clean them out. She'd gotten herself on one old guy's will as sole beneficiary. Next thing you know he died, suddenly, unexpectedly, inexplicably; she inherited a fortune even though his children's attorney contested the will. She sent his kids to their aunts to live, sold the house and all his property, and cleared out. It wasn't the first time she'd done that. She stopped short of admitting she'd killed the old gent."

I could point out the parallels between what Dupont or Whitman had done and what Caleb's parents had done. But I don't want to interrupt his confession.

"The children were the ones that suffered. She was stealing their home, their livelihood, their safety, and belief that right would always win. She had been doing this for years before a bad check caught up to her. By that time, she was worth about four million and the police knew nothing about it. Four million! I asked why she didn't quit and she said she liked it. The thrill of it.

"Susan was getting out at the end of the month and wanted to meet me. Give me a job. I prayed to a God I didn't believe in and decided to turn her down, but I started watching her and she led me to some others. She'd become a cop and was using her position to continue her stealing and killing. She killed a man in Utah while she was a cop. You didn't know she was a cop in Utah, did you? The house she lived in in Port Angeles was bought with dirty money. You surely didn't believe she'd used her own money."

I say, "So when she met you at Port Orchard Marina, she knew who you were from the time at the prison. How did you get her to go to her house?" She was a martial artist who had beaten up several men. Caleb is big, but that's not always enough.

Caleb laughs and the arm holding the club lowers. He's getting into this.

"I didn't meet her there. I broke into her house after she'd gone to pick up the note. She keeps a key under the mat on the front porch. She wasn't afraid of anyone. Thought she was top dog, but there's always one meaner. When she came home I ambushed her. From what I'd learned she was a real fighter. I didn't want to leave a big bloody scene behind. I know you found the root cellar. She wasn't so tough when I got her down there. She begged and cried and offered sex and then money. I gave her the ax."

"And you put a bloody meat cleaver in her boyfriend's apartment to frame him."

"I didn't want it to be too easy. Had you going though, didn't I? Of course, I knew you'd figure out he wasn't the one. Hell, she'd beat his ass in front of a bunch of people."

"He'd asked her to marry him," I say, and he chuckles. I make myself smile. We're getting along great. As soon as he drops the club, I'm going to bite his nuts off.

"I didn't know that. Now I'm glad I ambushed her."

Yeah. Good for you. Keep talking, asshole.

"This just keeps getting better. I thought you'd quit the cops and come with me. That maybe having someone on the inside would be a real hoot. You find them, I finish them. A team."

I've heard enough. "Not going to happen, kiddo. I won't ever work with you. I don't respect you or even like you. If I wasn't a cop, I'd hunt you. Don't you get it? Don't you see what you've become? You're worse than any of them."

He stares at me, face frozen, almost looking through me.

"You have no idea how right you are, Rylee."

SIXTY-EIGHT

"How far is it?" Sheriff Gray asks, keeping his eyes on the road. Ronnie is grateful for that. Multitasking at ninety miles an hour is never a good idea.

"About five miles," Ronnie says, looking at the pin on her map a little north of the blue dot that marks their position on the highway.

"You think they'll still be there?"

"I hope so. It's the only chance we've got."

She doesn't give voice to the other concern that overrides everything. The time. It took them too long to uncover Caleb Hunter's background. That it took too long to trace Dan's phone.

That they're going to be too late to save Megan.

SIXTY-NINE

It's do or die.

Do something.

Or literally die.

I keep him talking.

"Listen to me, Caleb," I say quickly. "You've done bad things. So have I. But I'm trying to make up for what I've done just like you wanted to do when you went to the priest college. I'm arresting these monsters, these evil creatures. Instead of killing them I'm helping to bring them to justice. Letting the courts deal with them." *When I can.* "You can do it too. You can stop this and become someone good. Fight evil a different way. Help me put them away. If you promise me you'll stop killers, I'll help you."

He rests his chin in his fingers. "Is that the best you can do, Rylee? I mean, really. I thought we were having a serious conversation. Lying is like breathing to you."

The makeshift club comes back up and he paces in a circle holding it over his head. His mouth is moving like he's having a conversation. I hope Alex Rader's ghost isn't telling him to kill me. He comes to a stop and grabs me, shoving me against the wall hard enough I fall to my rump and slide down.

"Stay there. If you think someone is coming to save you, you can forget it. The Rylee I knew wouldn't tell anyone where she was going. The Rylee I knew always wanted to do things by herself. She was indestructible. Fearless. That was then. Look at you now. Reduced to—to what? You're no match for me. You are definitely not the challenge I'd hoped for. I was going to make you my partner."

He goes to the cabinet under the sink and turns around with hatchet. The oak handle is stained and well used, and the metal is rusted except for the blade edge gleaming in the light coming through the kitchen window. I knew this day would come sooner or later. I would have liked for it to be later. When I came down hard on my butt, I felt something on my leg. I thought he'd taken my backup gun. I pull my legs in as far as possible and slide down farther. It will look like I'm going to kick at him. If I'm lucky, I'll be able to twist enough to reach it.

Keep him distracted.

I need him to stay just where he is until I'm ready.

"You've got me so leave everyone else alone. Promise me you won't hurt my friends. You want me to beg. I'll beg. You want to have sex, let's do it. You want money, I don't have much. I'm not worth much. I have some box wine in my fridge and you're welcome to that." While I say this, I slide a few inches at a time down the wall and bow my head like I'm beat. Done fighting. Legs bent. Past caring.

I'm ready.

"Go ahead," I finally say. "But remember one thing. You're a coward. I left you behind because I didn't want you with me. You're such a sissy you'd have gotten me killed. You've gotten big and you still have to sneak up on people. You were afraid to fight Dupont because you knew she'd kick your ass. I was going to pin Duggan's murder on you if I had to. You meant nothing to me but a possible romp in the hay. You pathetic piece of shit..."

He raises the hatchet over his head, his face contorts into a mask of insanity, and he steps toward me, then something drags his attention away from me.

Sirens.

Police sirens wail in the far-off distance. It sounds like they are near the bay. The area where Hayden and I spent many mornings hunting for pirate treasure or skipping flat stones across the water.

Sirens are music.

I take full advantage of Caleb's surprise.

I slide an inch farther, my hand finds my ankle, I can't draw the .38 so I lift my leg, point my foot at him and pull the trigger. It could have blown off the side of my foot, but it doesn't. The shot hits him in the lower stomach, and as he doubles over, I pull the trigger again and again and again. His throat blossoms, the next bullet takes part of his lower jaw off, and then his head explodes.

SEVENTY

The room smells like a pistol range and my sock and ankle are scorched black by the muzzle flashes. Six inches of skin on my leg and ankle are burned a bright red and already blistering. I scoot across the floor to the ax and use it to cut the bindings around my wrists then crawl on hands and knees to Caleb's body.

The first shot eviscerated him. Or maybe it was the fourth or fifth. All I know is the gun is empty and my spare bullets are in my Explorer and who knows where that is. Standing is harder than I thought. Maybe it's because of the goose egg on the back of my head. Could be because I've never killed anyone I truly cared about.

Dan's gift, the .38 backup revolver, is what saved my life and took Caleb's. When Dan and I became serious, he bought the backup gun and insisted I wear it because my job was dangerous. I couldn't argue. Maybe getting the gun was divine intervention or whatever but I don't believe in that stuff. I believe that it was Caleb's time to go and not mine.

Tears stand in my eyes and my throat is tight, but I'm not

going to cry. I won't waste the water. On the other hand, I head to the bathroom to pee.

Mistake.

The toilet seat is down, of course, and in my mind I can clearly see a seven-year-old Hayden pissing and missing the bowl but not the seat or the floor. Tears roll down my cheeks and I'm sucking down breath as my chest heaves. I can't stay in here. But I need a plan before I go outside where I'm sure neighbors will gather and a SWAT team will line up at the front door.

That's a stupid thought. I've done nothing wrong. Caleb kidnapped me and was going to kill me. I defended myself. Five times. But I'd have to explain why I sent the police on a wild goose chase and ended up here. Alone.

Why am I worried? Caleb won't have an attorney or sue me. His family are all dead. He killed them and many others and he confessed to me. But then, I killed him and the public will be thinking, "Isn't that convenient?" But they weren't here. They weren't threatened with the sharp edge of a hatchet. What was I supposed to do? I reasoned. I begged. I offered him sex. Let the assholes second guess me. What do I care?

I care because I don't want to be the subject of a deep investigation. Caleb was an old friend who threatened me, stalked, and acted on his threats. Ronnie knows almost everything now and she'll find out the rest. Clay and Patterson and Donna know a little. I can't risk them digging any deeper. They'll want to know why he came after me. Why he killed all the others to get my attention. He was killing dirty cops. Would they think I'm dirty too? And that leads back to them questioning why I sent them down a false trail.

The sirens are closer now.

They couldn't have found me unless my cell phone is nearby. I go back to the body—not Caleb now, but "the body"—and search his pockets. My hands get covered with sticky blood, and I move his intestines to get in his front pockets. I don't find a phone.

Instinct makes me survey the room to see what I've touched. I remind myself I've done nothing wrong, but Rylee says, *Erase all evidence*. I'll check the van for a phone, but first I'll check here and make sure I've not touched anything. There is nothing except for the ax handle and I peed in the toilet. I go back to the bathroom and using the bottom of my shirt I flush the toilet. Who kills someone and then goes to the bathroom? I'm being paranoid? Damn right. But why?

The sirens are getting closer still. Still a distance away but if the phone is here, Ronnie will find it. I need to think, but I'm feeling nauseated. *Concussion?* The van is in the garage. If I decide to run, I'll have transportation. *Why am I thinking of running?*

If the phone is there then... then what? I can't very well erase the fact the phone led them here. Shit!

I go to the garage. The back doors of the van and the driver's side door stand open. I don't have to go to the back of the van to see the blood from the dead animal is still pooled on the floor. Inside the cab there are numerous maps of Washington, Oregon and Idaho. Also maps of Indiana and Kentucky. I don't touch them. I feel under the seat and find a cell phone. Not mine. I flip it on and a background picture comes on the screen. It's me and Dan standing outside the Tides in Port Townsend. He has his arm around my shoulders and my head barely comes up to his pecs. We're both smiling stupidly. And speaking of stupid, *Caleb stupidly kept Dan's phone.*

I don't wipe my fingerprints off the device. Instead, I take it back inside and leave it near the body. Near Caleb's body. Near Wallace. Dead Wallace. Dead Caleb. The Wallace that will never bother me again. I can only hope my past has died with him. I can finally breathe. A little at least. Unless Ronnie or Donna start looking into my and Caleb's relationship and find the stupid picture of Rylee in the South Kitsap yearbook, the aptly named Rebel.

Now the sirens are circling ever closer in wide sweeps. The phone is their target. Fuck! Ronnie has the plate number of the van so even if I use it to run, my chance of slipping past the searchers is slim to none. *But I won't run. I'm in the right here. I'm the victim. I'm the guilty party.*

Caleb's apartment will be torn apart by Crime Scene and probably Mindy. Did Caleb leave something behind that can incriminate me? Was his plan to frame me for one or all of the murders if he couldn't recruit me? I can't very well leave here and go search his place. I can only hope there's nothing to find.

I pick Dan's phone up. He's got Ronnie's phone number in his contacts. I punch her number in and wait for my life to go up in flames.

SEVENTY-ONE

The hospital ER doctor says I have a mild concussion along with blistered skin on my ankle. She wants to keep me overnight for observation. I don't think so. She says I shouldn't go home alone with my injury. If someone stays with me, I can be released. Ronnie volunteers, of course, and I cry in front of the doctor and Ronnie and a nurse who puts her arms around me and I let her. And then Ronnie hugs me and... *What the hell is wrong with me?* The doc says the concussion might change my personality for a bit and my partner—my friend—Ronnie pipes in and asks, "What personality?" They all have a chuckle, but I'll get even when I'm better.

Ronnie is bringing me home, but I convince her to take me to Dan's room. We get there to be told Dan is still in a coma, but the young surgeon said Dan was doing much better. I told the surgeon Dan is a fighter, and I told Ronnie I wanted to stay in the room with him. She reminded me Sheriff Gray ordered me to go home. The .38 Dan gave me has been taken and I'm officially on suspension pending a shooting review board.

"Ronnie, I've got a head injury so Sheriff won't be surprised if I ignore the order to go home."

"You can stay here if I stay with you. I promised the doctor I would. And you can't ditch me again. Sheriff said I can detain you for the stunt you already pulled. And to tell you the truth, Megan, I'm leaning toward handcuffing you to the sofa. What the hell were you thinking? You could have been killed!"

"Caleb was after *me*, Ronnie. If I hadn't met him on his terms, he was going to kill Dan and you and the sheriff. You don't have eyes in the back of your head so don't tell me you could have taken care of yourself. Look at me. I'm exhibit A of what he could do. Thank you for your concern. It means the world to me. Honest. But I'm tired of talking about it. I've already told you and everyone else what I know, so if you'll excuse me, I just want to sit with Dan for a while." And I don't want to say anything that might incriminate me. I know my rights and I'm keeping silent.

"The ER doctor said not to let you go to sleep."

"There's no chance of that." My head won't stop pounding, and even with my eyes open, I see the ghosts of Caleb, my bio father, and others I've killed. They all have the same look. Dead.

Luckily the doc put my pounding heart down to a natural response to what I'd just been through.

"It was good of Sheriff to keep the ghouls at bay," Ronnie says, and I cringe at hearing the word "ghouls," reminded of what Caleb said about seeing ghosts. But she's talking about the news media. Every day is Halloween with them. *Trick or trick.*

"Yeah. That's good. I'm not up to talking to those idiots. I mean those professional journalists."

"Sheriff is putting out bulletins with Caleb's information and the victims' names to every agency here and surrounding states. Caleb's information will solve a lot of cold cases."

"I have a splitting headache, Ronnie." Literally splitting. "I need to shut my eyes for a bit."

"I brought my Taser in case you get sleepy."

Oh, Ronnie. You're so funny. Not. "Coffee. I need coffee stat, Doctor Ronnie."

"The doc said you shouldn't have stimulants and—"

"Hey. Who's injured here?"

"Sorry, Megan. One decaf coffee coming up."

Bitch. She's the best.

While she's down the hall, I turn on Dan's television. There are pictures of a young Caleb. I recognize the photo from the newspaper article about his parents dying. He looks nothing like that boy. The picture they put in the article of moi is one of me yelling at someone and making an ugly face. I was probably screaming at a reporter. I've pissed a lot of them off over the years and they have long memories. So do I.

I wonder if Dr. Albright is watching this? When this dies down I need to see her. I don't have unresolved issues. I have an unresolved life. She stopped seeing patients years ago, but she's always been available to me. And besides, she's a friend and I've learned that a person can't have too many of those. If Caleb had a friend, maybe he wouldn't have gone on a rampage.

My head feels like it's split in two and I sit back in the recliner and take Dan's hand. It's warm. A good sign. I can hear Ronnie down the hall talking to the dayshift nurse about, what else, computers. I lean back and squeeze Dan's hand. He's safe. Everyone's safe.

What I did wasn't horrible. How I felt and why I did it was horrible. I was protecting my own ass as much as stopping a murderer. I'd been on the verge of running. I can't blame that on the head injury. I've been thinking about calling it quits for quite some time. Running like a criminal, like who I was when I was Rylee. I've tried to change, but I'm not sure that part of me —the Rylee part—isn't still in charge at times. It's what I'm good at. Maybe it's what I was born to do. But I've fought that side of me until I'm exhausted. I want to be a force for good, but look what being good has gotten me. Killers out for revenge at every turn. Putting the people I've become close to in danger. Poor Dan almost died because of who I am. Or was. Not that there's much difference.

A tear zigzags down my cheek and I lay my head back, closing my eyes. I squeeze Dan's hand to let him know I'm here, and my eyes pop open when I feel a little squeeze back.

SEVENTY-TWO

The next few days flew by. Dan is out of danger and eating his Jell-O and other things hospitals are famous for. Instead of being pissed off at me for getting him hurt, he's asking *me* for forgiveness. He said he should have stayed in better contact. Being the compassionate sort, I forgave him. He acts like there's something on his mind, but he won't spit it out and I'm not going to pry.

Ronnie and Donna have forged—not exactly a friendship— more of a working bond. They are talking about starting a research company catering to missing persons. The sticking point is using police resources and equipment to aid in their searches. Knowing how good they both are at hacking, it shouldn't be a hurdle. They've talked Marley into a part-time position in their endeavor. If I'm honest, I'm a little put-off by Donna's quick friendship. I'm Ronnie's best friend. And one hell of a detective. But I guess after what I did I'm damaged goods.

Sheriff is basking in the glory of his department catching yet another serial killer, this time involving several states. It's a big deal since serial killers generally work limited hunting grounds.

They apparently didn't learn from the old saying, "Don't shit in your own milk." Caleb had learned the permanent way.

I've had dinner with Mindy several times and renewed our friendship while I pumped her for information on what was found in Caleb's apartment. She said that part was finished, and I didn't hear anything that should concern me.

Me, I've sanitized my apartment and packed what few things I need to take. I wish I could take Hayden in my bag, but he's gotten too damn big, and he's busy running Dan's business while Dan recovers.

I had lunch with Hayden yesterday and he hinted Dan was going to "pop the question." Dan has been making remarks for the last month about us moving in together and I'd resisted. He wants to marry me. I want to marry him. But I can't. I don't want to tell him. I'm a coward so I'll take the easy way out.

Last night I played several of the Albright tapes before I piled them up and burnt them in a back yard burn barrel. I've been cleared by the department and my .38 was returned along with my badge.

All sit like a museum display on the kitchen table.

My Explorer is parked on the street and the keys are on the table with my other sheriff department issue equipment.

Now I'm sitting in a beater I bought for five hundred dollars early this morning from Larry's Land of Used Vehicles. I haven't named the beater like Patterson seems to prefer. It's so ugly and worn looking I'd have to call it Rylee. I won't have it long before it disappears like everything in my life.

Larry took cash and made the title out to a name I have an ID for. Lexie Lawrence. The real Lexie is a dancer, but the ID was cheap.

I'm sitting on the street a block from Dr. Albright's house near Seattle. The massive forsythia bush is still by her front door but it has been cut back and looks depleted somehow. Her car is there and I saw her collect her newspaper an hour ago.

She looks exactly the same, maybe a little older. She favored her back when she bent to pick up the paper. I hope she's well.

Some of the past things Karen and I talked about play through my mind as if I'm in her house, at her kitchen table, sipping strong coffee or cabernet and being bathed in her warmth.

The last time I was here was after the multiple murders in Snow Creek. That was when I'd met Dan and he'd sparked feelings in me and I was lost at sea. I didn't think she would recognize me, but she'd immediately smiled and wrapped her arms around me. She still called me Rylee. I recall the conversation.

Karen: Rylee, you haven't changed a bit.

Me: I have changed. And I have you to thank for it.

And it's misery sometimes.

She laughed, and hearing her happiness at seeing me, I had felt like crying. I was afraid she'd slam the door in my face and call the police, but her warmth had tugged at my once cold heart.

Karen: You're a budding flower, Rylee. Beauty comes from the most unlikely places. You'll see.

She was right. I'd eventually opened my heart. Hayden had come back. Dan wormed his way into my life and if he was a worm, I was the apple and glad to have him. I have friends and I looked at my apartment as more than someplace to sleep. It became a home. Sheriff, Ronnie, Mindy, even Marley. Nan maybe not so much but she grows on you. Like a fungus. I was leaving them behind. It was better this way,

The beater's engine sputters but stays alive as I put it in gear. I hope Larry's Land of Crap Cars stays running long enough to get me where I'm going after I visit with Karen. Probably for the last time.

The curtain in the window twitches as I pull up her driveway. She comes out with a smile on her face as the engine shudders to a stop and I get out. Her white hair looks more like cloud than a halo now and her jowls are sagging more, but she's still beautiful.

"Hello, Rylee. I was waiting for you. I'm so glad you came. I saw you on the news. Come in."

She goes back inside and I hesitate a beat before following. I want to tell her the truth and probably will. I've spilled my guts nearly every time I've seen her, but this time is different. Caleb was a cold-blooded killer. Because of my new life I know the way I've lived my past life is wrong. But Caleb was doing what Rylee had done. What she believed in and that belief had driven her down dark passages. I can see both sides of that type of thinking, but killing him, making sure he was dead, feeling glad that I'd killed him; it brought me closer to Rylee than I had been in years.

Was Rylee really so bad? Or was she what this sick world needed? The public may claim she's a monster, but deep inside they secretly applaud what she's accomplished. Hypocrites. All. Back seat drivers with no drive of their own to right the wrongs in this world.

Karen invites me to have a seat in her kitchen where I can smell fresh baked bread. Two loaves sit on top of her stove and my mouth waters. She brings slices on a platter with blackberry honey butter and takes a seat.

"Eat," she says. "And tell me all about it."

I do, and I do.

A LETTER FROM GREGG

Dear reader,

I want to say a huge thank you for choosing to read *Final Victim*. If you enjoyed it and want to keep up to date with all my latest releases, just sign up at the following link. Your email address will never be shared and you can unsubscribe at any time.

www.bookouture.com/gregg-olsen

I hope you loved *Final Victim*. If you did, I would be very grateful if you could write a review. I'd love to hear what you think, and it makes such a difference helping new readers to discover one of my books for the first time.

I love hearing from my readers – you can get in touch through social media, or my website.

Thanks,

Gregg

facebook.com/GreggOlsenAuthor
x.com/Gregg_Olsen

PUBLISHING TEAM

Turning a manuscript into a book requires the efforts of many people. The publishing team at Bookouture would like to acknowledge everyone who contributed to this publication.

Audio
Alba Proko
Sinead O'Connor
Melissa Tran

Commercial
Lauren Morrissette
Hannah Richmond
Imogen Allport

Data and analysis
Mark Alder
Mohamed Bussuri

Editorial
Laura Deacon
Sinead O'Connor

Copyeditor
Janette Currie

Proofreader
Maddy Newquist

Marketing
Alex Crow
Melanie Price
Occy Carr
Cíara Rosney
Martyna Młynarska

Operations and distribution
Marina Valles
Stephanie Straub
Joe Morris

Production
Hannah Snetsinger
Mandy Kullar
Jen Shannon
Ria Clare

Publicity
Kim Nash
Noelle Holten
Jess Readett
Sarah Hardy

Rights and contracts
Peta Nightingale
Richard King
Saidah Graham